YOU NEED TO LEAVE

SARAH JULES

Proofread by Mary Hoyle & Susan Keillor

Published by Mark of the Witch Press

Dedicated to readers who frequently visit doesthedogdie.com
This book is for you.
Specs (and any other dog in my books) will always be okay.
I can't promise the same for the humans.

And to Buster, the inspiration behind Specs.

Author note: This book is written in British English.
Therefore, dear American readers, there may be fewer z's than you're
anticipating.
We Brits also spell some words differently too, don't worry about it. These
aren't typos, I promise. <3

TABLE OF CONTENTS

A QUICK RECAP OF YOU INVITED IT IN…

I know how annoying it is when the next book in a series comes out WAY after the last one you read. You have that internal debate about whether you should re-read the previous book, or if you should just dive into the latest book and hope for the best. Well, here I am to settle that debate for you. Below is a brief 'previously on': where I cover all the salient points of *YOU INVITED IT IN* to refresh your memory before you dive into *YOU NEED TO LEAVE*. There's no pressure to read this, of course, and I do recap the previous book throughout the first few chapters of *YOU NEED TO LEAVE*. Do with this what you will. It's here if you want it. Thank you for continuing on this journey with me and caring enough about the Eastwood family to find out what happened next.

Widowed father, Felix Eastwood, can see the spirits of the dead, a trait he inherited from his mother. When his brother, Eli, shows him a poorly designed advert for Lilith Lavelle's psychic cleansing services, Felix knows that she's preying on grieving and desperate families to make money. She's a charlatan, a fraud, and he decides to come up with a plan to take her down – a plan that backfires and places his own family in grave danger. Felix's twelve-year-old son, Asher, and Eli's rescue pup, Specs, find themselves entangled in Felix's plan.

The plan is, on the surface, simple: invite Lilith into his home, fake a haunting, and prove the psychic is a fraud.

Unfortunately for the Eastwoods, Lilith Lavelle isn't alone when she enters the house.

After Lilith leaves, Felix and Asher begin to experience the exact same (stereotypical) haunting they'd lied about and said they were experiencing.

The haunting intensifies, with terrible consequences.

Felix enlists his mother's help, but it's too late. Their family become the target of a demon (a spirit that never moved on to the next plane of existence and grew in strength and malice). No longer is it just shadow figures and cold spots. The demon Lilith inadvertently brought with her preys on the grieving family – pretending to be Asher's mother, who died when he was a baby.

Desperate for help, Felix forces Lilith to help clean up her mess. Sadly, Lilith knows *nothing* about demons. Lilith reaches out to other *experts* and only one responds: Emmanuel Stark (parapsychologist and arsehole). He says that, unfortunately, it's too late to do anything, but could they please film the haunting for posterity? The demon holds Asher in the air and breaks his limbs. Lilith videos it on her phone whilst Felix, Eli, and Specs desperately attempt to save Asher. Asher is released with no memory of the incident. He has no injuries. The demon possesses Felix and promises to use his body to slit Asher's throat, cut the flesh from his bone, and eat it raw.

The demon allows Lilith to remember where they met, at a psychic cleansing of a dying child the demon had been feeding on. The demon is named Nicolas Damont and, when he was alive, he was known as the Werewolf of Châlons. He sexually abused children, murdered them, and ate them, something he continued to do after his death.

In order to prevent Nicolas from using Felix's body to kill Asher, Lilith stabs him in the neck and kills him. *Kill the host, kill the demon.*

The ordeal is far from over. Lilith is arrested. Felix is dead. Eli and Asher find the body of Asher's grandmother (Felix and Eli's mother) hanged in her retirement home. She'd attempted to sacrifice herself to save them, but the demon wouldn't accept her sacrifice.

Where we left off, Lilith was awaiting trial for Felix's murder, but she feared she wasn't alone in prison.

And there's your whistle-stop tour of the first book.

Happy reading, and thank you for coming back for the sequel.

I'm sorry for what comes next.

BAD NEWS

'In accepting my sacrifice, your kind will never be able to feed from her again. She will be deemed untouchable to you. I sacrifice my life so that hers remains untouched.'

The words stared back at Eli through the screen of his tablet. Each syllable was a gut punch, forcing the wind from his lungs and bending him in two. The handwritten note from 1970 had been tucked into the pages of his mum's diary. The diary her suicide note had instructed him to read. Her death was still raw. Every time he closed his eyes, the image of her swinging from the ceiling light vied for his attention against the barrage of other memories that threatened his sanity. The words at the bottom of the letter had been unreadable to the naked eye, smudged by his grandfather's bloody fingers, probably when he tucked it into his back pocket before slitting his throat at the altar of the local church.

Eli dropped the tablet into his lap and lay his head back on the thick pillows of his bed. Every day of the last six months had felt impossible. Every day, he got up for Asher's benefit. Taking care of his nephew was the *only thing* that got him through the days. Eli released a long exhale and turned to look at the clock on his bedside table. Not *his* bedside table. Felix's. After Felix had died in Eli's living room, there was no way he could have expected Asher to move in with him, and so Eli had found himself living in Felix's house and playing father to Felix's son. Thankfully, his brother had life insurance, and the policy had paid off the remainder of the mortgage. Technically, Asher owned the house, and Eli was just taking care of it until Asher was of age.

The clock blinked 7:04 AM.

His phone pinged: an email notification to his work account. It was a soulless noise that never failed to irritate him. Picking up his phone, he clicked on the notification.

'Just what I needed,' Eli said under his breath. An email from Emmanuel Stark; world-famous parapsychologist and all round arsehole. Whenever he saw the pretentious twat's name, anger flooded through his system. Lilith Lavelle had reached out to Emmanuel as a last-ditch attempt to save Eli's family from the demon that was Nicolas Damont, whom she had unknowingly brought into Felix's home. Eli would never forgive Emmanuel Stark for the way he behaved that day. Damont had been torturing Asher, breaking the bones in the boy's body whilst he hung in the air, and Emmanuel Stark had nonchalantly said there was nothing he could do to help, but could he please have a video of it?

He should ignore the email. He knew that. Reading it would only anger him further, but the self-sabotaging part of his brain, the part that knew being angry was easier than being sad, forced him to open it.

Eli,

It has been six months since your brother's passing. I do hope that you and Asher have been able to find some happiness. Grief is a terrible thing. It is disappointing that you haven't been responding to my attempts to contact you. I thought that what I was suggesting would be mutually beneficial, but apparently, you don't share that view. You need to talk through what happened that day with somebody who doesn't think you're crazy. It is the only way to help you to move on, and I have questions. The video Lilith sent to me is definitive proof of the supernatural. It is proof of life after death. All I want is to talk to you about what happened. A case study. Without sounding too blasé, I need you and Asher as case studies. This is my big break – the highlight of my career. Lilith is also refusing to return my calls. I can anonymise everything, but just think of the ways in which this could change the world. Life beyond death exists! Your family is living proof that our minds don't simply cease to exist after we die. You could be rich, famous, if you wanted. This is your last chance, Eli. I want your side of the story, but I will go live with my findings (and the video) without you. I have been more than patient, given the circumstances. You have 48 hours. If you fail to answer me within that time, the video gets uploaded on my social media. I am not the kind of person to make threats, but you have left me no choice. I have waited long enough.

Regards,

Dr Emmanuel Stark – Parapsychologist

Eli had responded to the first couple of emails Emmanuel had sent asking, politely and then not so politely, for Emmanuel to leave him alone and to never contact him again. After that, he'd stopped answering. He sighed, trying to figure out what to do. To answer or not to answer, that was the question. He had forty-eight hours anyway, no use replying in the heat of the moment. He placed his phone back on the bedside table and laid back down. He closed his eyes. The light hadn't yet begun to seep through the curtain. It was one of those oppressive late January mornings. It did nothing to lift his mood. Plus, he needed to tell Lilith about what the note from his mum's diary had said. It answered their questions about why her sacrifice hadn't worked: the question they'd been pondering for months. Eli, from the comfort of his dead brother's house. Lilith, from her prison cell at New Manor, the local women's prison where she was being held on remand while waiting for her case to go to trial. She had officially been charged with first-degree murder, although her solicitors were fairly confident that, should it actually go to trial (because apparently the case could still be dropped by the Crown Prosecution Service), they could prove she acted in self-defence against Felix. However, in order to do that, Eli's brother would have to be ripped apart in front of a jury. The party line was that he'd been in the throes of a psychotic break when Lilith had killed him, in order to save Asher. In reality, he'd been possessed by Nicolas Damont, a 500-year-old demon who had a taste for young children. Fucking insanity.

'What has my life become?' Eli muttered, pushing the heels of his hands into his eyes.

There was no time like the present to get in contact with Lilith. Managing to speak to her in real time required planning and usually a few days' notice. Lilith could call him whenever she wanted, but he had no way to phone her. The Prison Voicemail app was a lifesaver. All he had to do was use the app to leave her a voicemail, and when Lilith checked her voicemail using the prison phone (which she did every day) she'd know to call him back. Eli opened the app on his phone and tapped 'record'.

'Lilith, it's Eli,' he spoke into the phone. 'There's been an update on that puzzle we've been trying to solve about my mother. I know why what she did didn't work. I need you to call me back ASAP.' He paused, and then added, 'I hope you're doing okay in there.'

'Who are you talking to?' Asher's head poked around the door.

'I was leaving a voicemail for Lilith,' Eli explained. Asher was almost thirteen years old. He'd always been young for his age, but recently he'd changed. He seemed far older than his years. That was the price of trauma. It forced children to grow up before their time. Whatever innocence Asher had before Nicolas Damont came into their lives had vanished without a trace.

'What about?' Asher asked. He padded into the room on bare feet and sat at the foot of the bed. The creak of the springs elicited a grumble from Asher's room. He heard Specs jump down from Asher's bed and walk into the room, where he promptly jumped up beside Asher and sighed a big, Staffy sigh.

'You know that I told you Nanna did what she did to try and save us from Nicolas Damont?' Eli said. He didn't shy away from difficult conversations with Asher. He wanted Asher to trust him completely, but there was no way he could say the phrase *killed herself* when referring to what his mother had done.

'Yeah,' Asher said, placing his hand on the scruff of Specs's neck and ruffling the fur there. Specs yawned gratefully.

'I know why it didn't work now. Here, look at this,' he said. Unlocking his tablet, he showed Asher the letter. 'I managed to clear up the words at the bottom of the letter that had been smudged with blood.'

He waited for Asher to read, studying his face carefully for any signs that it was too much for him to handle. Asher's face remained blank, and then his eyebrows raised slightly in question.

'So, it didn't work because of the deal my great grandad made, which Nanna didn't know about?'

Eli nodded.

'So, she died for nothing.' Asher blinked at him. His words stung.

'No. She died trying to save the person she loved the most in the whole world. I know she would do it again in a heartbeat. You were everything to her, Asher. She wouldn't regret trying to save you.' Eli leaned forwards, meaning to wrap Asher in a hug, but Asher edged back. Specs readily jumped between them, accepting the hug that had been intended for Asher.

'I fucking hate this,' Asher said. Since Felix's death, Asher's language had become far more colourful. Eli could never bring himself to reprimand him. After all, Eli was fucking angry, too.

'Me too, Ash. I'm sorry I can't fix it.'

'It's your fault. You showed Dad Lilith's advert. If you hadn't done that, none of this would have happened.'

Eli felt like he'd been slapped. 'I know. I'm sorry. If I could take it back, I would. I wish I hadn't. God, I wish I hadn't.' Eli pinched the skin of his thigh under the quilt to stop himself from crying. This wasn't about him. This was about Asher. He wanted to be there for his nephew no matter what, even if Asher was lashing out. He needed somebody to blame, and he couldn't blame his dead dad. Plus, he was right. Eli blamed himself too. The feeling of regret often overwhelmed him completely, washing away the boiling pot of anger, the grief, the depression he felt.

'I don't understand why this happened to me,' Asher whispered.

'It's not fair, Ash. It should never have happened. Things like that should not happen.'

Asher had been through so much in his short life. He'd lost his mum when he was still a baby. The demon had used Asher's anguish and confusion about her death to torment him. It had been heartbreaking to watch. And then he'd witnessed his dad's death. And his grandmother had died too, attempting to exchange her life for his, all in the space of a day. It was an impossible amount of grief for a person to handle, never mind someone so young.

Asher patted the space next to him and Specs launched himself onto it, turning upside down so that Asher could scratch his tummy. The dog always seemed to know exactly what Asher wanted from him. Specs had been an invaluable part of the grieving process for both of them. He'd been a comfort, a distraction, and a constant support. The rescue pup was the best decision Eli had ever made. Without him, Eli wasn't sure he or Asher would have survived the last six months.

'You'll get through this, Asher. I know it doesn't feel like that now, but you will. Your dad would want you to be happy. I know you don't feel happy right now, and maybe you won't for a long while, but you will be happy again. Remember what Simone said about growing around the grief? You'll do that. We'll do it together. I miss your dad, too. And Nanna, but I am here, and I will never leave you.'

Simone was Asher's therapist, and an absolute godsend.

'You can't promise that,' Asher said, a single tear snaking down his cheek.

'I can. I am not going anywhere. No matter what. We know the other side, the beyond, whatever you want to call it, exists. I would haunt the hell out of you if anything happened to me. You'd never be alone again.' He tried to elicit a smile from his nephew. It worked, somewhat. Asher wiped the tears away.

'Do you think Dad is here? And Nanna?' he asked, looking around the room.

'I do. Sometimes I think I can feel them watching over us.' It was the truth. Often, Eli felt like he was being watched. He had caught the ghost of the scent of Felix's aftershave or felt a hand against his skin.

'I don't,' Asher said. 'I wish I could see spirits. Then it would be like he'd never left.'

Eli wasn't sure what to say to that. Felix had pretty much pretended he couldn't see spirits, a gift he'd inherited from their mum. The only spirit Eli had seen was Nicolas Damont, and that was only because Damont was an old and powerful demon, and he wanted to be seen. The longer a spirit stayed on this plane of existence without passing on, the more powerful it became, which was why it sucked when one targeted your family.

'Shall we get breakfast?' Eli asked. 'We can go out; get something unhealthy and full of sugar?'

A spectre of a smile tugged at Asher's lips. 'Waffles?'

'Waffles it is. Meet you downstairs in twenty?'

'Deal,' Asher said. He flung himself off the bed, the old dog following behind him. Specs behaved like a puppy. Even at ten years old, going on eleven, he was showing no signs of slowing down. 'See you downstairs!'

It was in moments like this that Eli could see glimmers of the old Asher.

The call came at 3 PM. Eli and Asher were watching reruns of the American sitcom *Superstore*. It had become their comfort programme, never failing to brighten their mood. The caller ID said 'NEW MANOR'.

Eli left the sofa and went into the kitchen. 'Lilith,' he said as he answered the phone.

An unfamiliar voice responded. 'Am I speaking with Elijah Eastwood?'

'Yes, who is this?' he asked.

'Deputy Governor Stefanie O'Connor. I am calling because Miss Lilith Lavelle put you as her emergency contact.'

'Is she okay?' Eli asked, knowing the answer already. Dread needled his skin.

'No, Mr Eastwood. Unfortunately, Lilith was found dead in her cell this morning.'

Eli collapsed into a chair.

'What do you mean, dead?' he asked, breath catching in his throat.

'She committed suicide.'

'How?' He said the word like a prayer.

'We are conducting an investi-'

'HOW?' Eli yelled, blood rising to his temples and blurring his vision.

'It appears that she hanged herself using her bedsheet. I am sorry for your loss, Mr Eastwood.'

A STRANGE MESSAGE

Eli stared at his phone like it was a bomb primed to explode in his hand. He blinked against the realisation of what had just happened. There would be no telling Lilith about what he'd read in his mum's diary because Lilith was dead. Lilith Lavelle was dead. There had been no note. No explanation. The guards had found her hanging that morning and that was that.

'What is it?' Asher stood in the doorway, Specs at his heel. Eli hadn't even heard him move from the sofa.

'Come here,' Eli said, gesturing to the dining table. Asher took his usual seat at the right-hand side of the table, facing the kitchen window.

Asher didn't speak, but Eli could see a question forming on his lips. He didn't want to make Asher ask.

'That was the Deputy Governor of New Manor. She called to let us know that Lilith died this morning.'

Asher's brows furrowed as though he was trying to put the pieces of the puzzle together and a piece was missing.

'She said that Lilith killed herself.' There was no point sugarcoating it. As much as Eli wanted to protect Asher from further trauma, he deserved to know the truth.

'Lilith wouldn't do that.' Asher folded his arms across his torso. Eli noticed that his nephew was losing his boyish frame, filling out. A stab of anguish pierced his heart that Felix wouldn't be there to see Asher grow into a man.

'They're looking into it, Asher, but they have no reason to lie.'

'I didn't think they were lying,' Asher said, the words barely audible under his breath. 'Maybe they just don't know the truth.'

'The truth?' Eli pushed.

'What if it was Nicolas Damont?' Asher stared at Eli through glistening eyes.

'Damont is dead. Lilith killed him.' Eli hoped he sounded sure. In truth, he'd had the same concern. Lilith had never seemed suicidal, although he knew that suicidal people didn't always appear suicidal. She'd spent the last few months making the most of prison life. And, as far as her solicitor had assured them, the chances of her release were extremely high. She had everything to live for.

But she said that something was in there with her, Eli's brain reminded him.

It was back when Lilith first went to prison. Maybe a few weeks in. Lilith had sounded *off*. She'd said something along the lines of *'What if we didn't kill Damont? What if he's here?'* But then she'd never mentioned it again, and Eli had chalked it up to her struggling to adjust to life in prison and the possibility of spending the rest of her years behind bars. That had to take a toll on a person's sanity.

'Will there be a funeral?' Asher asked.

'Maybe. I don't know. Why?'

'Because we should go. Lilith saved us.' Asher bit his lip in thought. 'And, I don't think she had any family or friends, so who would go?'

Asher was right. Eli had never heard Lilith talk about friends or family, and she'd put Eli down as her emergency contact.

'We can go, if there's a funeral,' Eli promised.

'What if there isn't? What happens to a body if nobody wants it?' Asher studied his hands as he spoke, a trait he'd picked up from Felix, who used to do the same thing when he was upset.

'Do you know what? I don't know. We can look into it if you want,' Eli tried to appease Asher. The last thing he wanted to do was think about Lilith's body lying unclaimed in a morgue. While on some basic level he knew that those without living relatives would be given paupers' funerals by the local council, he didn't know enough about the procedures and legalities to attempt to explain it to Asher.

'Maybe she's here with us, too. You said you could feel Dad and Nanna. Can you feel Lilith?'

'No,' Eli said, reaching out and placing his hand on Asher's, 'but that doesn't mean she isn't here.'

'I never said thank you,' Asher muttered under his breath. He glanced up at Eli's face and saw his questioning glance. 'For saving us, I mean,' he added.

Lilith bore the brunt of what had happened that day. She'd taken the fall and had done so readily and with such authority it had given Eli whiplash.

'She knew how grateful you are.' The complex web of emotion that Asher had to feel towards Lilith was too much for Eli to begin to comprehend. She'd been the one to bring the demon into the house and had subsequently refused to help them get rid of it. It transpired that Lilith was a fraud, as Felix had expected when he'd invited her into their home, and that she'd brought the demon there unknowingly. There wasn't a cat in hell's chance that Eli would be able to unpack that emotional baggage.

'I hope so.' Asher looked back down at his hands forlornly.

'Just in case she is here, you could tell her how you feel. Or maybe you could write a note to her and if she is here, she'd be able to read it over your shoulder.'

Parenting didn't come easy to Eli. He was supposed to be the fun uncle. He loved Asher so much it hurt, but he was never supposed to be the primary parent. He was acutely aware that every decision he made would impact Asher's life, his future.

'Yeah, that's a good idea,' Asher said. Eli had the distinct feeling that Asher was only saying that for his benefit. 'I'm going to do that now. Come on, Specs.' Specs didn't need telling twice;

he followed Asher out of the room. The telltale creak of the stairs gave away their intended destination: Asher's bedroom.

When he was certain Asher was out of earshot, Eli placed his forehead on the table and allowed the tears to fall.

His phone pinged the message tone.

Eli groaned audibly. There was only one person who messaged him. Craig. Prior to Felix's death and all the other crazy shit that happened, Eli and Craig had been dating. It had been going well. Craig was a librarian. Nice. Good looking. Liked dogs. He had the dry sense of humour that Eli loved, but they'd only been on five or six dates before Eli's life had gone tits up. When Felix had died, Craig had tried to be there for him, but it had been too much, too soon, and Eli had withdrawn. He was ashamed of his behaviour. He wasn't the type to ghost somebody, but he felt like he was being ripped apart at the seams, and he just couldn't do the whole dating thing and hold himself together. He didn't want to. Craig had been so understanding, and it made Eli feel a thousand times worse. The *'I'll be here when you're ready'* messages were agonising to read.

Just checking in with you. I hope you and Asher are okay. You know where I am if you need anything,' the text read.

'Damn it,' Eli said. Damn him for being so fucking nice.

'I still need space,' Eli typed back, hating himself more and more with every single letter he typed.

Asher sat on his bed. Specs snored his thunderous snores from by his feet. He loved that sound. It was the sound of comfort. Specs was his best friend. The only good thing that came out of his dad's death was that he got to live with Specs all the time now. It was the silver lining his counsellor Simone had told him to look for.

Asher's spiralbound notebook rested on his knee. A green felt tip lay on top of it. He had no idea what to write to Lilith.

Pulling the cap off the pen with his teeth, Asher wrote, *'I'm sorry you're dead.'* He didn't realise he was crying until a tear splashed on the paper, causing the ink to bloom outwards like a flower.

'Lilith,' he whispered into the empty room. Specs grumbled and looked at him with an expression that said, *'Are you talking to me?',* before placing his chin back down on his paws. 'I'm really sorry you're dead. I don't believe you killed yourself. And if you did, I believe you had a really good reason. I hope that you're safe now on the other side. Thank you for looking after us.' He sighed. The air shook as it left his throat. 'I'm sorry this whole thing happened. I don't blame you for bringing Nicolas Damont into our house.' *I blame my dad for that,* he didn't add. *If my dad hadn't…*

STOP, he thought. Wishful thinking didn't help. Dad invited Lilith. Lilith brought a demon with her. That's what happened and he couldn't change the past. He tried to put what he'd been taught in counselling to good use. He couldn't tell Simone everything, of course, but he told her enough that she was helping. She worked out of a Wendy house at the bottom of her garden, and she always had summer fruits dilute-pop because that was his favourite. It was good to talk to somebody who wasn't Uncle Eli or Specs, and she'd taught him loads of techniques to help him manage his grief and anxiety. She said that, in time, he'd grow around the grief, although he wasn't entirely sure what that meant.

'Lilith, if you're here, can you give me a sign, so I know I'm not talking to myself?'

He looked around the room.

Nothing.

But that made sense. Lilith had only just died. If she was here, she wouldn't be strong enough to manipulate the surroundings yet. The same went, theoretically, for his dad. Asher would kill to see his dad again, even in spirit form. How was it fair that the gift to see the dead hadn't passed onto him?

Life wasn't fair.

He sighed. 'Lilith, if you are here, I'm really sorry.'

He stood up and grabbed his dad's old Gameboy Color, pressing the on button. *Pokémon Crystal* came to life before his eyes. The Gameboy was chunky and bright yellow. The picture was terrible too, but he preferred it to his Switch. It made him feel closer to his dad. Asher's character in the game, named after himself, was wandering through the tall grass near Golden Rod City, when the screen glitched. Lines pulsed across the image, distorting and altering it. The familiar music shifted and stretched until it was unrecognisable. Asher held his breath as the picture continued to change, slowly turning into a whirlpool. The details were being sucked away. The sound vanished with it, leaving behind a blank screen.

'No, no, no, please don't break!' Asher said. His chest warmed, and a lump grew in his throat. He tapped the screen with his finger and then moved his hand to press the power button. Before he could, words flashed across the screen.

'THEY'RE COMING FOR YOU.'

LEAKED VIDEO

Monday had rolled around quickly. Eli had spent the remainder of the weekend trying and failing to distract his sullen nephew. News of Lilith's death had knocked Asher's progress back significantly. Asher had reverted into himself; turned distant. All he'd wanted was to stay in his room and play on Felix's Gameboy. Was Eli supposed to let him do that? Or should he encourage him to put it down and go outside into the frigid January weather to get some fresh air? In the end, Eli had settled for encouraging Asher to come and play the Gameboy in the living room. At least that way they were together. It felt like a half-win. Throughout the remainder of Sunday, they sat in the same room, occasionally talking, but mostly silent. When Asher went to bed that evening, Eli hated himself for the relief he felt that the day was over.

Eli had taken Asher to school on Monday morning and dropped him near the gates, as he'd done every school day for the last few months. Asher climbed out of the car and walked away, muttering, 'Thanks.' That downhearted thanks was all Eli had been able to think about all morning. He was failing Asher. He didn't know what he was supposed to do. How the hell do you support a child who'd experienced what Asher had been through? Simone had been helpful. She'd given him some books to read and some websites to explore, but the information was conflicting…

Try to distract the grieving child.

Give them space.

Talk to them about their loved one.

Don't talk to them about their loved one. Let them talk to you when they're ready.

The morose way Asher had thanked him that morning ached like a broken limb. He should have called Asher back. Told him he didn't have to go to school that day. They could lie around and watch films until he was feeling more like himself. But maybe that was the wrong thing too. Maybe school was the best place for Asher. A welcome distraction. He had a close group of friends around him. 'The Geek Squad', Felix had called the boys. Asher thought the name was hilarious, and it stuck. Hopefully, they'd put some pep back in Asher's step.

Eli turned his attention back to the task at hand. Freelancing meant that he had some flexibility in his job, but he had to work in order to afford to live. Time spent not working was time spent not earning. His savings, and the little bit of money that Felix had left to him, were a finite resource. He was working on the branding for an independent bookshop in town. The client had been vague in their desires and so Eli was making educated guesses based on what, in his experience, would suit the business. Often, in his role as graphic designer, Eli had to be a mind-reader.

Specs's bark signalled to Eli that he'd been working for too long without taking a break.

'You want to go out?' he asked.

Specs barked once, telling Eli that yes, he did, in fact, want to go out.

Eli went to open the back door and Specs bolted out to his favourite patch of dead grass.

Leaning against the door jamb, the cold bit his skin. It was going to snow over the next few days. A couple of snow days could be just what Asher needed. They could do all the things they used to do on snow days: build snowmen, have snowball fights, drink hot chocolate, and watch movies huddled under blankets.

All of it without Felix.

That was his life now. Everything moving forwards would be without Felix. For him and for Asher. He closed his eyes and let the icy wind nip at his face.

You'll get through this. It won't feel so raw forever, he kept telling himself.

Six months. He'd never lost somebody close to him before. To lose your brother and your mum in the space of a day, as a result of the same insidious creature, was unimaginable. If he thought about what he'd lost for a moment too long, Eli would find himself unable to function. His mother's death had been difficult, especially the manner in which she'd died, and the fact that he'd found her. But, given her age, her death was still easier to swallow than his brother's. It was more *expected*. It had also been her choice. Felix was different. Felix should have been by his side until they were ancient. And now he faced a life without him. The pain of mourning the life his brother would have had… He had to push it aside for Asher.

Opening his eyes, Eli watched Specs trot back up the garden. Noticing Eli's mood, Specs jumped and placed his two front paws on Eli's hips, using him as a post to stretch against.

'How about some lunch?' Eli asked, ruffling Specs's head.

Specs answered and walked over to his bowl, looking back over his shoulder to check that Eli was following through on his promise.

'Dumb dog,' Eli said, grinning.

Specs sat patiently while Eli spooned wet food from the tin into his bowl. The dog waited for the command, 'Get it,' to start eating. Eli couldn't take any responsibility for Specs's behaviour. He'd been an angel from the start. He picked up commands with very little effort, and he was sweet as pie with people and animals alike. The image of Specs ripping into the backs of Felix's legs, trying to stop him from reaching Asher, flashed across Eli's mind in a visceral, agonising, vision.

A panic attack.

His heart rate spiked. His breath shortened. Knowing what it was didn't make it any easier.

Gripping the countertop to keep himself from collapsing to the floor, Eli began to slow his breaths, counting each one.

PTSD, he was pretty sure, as was his GP, triggered the flashbacks, which in turn triggered the panic attacks. Although the waiting list to see a psychiatrist was eighteen months long, and then a formal diagnosis could take even longer. A diagnosis wouldn't help him. He didn't need a label to tell him that he was unwell. The anti-depressants kept most of the symptoms at bay. He should see a psychiatrist or a therapist or somebody qualified, he knew, but telling them half-truths wouldn't help. *My brother was possessed by a French fucking demon and the demon used his body to try and murder my nephew*, would get him sectioned, and leave Asher alone. No. He had to deal with the trauma alone, with his dog and a boatload of anti-depressants as a crutch.

He counted each breath, focusing on taking long inhales and filling up his lungs to the point they felt like they might burst, before slowly exhaling. By the time he got to number sixty-two, he felt calm and able to move from the counter.

His phone rang. A jarring noise that almost thrust him back into the panic attack.

He looked at the Caller ID.

Holstone School.

'Hello,' Eli said, swiping up to answer the phone, and putting it against his ear.

'Mr Eastwood?' a woman's voice responded.

'Yes,' Eli said.

'I'm Miss Deane, the school nurse. I have Asher in with me. He says he doesn't feel well. Are you able to come and pick him up?'

'Yes, of course. Is he okay?' Eli walked into the hall, slipping on his shoes and grabbing his car keys.

'Well, he's a little upset. He says he feels too ill to be at school.' She lowered her voice. 'To be honest with you, I'm not sure he's ill. He says he feels sick and has a headache. I think something might have happened to upset him, but he won't tell me what. He's in no state to be in school. I have him in the nurse's office.'

'I'm on my way,' Eli said.

'I'll keep him in my office until then,' she replied.

'Thank you.' Eli hung up the phone. 'Specs. Want to go get Asher?'

Specs bounded over, ears standing to attention. The residual effects of the panic attack still prickled at Eli's skin, feeling like a warm electric current. With a final deep breath, he packed Specs into the car and headed to pick up his nephew.

The school nurse shot Eli a sympathetic look as she deposited Asher into his care. Asher shuffled alongside Eli, looking at his feet with rapt attention. Placing an arm around Asher's shoulder, Eli guided him towards the car. Asher didn't notice Specs until a wet tongue wiped across his ear as he sat down in the passenger seat. Buckled into the backseat, a quick lick of greeting was all Specs could manage.

'Hey, Specs,' Asher muttered.

Eli put the car into gear and set off home. After a couple of minutes, the silence became unbearable.

'What happened, Ash?' he asked. Asher's face was a roadmap of tear stains.

Asher didn't answer. His breath hitched, and he began to sob. In the backseat, Specs began to whine.

'Ash, hey, come on,' Eli said, pulling the car over into a side street. He stopped the car, turned off the ignition, and turned to look at Asher. His fists were balled in his lap. Tears fell unbridled onto his cheeks. 'You can tell me anything. Whatever happened, we'll sort it together, okay?'

Squeezing Asher's shoulder, Eli adjusted himself, so he was facing Asher.

'There's a video of me online.'

Eli's skin turned to ice as he remembered Emmanuel's final email and the threats that he'd made.

'The one of you…' Eli didn't know how to finish that sentence.

'The one of me floating in mid-air. Ethan showed it to me. My bones…' Asher stopped, gulping air and shaking his head.

Eli remembered what happened to Asher's bones with vivid clarity. How Nicolas Damont had snapped them like twigs while he hung in the air. Eli had never asked Asher if he remembered what had happened when Damont had done that to him. Asher had never mentioned it, which Eli had taken as a good sign. But…

'Why don't I remember that happening?' Asher said between sobs.

'I think it's a blessing that you don't,' Eli said. 'Asher, we did everything we could to stop it.'

'I know. I watched the video.' Asher's voice turned cold, accusatory. 'You didn't tell me it had happened.'

'I hoped you didn't remember, Ash. It looked so painful, and then when it was over and you didn't talk about it, I just hoped...'

'You lied to me.' His words were thick with anger.

'Asher, I-' Eli started.

'I thought you were honest with me. You told me you were. That video...' Asher's body pulsed. He flung the car door open and began to heave onto the pavement. Eli's hand floated to Asher's back by instinct and began to lightly rub over the top of his black school blazer.

'Asher, I'm sorry. If you didn't remember that, I didn't want to remind you. It was... It was fucking awful.'

Asher pulled himself back into the car and shut the door, wiping his hand across his mouth.

Specs's whines intensified.

'I'm okay.' Asher directed the words at Specs, turning to stroke the dog's ears. The whines stopped immediately.

'Asher...' Eli said. A hot flush erupted across his skin. He was failing at every opportunity. 'I thought I was doing the right thing.'

'I know,' Asher said. After a beat, he continued, 'The video. It was awful. I couldn't believe it was me. And seeing you and Dad, and Specs…' Asher made a noise that was a cross between a laugh and a cough.

'You should never have seen the video. I never thought he'd post it.'

'Emmanuel Stark?' Asher said.

Eli shot him a questioning glance.

'Lilith recorded a video that night. She sent it to him,' Asher continued. His voice was rough, broken. 'She wanted him to believe her?'

Eli nodded, watching Asher piece together what had happened.

'You said that you didn't think he'd post it?' Asher said. He looked at Eli with pleading eyes.

'He's emailed me a few times asking to speak to us about that night. I refused.' He had a choice: to confess to Asher that he knew Emmanuel would release the video, or not. He'd fucked up parenting at every possible juncture thus far, and he couldn't trust his own instincts. 'Emmanuel told me that he would release the video if we didn't speak to him, but I didn't think he'd actually do it.'

Asher's jaw fell open. Tears sprang back into his eyes. Fear furrowed his brow. His lip shook. Betrayal. Asher felt betrayed.

'Asher, I'm sorry.' He was doing a lot of apologising, and it was helping no one.

'Why would he do that?' Asher asked. 'Why would he share that? He wrote a blog post alongside it, including screenshots of Lilith's messages to him. It changes everything.'

'Lilith,' Eli said aloud. Her death had not yet become public information. It hadn't even made the local news. Eli had checked. Many times. Felix's death had very briefly made national news and had then been relegated to local news for a couple of weeks, with the focus being on the social media psychic accused of murdering a client. After that, the murder had vanished from the news, and all attention died away.

'Everyone at school saw the video?' Eli asked. His throat was so tight he could barely speak.

The car windows had misted over, cocooning them both inside, hiding them from the world.

Asher nodded, another sob shaking his body.

'Were kids saying shit to you? Is that why you wanted to come home?'

Asher nodded again, not meeting Eli's eye.

'Were they being arseholes?'

'They said that Dad was crazy. That the video was fake. That we did it for attention.' Each word felt like Asher had to force it from his mouth. 'They said I was mental. That you were too. That Lilith should have killed all of us.'

Blood thumped against Eli's skull. Rage slammed into him like a tidal wave.

'Kids can be mean, Ash. They shouldn't have… I'm sorry they said that to you. I'll speak to the school.'

'Don't. It will make it worse. I just, I don't want to go back. Not yet. Please don't make me go back,' Asher begged.

'Okay. I won't make you go back until you're ready.'

Asher was a couple of weeks away from being thirteen. Missing a few days or weeks of school wouldn't impact him too much, but Eli was sure as shit going to phone the head teacher and tell her what the arsehole kids were saying to his nephew.

'Can we go home now?' Asher said.

'Yeah, let's go.' Eli turned the engine back on and put on the heat to clear the windows. 'It'll be okay. Don't worry. We'll figure it out.'

Asher didn't respond.

Not knowing what else to say, Eli put the car into gear and drove home, his hands gripping the wheel so tightly that his knuckles turned ghost white.

GETTING RID OF IT

With Asher in front of the TV, wrapped in a grey fleecy blanket covered in little white Staffies, Eli excused himself under the guise of needing the bathroom. Asher had calmed down, and Specs had taken it upon himself to supervise him. Once in the toilet under the stairs, Eli sat on the closed toilet lid and pulled out his phone. He typed 'Emmanuel Stark' into Google. The first link was for Emmanuel's website. The following were links to Facebook pages, Instagram and TikTok accounts, and every other social media platform you could think of that gave the user the ability to post or share a video. Eli scrolled. Some of the links had captions.

'PROOF OF GHOSTS!'

'Demonic possession video REAL!'

'BOY GETS POSSESSED BY DEMON - VIDEO EVIDENCE!'

'Shit,' Eli said.

He gritted his teeth and clicked on the link to Emmanuel's website. The banner at the top of the webpage read: *'LATEST BLOG POST: PROOF OF THE SUPERNATURAL.'*

'You bastard,' Eli snarled.

The banner took Eli to the blog post. The title, written in bold, said, *BOY POSSESSED BY DEMON: PROOF OF THE SUPERNATURAL.'* Below the title, was an embedded YouTube video. The freeze frame was of Asher, hanging in mid-air, his arms bent at odd angles, broken and grotesque. Bile burned in Eli's throat. He clicked the video, steadying himself for the nightmare he was about to relive.

The first thing he heard was Specs's barking. Loud and panicked. He dove for the volume dial and turned it down. The video was filmed from the kitchen door. Lilith's unsteady hand held her phone, hidden behind the camera. Asher's body rested seven feet above the ground, hanging limp and lifeless. His head fell backwards, chin jutting upwards, mouth opened in a silent scream. Blood ran from the side of his mouth in clumps, knotting his hair, and dripping down his forehead. Eli had his hands wrapped around Asher's wrist.

'Get the other,' he heard himself say.

Felix moved instantly, doing as asked, grasping Asher's other wrist.

'On three,' Eli said. 'One, two, three.' His voice was clear, despite Specs's barking. From the angle Lilith filmed, Specs was visible only when he jumped up, trying to latch on to any part of Asher to pull him down.

Together, Eli and Felix put their entire body weights into trying to pull Asher to the floor.

CRACK. Even through the phone, the noise sent shock waves through Eli. Asher's shoulder blades dislocated before his eyes. His arms lolled too far around his back.

Eli and Felix both staggered back. Neither had realised that Lilith was filming them, not yet.

'Oh my God, oh my God, oh my God.' Felix said the words like a prayer, over and over.

Blood bloomed from Asher's shoulder blades.

'Where's that blood coming from?' Eli said, looking to Felix for an answer. Felix didn't speak. His head was angled upwards, studying his son.

Eli pulled back Asher's t-shirt and blood gushed from within it with enough force to knock him off his feet. Eli slipped on the blood-slicked floor, landing with a bang. He remembered vividly the headache that had pulsed within his skull then. The result of multiple concussions.

Asher's body began to shake. It was barely perceptible at first but then became more vigorous. His scream was fierce. His head snapped backwards at an impossible angle, the back of it pushing against his dislocated shoulders. The scream did not stop. It echoed.

This was when Eli noticed Lilith was recording them.

'What the fuck are you doing?' Eli yelled, rushing toward her to snatch the phone.

'He told me to record it. I told you that,' Lilith said. Her voice shook.

'And you decided that was a good idea?' the Eli from the video yelled. 'Fucking hell, Lilith, this is our family, not something to be studied! What? Do you think this is going to get you taken seriously? *Lilith Lavelle witnessed a real haunting, a real possession, she deserves our respect.* You said it yourself, they all think you're a fraud!'

Eli snatched the phone from her hand and threw it across the room.

The picture blurred as it flew across the room. It bounded off the wall and landed behind the sofa, propped up against the wall. From the angle, you could only see their feet.

When Lilith spoke, the words were unclear. Taking a chance, Eli turned up the volume. Her words were rushed, panicked, making them even more difficult to discern. "This is it… real deal… record it? This could change… history… think of the consequences!'

Eli's feet stepped closer to her. He remembered being so close that his nose was almost touching hers. His words were louder than hers, more frantic. 'You listen to me,' Eli demanded. 'My family will not be the one to prove that this is real. My family will not be the sacrifice.'

'Eli, something's happening.' It was Felix's voice. His feet were in view. They hadn't moved.

Specs's barking kicked up a gear – a heart-breaking fusion of crying and barking.

Although the video didn't show it, Eli remembered Asher's body writhing. The SNAPPING noise forced tears to form behind his eyes. He said a silent prayer that the video didn't show Asher's arms snapping at the elbows until his forearms fell at 90 degrees. Asher's wrists had been next.

SNAP.

Then each of his fingers had been pushed back by an invisible force towards the top of his hands. The memory of blood running from Asher's eyes while his body was being broken felt like a truck slamming into him.

Eli gripped his phone tighter as he watched, his plastic case slicing his fingers.

'Where is the blood coming from?' Felix asked again, sobbing.

'Asher, Asher,' Felix said. 'If you can hear me, I'm here. I'm here. We'll figure this out. We will.'

'What the fuck do you want?' Lilith screamed. 'What do you want from us?' Her voice was drowned out by Specs's desperate barks.

'Daddy,' Asher's voice said.

Specs was silenced.

And then Asher spoke again, 'Don't worry, Kitty. It's not over just yet. I want to savour this feeling.'

Asher's body dropped like a stone, landed in a crumpled pile on the floor, and fell into the camera's shot. Felix and Eli dropped to their knees, their hands exploring his body, checking for damage. Eli could remember the relief he'd felt, knowing that Asher's body was whole. There were no breaks. No cuts. It was like nothing had happened to him.

'This is your fault, Daddy. Mummy said it was all your fault.' Asher's words were painfully clear.

'Mummy said that?' Felix said. His hands were clasped tightly on either side of Asher's face.

'Yeah. She's always telling me that. She said that you're trying to kill me, and if you loved me, you wouldn't have told Lilith to come and bring a demon with her. She says she's going to take me with her, but I don't want to go. I don't want to die. I want to stay with you.' Asher stopped speaking and pulled in a deep breath. Eli couldn't see his face in the video. He had knelt in the way. He knew what words were coming next and braced against them. 'She's going to make you watch her kill me.'

'Hey, Asher, no. Your mum isn't here. And, if she was, she wouldn't say things like that. She loved us both. She knew how much I love you. She would never hurt you, and neither would I,' Felix promised.

'No, she said that you failed us. You failed her, and now she won't stop crying.'

'You can hear her now?' Lilith asked off camera.

'You can't hear her?' Asher's voice shook.

'I can't hear her, Ash,' Eli said, warily.

'I don't think any of us can,' Lilith said, stepping into view. Her once white Converse were now a dirty brown.

'Wait,' Asher said. 'She's not crying. She's laughing. Why is she laughing?'

'It isn't your mum, Ash,' Eli said. 'You have to know that. Whatever this thing is, it isn't your mum.'

Felix pulled Asher against him, hugging him tightly.

Specs padded to Eli. 'It's okay Specs. It's okay. Shhh, it's okay,' he said into Specs's neck.

'I'm sorry,' Lilith said.

'You're what?' Eli snapped.

'I'm sorry. I didn't mean to. I didn't know it would. It shouldn't have been like this. I didn't believe it was real. I didn't. I promise.'

Eli didn't answer her. He wished he had. He wished he hadn't been so cruel to her.

'Has it stopped? Do you think it's over for now?' Felix asked.

The video turned to black as Lilith picked her phone up. There was a brief flash of her face, mascara running down her pale cheeks, and then she stopped the recording.

Eli stayed where he was.

Most of Asher's friends had seen the video. Most of the school had if Asher hadn't been over-exaggerating. What did that mean for them? What would happen next?

Clicking out of the video, Eli read the blog post.

The events in the video above took place on July 28th, 2024, in Yorkshire, England. It features the Eastwood family. Father, Felix. Son, Asher. Uncle, Eli. Dog, Specs. And Lilith Lavelle, self-labelled psychic who offers 'cleansing' services to those experiencing supernatural events. Felix Eastwood invited her into his home with the intention of proving her to be a fraud. It seems that in doing so, he inadvertently welcomed a demon into his home. For those of you who are new to my blog, the current prevalent theory is that demons are evil spirits. The theory is that most spirits pass on to the next life shortly after death. Some stay around for a while but then move on. Some spirits are evil: those of people who have done terrible things. These spirits become demons, or evil spirits. If they choose not to move on to the next plane of existence, they become stronger and stronger, and become less spirit-like. They lose the last of whatever humanity they have and become demons. Many continue to commit the hateful acts they did when they were alive. They are not ghosts. We theorise that ghosts are left-over energy and are not sentient. These beings ARE SENTIENT.

Lilith reached out to me via social media to ask for advice. She informed me that she had witnessed some supernatural activity in the home and that she suspected it was being caused by a demon. Could I give advice on how to 'get rid of it'? I told her that if it was, in fact, a demon, then the demon would possess somebody before long because that's what demons do. They crave a physical body to enact their evil deeds. This was before the child was held in the air and tortured, of course. I advised that, despite there being no concrete proof of what to do in order to combat a demon, the current theory was that exorcisms work, but only if those involved subscribe to a religious theology that aligns with exorcism. The alternative would be to wait for the demon to possess one of them, and then kill the vessel, thus killing the demon. We have various records and accounts supporting this theory. I requested that she record anything they attempted as it would be invaluable to my research. What we see in the video is the first irrefutable evidence of demonic possession.

Sadly, Felix Eastwood died on this night. The exact circumstances surrounding his death are uncertain. Lilith Lavelle was arrested and charged with murder. She is currently awaiting trial. It is my opinion that Lilith Lavelle did what I suggested. She killed the host, therefore killing the demon. Felix Eastwood was not mentally ill, as it has been suggested by his family; he was possessed by a demon. I have reached out on numerous occasions asking to speak with Elijah Eastwood regarding his brother's death and the events of that night, and he has refused to speak to me. Elijah has information that could prove crucial to our understanding of the universe. Lilith Lavelle has also refused to speak with me. They left me with no choice but to release this blog post, and the video, without their contribution. It is a great shame that this couldn't be a collaborative process, given their unique insight into the phenomenon.

What I share with you is life-shattering. It alters our understanding of the universe more than any previous discovery. This is proof of the supernatural, of forces beyond our previous understanding and, dare I say, proof of life after death.

Emmanuel then went on to give a timestamped account of the video he'd uploaded. The words read with detached indifference.

The blog post had been uploaded last night. It had taken just over twelve hours for the video to circulate enough that the majority of Asher's school had seen it. The magnitude of that began to dawn on Eli. The majority of Asher's school had seen him floating in mid-air. Had seen his dad and uncle trying to pull him down from the ceiling. Had seen blood pour from his body. Had seen one of the most painful and private moments of their lives.

'Fuck this.' Eli clicked on Emmanuel's last email and then tapped the phone number included in the signature. Asher would hear him if he called Emmanuel from the downstairs toilet. In a weak attempt to cover his tracks, he flushed the toilet and called to Asher, 'I'm going outside.'

Asher mumbled an acknowledgement.

Once outside, with the back door shut firmly behind him, he called Emmanuel's phone number.

A voice answered after two rings. 'Doctor Emmanuel Stark.'

'What the fuck did you do?' Eli growled, unable to control himself.

'Elijah?' Emmanuel asked.

'Yes, of course it is. I've just had to pick my grieving nephew up from school because every single kid has seen the video you put on the fucking internet.'

'I'm sorry that uploading the video impacted Asher. That was not my intention.' Emmanuel's voice was frustratingly calm.

'Your intention? What was your intention? The kid lost his dad, and now a video of him being strung from the ceiling by a demon is on the internet.' Eli pinched his thigh with his free hand to give him something to focus his anger on.

'I gave you plenty of opportunity to-'

'Don't you dare blame me for this. I told you that my family wanted nothing to do with you. You had no right to upload that video.'

'I had every right.'

Emmanuel's calm tone sent shock waves of rage through Eli. 'No, you didn't. You've ruined a kid's life. How do you think he's going to go back to school now? How is he going to live a normal life with that following him around? Don't you think he's been through enough?'

'This is much bigger than one child. I don't think you're quite grasping the magnitude of-'

'Take the video down,' Eli demanded.

'I can't do that. The video forms a fundamental aspect of my research into the field of demonology; this is the biggest thing to happen in parapsychology since its conception.'

'You're willing to ruin our lives for your big break?'

'Quite frankly, yes, I am. This isn't about you. It is about what the video proves. I would love for you and Asher to be part of this, rather than a hindrance. Your insight would be invaluable. I'm in the UK now. Sheffield, actually, so not far from you. I would love to meet up so we can-'

'If you ever come within ten feet of Asher I will kill you,' Eli threatened. He'd never said such a thing in his life. He was taken aback by the fact that he meant it. He would kill Emmanuel Stark if given half a chance.

'Think on it. Not on murdering me, obviously, don't think on that too hard. Think about what I'm offering you. I'm offering you the chance to be part of history. Your names and faces are out there now. You may as well make the best of a bad situation, don't you think?'

'Never contact me again. I'll be speaking with my lawyer and the police. The video you released is tied to a murder investigation.'

'The video I released proves that you were less than honest with the police. The outcome of Lilith's trial doesn't concern you. The repercussions for *you* are what concerns you. That being said, if you can get Lilith on board too, maybe we can all work together to assuage her guilt. The case would be unprecedented. I'm going to make an assumption that Felix was possessed when Lilith killed him. If that doesn't prove self-defence, I don't know what does.'

Eli's breath hitched in his throat. 'You don't know,' Eli said, blinking against the weight of understanding.

'Know what?' Emmanuel asked, a tone of exasperation in his voice.

'Lilith is dead. There'll be no fucking trial.'

'What are you talking about?' Emmanuel's voice was low, uncertain.

'She hanged herself in her cell.'

'That can't be true,' Emmanuel said.

'Take the video down, Emmanuel. This is your last warning. And leave me and my family alone. We want nothing to do with you and your research.' Eli ended the call and stared at the phone. He didn't feel any sense of relief after talking to Emmanuel.

'Who was that?' Asher said.

Eli closed his eyes and sighed. He'd been caught in the act.

'Emmanuel Stark,' he said, turning to look at Asher.

Understanding moved across Asher's features. 'Thank you.'

AND SO IT BEGINS

Asher watched the video for the fifth time in a row. He sat under the quilt of his single bed, his hands like a vice grip around his tablet. With the light off, his room was a tomb. He wasn't sure how he was supposed to feel about the video. It was the last video of his dad that existed. It looked fake. If Asher had seen the video online, he'd have laughed and scrolled on. But it had gone viral. It was, quite literally, everywhere. Billions of people had seen it. The comment sections were the worst. Strangers on the internet, safe behind the protection of their screens, ripped them apart. Their *bad acting,* their *bad special effects,* the *animal abuse* for causing so much upset to the dog *('Somebody should take the dog away from them. They don't deserve a dog.').* One commenter said that the video was a *'shite version of Blair Witch'.* These comments weren't as bad as the ones from people who believed the video was real. Those comments were feral.

'Kill the host, kill the demon. Somebody should have put a bullet through the kid's brains!'

'I wonder what kind of satanic shit the family were into if this happened!'

'If they'd only welcomed Jesus into their hearts, none of this would have happened.'

'Your sins always catch up with you, eventually.'

'The unclean of spirit always get what they deserve.'

'What an ugly child. I hope the demon finished him off, stop him breeding.'

'It's like his family weren't even trying. They clearly don't give a shit about him.'

'He should have drowned on that blood. Done the world a favour.'

Uncle Eli didn't know Asher had social media. But he was nearly thirteen and all his friends did. He had it under a fake name and birthday and had the privacy settings ramped up, so he was already a thousand times better off than other kids his age. He mostly used social media to join Facebook groups about Pokémon, but it meant that he could access pretty much everything social media had to offer.

A few of the comments were different. They were from people wanting more information about the haunting and the aftermath. It had been linked to Lilith Lavelle, *'ACCUSED MURDERER'*, but nobody seemed to know that she was dead yet.

The rabbit hole he'd gone down led him to a YouTube video called *'DEBUNKING THE FLOATING BOY VIDEO.'*

He debated playing the video. He *knew* he shouldn't. He also knew that he *would*. After connecting his headphones, he pressed 'PLAY' on the video. It was by a creator called Debunking the

Dead. Asher hadn't heard of him before, but it didn't seem like a jump to assume that he made a living debunking ghost videos.

A guy with long black hair filled the screen. Behind him was a bookcase filled with horror DVDs.

'Hello and welcome back to Debunking the Dead. If you're new here, hi, I'm Alexander Deadovich and I am a special effects artist. I debunk videos of *paranormal activity* caught on camera. Today's episode is a doozy. It comes from across the ocean in the UK. Specifically, Yorkshire.' In his American accent, he said *shire* like it was a Lord of the Rings reference, rather than sh-er, like it should be pronounced. 'The video isn't long. In fact, it's only a few minutes in total, but it is creepy A F. I'll start by saying this: this video is linked to a murder investigation, and that is not something I want to provide commentary on. I will not talk about any ongoing investigations. I'm focusing solely on the floating boy video, as it has come to be known. The video was released a couple of days ago, and it has already gone viral. The question is: is the video real? Is this a genuine haunting caught on camera? Let's watch the video together first.'

Alexander played the video. His face popped up in the corner of the screen in a little square. He squinted at the computer screen in front of him, watching it closely. Asher could imagine his audience leaning into their screens, trying to see every single detail of his suffering up close and personal.

'What do you think? Real or fake?'

He paused for dramatic effect, raising his eyebrows, letting the viewer think about their answer.

'Let's start with the fake blood, shall we?' He zoomed into Asher's face, to the blood pooling out from his mouth. 'You can tell from the viscosity of it that it's corn syrup and red food dye.' He smiled a charismatic smile. It made Asher want to scream. 'You see how it spreads as it pools, real blood doesn't do that. Real blood would clump as it ran…'

Asher clicked off the video. He couldn't take it anymore.

A grunting snore sounded from the bottom of the bed. Specs stretched in his sleep and sighed.

'Dumb dog,' Asher said, leaning over to ruffle Specs's head. The dog blinked at Asher and then rolled onto his back, exposing his tummy.

'You want belly scritches?' Asher placed his tablet down, crawled beside Specs, and did as the dog requested.

'*Ash.*'

Asher sat up straight. Specs's ears pricked to attention, and he rolled back to his feet. The fur on his back stood on end. He'd heard the voice too.

Asher sat still, listening as hard as he could, straining to hear. Sliding back into bed, he pulled the covers up to his chin. Specs remained at the foot of the bed, standing guard. His ears twitched, trying to catch the source of the sound.

'I'm hearing things,' Asher whispered to Specs.

Specs didn't move from his spot.

Asher didn't want to admit to himself whose voice he'd heard. His therapist had told him that people who were grieving often saw their loved ones in crowds or heard their voices randomly. The thing was that Asher knew that there was life after death. Hearing his dad's voice meant there was a chance it really was his spirit.

'Dad, are you here?' Asher whispered.

There was a sound of something small and light falling from his chest of drawers and hitting the floor. He didn't want to take his arms out of the covers. As silly as he knew it was, it would leave him vulnerable. Vulnerable to what? He didn't want to think about that.

After steeling himself, he flung his hand out of the covers as quickly as he could and tapped the lamp on his bedside table. Light flooded the room. He blinked against it.

As his vision righted itself, Asher looked at the floor under the dresser. There, on the rug, was the *Goosebumps* book he'd been reading with his dad. He hadn't been able to face reading any more of it since his dad had died, and so it had sat on top of the chest of drawers for months. Unread, last dog-eared by his dad. A timestamp of his life before.

'Was that you, Dad?'

The lamp flared, burning bright, and then popped. The room plunged into darkness.

Asher screamed. Specs's panicked barks snapped through the air.

Eli was there in seconds, bursting into the room.

He turned on the light switch and looked frantically around the room. 'What is it?' he asked. He was beside Asher before the kid had even registered he was there. 'What happened?'

Asher was sitting up in bed, folded over his knees.

'What's wrong, Ash?' Eli placed one hand on Asher's knee and the other on his shoulder. Asher peered up at him with wide eyes.

'The bulb in the lamp broke. I'm sorry,' he said.

'It's okay. It scared you?' Eli asked, trying to make sense of the scream.

'Yeah. It made me jump.' Asher's breathing was calming. His chest stilling.

'You're okay. These things happen. What were you doing up?'

'Couldn't sleep,' Asher said. 'I was watching YouTube videos on my tablet.'

Asher had been watching the same videos Eli had, he assumed. The ones where greasy-haired teenagers said that the video Emmanuel posted was fake and gave a million stupid reasons why.

'Come on, let's go get a biscuit and a glass of milk. Nanna always said that helps when you can't sleep.' As a kid, Eli had been a terrible sleeper. Some of his favourite memories of his mum were of them sitting at the kitchen table at two in the morning eating a digestive biscuit and drinking a glass of milk. It was the only time he'd had her full, undivided attention. With only a year between Eli and Felix, they'd spent their entire lives together, people often mistaking them for twins, despite the fact that they looked completely different. Eli was blonde-haired and blue-eyed. Felix had been dark-haired and brown-eyed, a grown-up, slightly paler version of Asher. But on those nights, the nights when he couldn't drift off, he got his mum all to himself and he loved that. It was their time. He couldn't see the dead like Felix. He didn't have that in common with their mum. What he shared with his mum, was insomnia.

Asher padded along behind Eli, Specs trailing in their wake. Asher sat at the table while Eli poured two glasses of milk and grabbed the packet of biscuits from the cupboard.

'Nanna used to do this for me when I was little,' Eli said. 'It works. I don't know why, but it does. Tomorrow's a new day, Ash. We'll get through this together. You, me, and Specs. I promise you.'

Asher nodded, dunking his biscuit into his milk and then slotting it into his mouth.

Eli couldn't promise that everything would be okay, but he could promise that they would get through it. They had to. His one job was to keep Asher safe, and he intended to do everything in his power to make sure he did that.

'I think I heard Dad,' Asher said, after swallowing his first biscuit.

'Yeah?' Eli replied, not wanting to push too hard.

'Yeah. He said my name. I think that means he's okay.' Asher picked up another biscuit.

'I think so too,' Eli said. He wanted to believe that Felix was there. He knew that if Felix could be there, he would be. He also knew that the afterlife wasn't as simple as his mum and Felix had originally convinced him it was. They always said that spirits hung around for a brief period of time and then passed over. *Yeah right.*

A long silence followed Eli's words. He kept waiting for Asher to fill it. Talking about what was bothering you helped; why else would the prevalence of private therapists and counsellors have sky-rocketed in recent years? Asher used to be the kid who would never shut up around those he was comfortable with. Eli missed that version of him.

'Do you want to talk about what's keeping you up?' Eli asked after he was unable to take the silence any longer. Felix was the one who was comfortable with silence. For Eli, it ate at him until he eventually filled the gaping void with a mess of pointless empty words.

Asher shook his head.

'What about if we had a sleepover downstairs? We could get the blow-up mattresses out and have the TV on?' Eli was desperate, grasping at straws. He didn't expect Asher to take him up on the offer.

'Okay,' he said. His voice was childlike. Something had really done a number on him.

'You go and put a film on. I'll get the mattresses.' Eli went to find the blow-up mattresses that lived in the cupboard under the stairs. They were the fancy self-inflating kind. Felix had bought them when Asher had shown a significant, but short-lived, interest in camping. Eli laid them out in the living room, pushing the coffee table to one side to make space. Butting the two single mattresses up against the sofa, he made the executive decision not to bother with proper bedding. Throw blankets and sofa cushions would do just fine for one night.

The second Eli placed the blankets on the mattresses, Specs climbed aboard, sighing deeply and settling his head between his paws. Asher scrolled through the film options on the TV, completely absorbed with the task. He finally decided on *Hotel Transylvania* and then hopped onto the mattress Specs had chosen.

Eli sat on the other, propping his back against the sofa so that he was upright.

Neither of them spoke.

Eli opened his mouth to speak a few times, but swallowed the words back in. He remembered the wise words his mum had said to Felix after Jenna (his wife, and Asher's mum) had died, and Felix had spiralled about whether he was good enough to be a single father. *All children want to know is that you're there for them. Just show up, and they'll be fine.* Eli was showing up. He might not be able to guarantee that he was doing the right thing - navigating his own grief alongside his nephew's felt like an impossible task - but he was damn well showing up.

Halfway through the film, Asher slumped down, and his breathing slowed. Eli studied his nephew. He would be thirteen in a couple of weeks. A fully fledged teenager. Asleep, he looked so young, so innocent. Sleep wiped away all evidence that this was a boy who had lived through true horror; a boy who was dealing with the loss of his parents; a boy who had faced evil that most human beings would never believe existed.

Eli laid his head down on the sofa cushion, pulled the throw up to his neck, and tried to sleep. He stayed that way until the sun began to rise.

VIRAL

The emails started coming later that day. Eli's real name had been included in Emmanuel Stark's blog post. It didn't take a genius to do a Google search for it and link it to Elijah Eastwood Graphic Design. As a freelancer, he had to have his contact information online. It was the only way to get new clients. His website, which was expertly made, if he said so himself, led the vultures straight to him. They came in swarms, each one a variant of...

Dear Mr Eastwood,

I am writing regarding the video Emmanuel Stark shared online featuring you and your family. As a [true crime podcaster/ researcher/ doctoral student/ Redditor/ blogger] I would love to speak to you about the subject in more detail.

They all ended with the afterthought of apologising for the loss of his brother.

I was sorry to hear of your brother's passing.

And then the promise that from his death something good could come.

I believe we could learn something from the incident, and that it could have significant [academic/psychological/ethical/theological] implications which would impact generations to come and greatly improve our understanding of the universe.

They continued throughout the day. Eli had decided to leave Asher to his own devices. He'd barely moved from his spot on the blow-up bed in front of the TV, only getting up to go to the bathroom or get a snack. Eli holed himself up at the kitchen table under the guise that he was working. Instead, he was scrolling through webpage after webpage, social media account after social media account. The video had officially gone viral. It was everywhere. The straw that broke the camel's back came in the form of a follow-up blog post from Emmanuel Stark.

Thank you all for your wonderful outpouring of support since the release of the video yesterday. This is a career-altering, nay, life-altering, discovery, one which I would not have been privy to without Lilith Lavelle reaching out to me for support during this episode. Lilith Lavelle was, as you are aware, in the thick of it. She witnessed the event firsthand. Lilith Lavelle was not an academic. She was not a paranormal researcher with any credibility. In fact, I have it on good authority that she was not a believer. Lilith Lavelle was a charlatan. She offered 'psychic cleansing services' to the grieving, the ill, and the desperate. I am not sharing this information to discredit her further.

I share this with the aim that you understand that Lilith was not equipped to deal with the paranormal phenomenon as it arose, much less a demon. My understanding of a demon, and this is purely circumstantial, is that a demon is a spirit that never moved on. The spirit must be incredibly old and powerful to inflict such harm. As you know, the Eastwood family has not been forthcoming regarding the events of that night, but I believe they have further information regarding the name of the demon, and how they banished it. It is in the interest of humanity that I have access to this information in order to expand our understanding of life after death.

I must end this blog post with some sad news. Lilith Lavelle passed away on Friday 17th January in New Manor Women's Prison, where she was awaiting trial for the murder of Felix Eastwood. It is my great suspicion, and I believe there is significant evidence to support this claim, that Lilith murdered Felix Eastwood in order to murder the demon possessing him. You've all heard the phrase, 'Kill the host, kill the demon.' Had this gone to court, and had this been proven, this would have had an unprecedented impact on the judicial system. Many of you will be aware of The Devil on Trial/The Devil Made Me Do It, *which refers to the real-life trial of Arne Cheyenne Johnson, who was charged (and later found guilty of) the murder of Alan Bono in 1981. The case was made famous by none other than problematic demonologists Ed and Lorraine Warren (who went mainstream in recent years as a result of* The Conjuring *film franchise). While I am unable to comment on the guilt of Johnson and the details of that murder, I can say with absolute certainty that I could have proven to a judge that Felix Eastwood was possessed, and that Lilith Lavelle murdered him in order to kill the demon possessing his body. If anybody has a relationship with the Eastwood family* *and could possibly convince them to speak with me, that would be very much appreciated. Thank you.*

You can catch me on The Brunch Club *tomorrow at 10 am.*

He was going on daytime TV. The bastard was going on daytime TV.

Eli ignored every single email that went his way.

His phone rang. He looked at the caller ID. Craig.

He declined the call.

The text came through almost immediately.

'I need to talk to you now. This is urgent.'

The phone rang again. This time, Eli answered the call. 'Hi,' he said.

'Who the hell is Emmanuel Stark? What's going on with that video?'

'I don't even know where to start,' Eli said honestly.

'People are messaging me asking about it.'

'Who?' There was no reason for people to be messaging Craig. They were never *together.*

'Friends, for one. Friends that I told we were dating. And I'm getting emails and DMs from strangers asking for your phone number, your address. What the hell is going on, Eli?'

'You wouldn't believe me even if I told you,' Eli said.

'Try me.' There was a command to Craig's voice that Eli hadn't heard before.

'Fine,' Eli said. 'But if you think I'm crazy, that's on you.'

'I won't think you're crazy,' Craig answered. His voice softened. Eli wasn't sure Craig could promise that.

Eli gave him the whistle-stop tour of everything, Nicolas Damont and all.

'Well, shit,' Craig breathed after Eli had finished.

'So, on a scale from one to ten, how crazy do you think I am?' Eli tried to keep his voice light.

'I don't know how to answer that,' Craig said. His words were stilted.

'Do you believe me?' Eli asked, scared to know the answer.

'I don't know.' The clipped tone of his voice told Eli that he *did* know.

Eli pursed his lips. As disappointing as it was, it was a fair enough response.

'Just, don't give anybody my information and ignore the emails. I'm sorry this is impacting you, it's not fair.'

'Eli, I told you I was in this with you, that I was there for you if you needed. I wanted it to impact me. I wouldn't mind if it impacted me more, at least I would be involved.' He stopped, and his voice lowered, 'At least I'd be able to see you.'

'Craig, I…' Eli felt like a weight had been dropped on his chest.

'It's okay. I know that's not what you want. I just thought…' He laughed. It sounded sad. 'I just thought that we were heading somewhere.'

'I'm sorry,' Eli said, offering no explanation.

'I know you are,' he said. 'Me too. Just, stay safe, okay? Look after yourself. If you want me, you know where I am.'

If you want me…

'Thank you, Craig.'

Eli hung up the phone and stared at it. He wanted so badly to throw it against the wall. It wasn't all that long ago that he'd thought there was a chance that Craig could have been his future. Now, he couldn't even contemplate the idea of romance.

The deluge of comments on his social media followed the unsolicited emails. He'd, stupidly, thought that his social media (which was under a random username) wouldn't be found. He didn't use Facebook, only Instagram. He liked posting photos, not essays. The comments ranged from: *'Please message me.'* To, *'You fucking monster. Why would you fake such a thing? And putting a child in the video. Sick! You should kill yourself.'*

He shut it down immediately, making it private, but a barrage of commenters had already found their way there. The damage had been done.

He didn't see Asher looking over his shoulder until he spoke.

'Why do people hate us?' he said.

'They don't hate us,' Eli lied.

Asher widened his eyes and didn't bother rebutting his words. They both knew it was a lie.

'People are scared of what they don't understand,' Eli said. 'People have really strong feelings about life and death and if somebody disagrees with them, then they respond with hate.'

'I don't get why people are like that,' Asher said, his brow furrowing. 'I would never say something like that to somebody I didn't know.'

'That's because you're a good person, Ash.'

'Why are they saying this to us and not to Emmanuel? He posted the video.'

'It's *our* faces. They think that we're the ones who faked it, and that Emmanuel is just stupid enough to fall for it. It doesn't help that my job makes people think I'm capable of doing the special effects.' A few of the comments, and commentary videos, had not so subtly alluded to Eli's job as a graphic designer.

Asher nodded, accepting Eli's explanation.

Eli's phone rang. Asher looked at the screen. It said a number that Eli didn't recognise.

'Are you going to answer that? What if it's the prison or something, about Lilith?' There was resignation in Asher's voice.

'You're right,' Eli said. He'd had no intention of answering until Asher had spoken. He was the adult in the situation, he reminded himself. He had to behave like one. He answered the call and said, 'Hello.'

'Is that Eli Eastwood?' a male voice said.

'Who's speaking please?' Eli said.

'My name is Joe Russell.' He waited, as though Eli should know the name. 'I'm a paranormal investigator in the UK. I write books about paranormal incidents, and I have a YouTube-'

'I'm not interested,' Eli said. 'How did you get my number?'

'I have a really good research assistant,' Joe said.

'Please don't contact me again.'

'I think we could come to a mutually beneficial agreement. Now is the time to capitalise on it. I get the impression you don't want to work with Emmanuel Stark, and I don't blame you, the guy is… Anyway, I want to help you. My last book ranked in the top twenty of the New York Times Bestsellers List. You could make a lot of money from this.'

'No, thank you. Asher and I want to forget this ever happened. I lost my brother. Asher lost his father, don't you people understand that? This isn't a money-making scheme. We don't want to profit off death. Never contact me again.'

'Eli-' Joe protested as Eli ended the call.

Asher looked at Eli, trying to gauge what he was thinking. Eli felt like he was about to explode. The pressure in his chest built to dangerous heights. He felt a panic attack building inside him. He couldn't let Asher see.

'It's okay,' Asher said. 'Take a deep breath in, and a really slow breath out.'

Eli looked at Asher. He could feel tears building behind his eyes. His twelve-year-old nephew was attempting to talk him down from a panic attack. It wasn't the way it should be. The dynamic was reversed. How was that fair on him? The panic continued to rise. His heart rate soared. He could feel his pulse pounding against his temples.

'Name something blue that you can see,' Asher said.

Eli searched the room. 'The mug,' he managed to squeeze through his tight throat.

'Something red?' Asher said.

'The kettle,' Eli said.

'Green?' That was harder. Eli had to search for a while. Eventually, he noticed a green magnet on the fridge. He told Asher what he saw. His chest felt like it was releasing enough that he could grab hold of his thoughts and bring himself back down. Deep breath in. One. Two. Three. Four. Five. Hold it. One. Two. Three. Four. Five. Breath out. One. Two. Three. Four. Five. Six. Seven. Eight. Nine. Ten.

Rinse and repeat.

'You had a panic attack,' Asher spoke after a few minutes. It wasn't a question.

'I did,' Eli said.

'I didn't know you had panic attacks.'

'They're new.'

'Since Dad died?' Asher asked.

'Yeah.'

'Why didn't you tell me?' Asher asked. He took a seat next to Eli.

'Because it's my job to look after you,' Eli said. 'I didn't want you to think I couldn't look after you. I didn't want you to think that I was weak.'

'It doesn't make you weak. Simone told me that people with anxiety are the strongest people in the world because they have to fight every single day for things that other people do without thinking.' Asher paused and then added, 'Was it the phone call that triggered it?'

'Yeah.' It was a half-truth. In reality, Eli was worried that this was just the start of it. A random guy had his phone number now, a number that he only gave to friends and clients. What if the number got leaked? What if people hounded them for weeks and months? What if the video never died down? He'd never before given any thought to the participants in viral videos. What happened to them after their videos were seen by the whole world?

THEY'RE COMING FOR YOU

Emmanuel's annoyingly perfect face was everywhere Eli looked. His grey hair was styled long on top, pushed back from his face. He wore wire-framed glasses, perched on his nose. Everywhere Eli saw him, Emmanuel wore an immaculately pressed suit. Here, Eli's life was falling apart. Out there, Emmanuel was living the high life. He'd somehow got himself invited onto every news outlet to discuss the implications of the video. He also seemed to be doing a tour of podcasters and YouTubers, where he answered the same questions and said the same things. He emphasised how significant the video was in terms of proving both demons and spirits existed, and also that there was, therefore, an afterlife. Every single religious organisation with a social media platform (a surprising number of them) wrote him off as a fraud. Yes, the afterlife did exist, they said, but the video was fake. The Church of England's official spokesperson said to believe the video was real was blasphemous. All throughout history, demons had plagued humanity and only the Church's top demonologists (because they were still a thing in modern society, apparently) could banish them. Killing the host, the Church said, should never be attempted and was false information. *Killing the host did not kill the demon and was still murder…* they said.

Eli was almost certain that Asher was consuming the content Emmanuel was putting out there, but neither of them mentioned it. It was like they'd taken a silent vow to protect the other. Eli's work email had exploded. It was getting nearly impossible to sift through the emails to find genuine potential new clients. Emmanuel's name popped up now and again, but Eli didn't bother to open his emails. He wasn't interested in anything that Emmanuel could possibly say to him.

It was getting late in the day and Asher hadn't moved off of the blow-up bed. Specs was growing restless.

'We're going for a walk,' Eli said, leaving no room for objections.

Asher looked up from his spot with an expression that read *'Seriously?'*

'Put some joggers on and grab your coat,' Eli said. 'Specs, do you want to go on a walk?'

Specs ran to where his lead was stored in the hallway cupboard and sat patiently, his tail thumping the ground at steady intervals.

'Good lad,' Eli said. He clipped Specs's lead to his collar and slipped his own shoes on. He freed his and Asher's coats from their hooks, putting his own on and holding Asher's out ready for him to grab it on his way past.

Asher walked down the stairs a second later, jogging bottoms on, and trainers on his feet. He took the black puffy coat from Eli. 'Where are we going?'

'Let's go to the park, eh? It should be fairly empty right now so we can let Specs have a good run around. Grab his ball.'

The park was just around the corner from the house. Specs happily trotted beside them the whole way, making the lead seem redundant. The smell of wet leaves filled the crisp air. Eli stuffed his hands in his pockets, breathing out white puffs of air. They walked in silence, the cold pinking Asher's cheeks, giving him a healthy look.

When they reached the park, Asher unclipped Specs. The dog sat at Asher's feet and stared at the ball in his hand. The park was mostly wide-open space, full of sludgy grass. Asher and Specs settled into a rhythm of playing fetch. Each time, Specs ran back over with the ball proudly held in his mouth, before dropping it dutifully at Asher's feet.

'Eli?'

Eli turned to look in the direction of the unfamiliar voice. A man with greying hair and stubble looked back at him, crooked grin on his face.

'What a coincidence,' the man said. Eli was sure he'd never seen him before. Eli turned his gaze to Asher and Specs, a feeling of dread pooling in his stomach. They were still playing as normal; neither had noticed the man.

'Do I know you?' Eli said. An instinct that he didn't know he possessed told him to remove his hands from his pockets.

'No, but I've been trying to track you down. You haven't answered any of my emails.'

'I've been getting a lot of unsolicited emails,' Eli said. His words were clipped. Cold.

'My name is George Smith. I work for *The Mirror.*'

Eli didn't answer. He was trying to reconcile the fact that a reporter had actually tracked him down near his own home.

'I was actually just heading to your house when I saw you walking.'

'You were going to my house?' Eli's face felt both too warm and too cold.

'I was. I wanted to talk to you, and you weren't responding to my emails.'

'So, you thought it was okay to show up at my house?' Eli couldn't keep the tremor of anger from his voice.

'You weren't answering my messages,' George said, like it was a valid reason to show up at a stranger's house.

'How did you get my address?' he asked.

'I'm a journalist,' he said.

'That didn't answer my question.' Eli balled his hands into fists.

'I was able to access the police reports regarding your brother's murder. I didn't know for sure that you lived there, but I hoped to at least find a forwarding address.' He didn't even have the decency to look apologetic.

'You had no right to do that. You can't just show up at somebody's house…'

'You can. There's no law against it. Look, I'll level with you, I've been given the authority to pay you a large sum of money to speak with me. We can talk figures now if you want or-'

'Get the fuck away from me.'

Specs's growl grew louder as the dog approached. He put himself between Eli and George, hackles raised, a snarl leaking from his teeth.

George held up his hands in a signal of surrender.

'I was just doing my job. I haven't done anything wrong. There's no need for that.' He looked down at Specs with a face full of hatred.

'Leave me and my family alone before I call the police.'

'And tell them what?'

'That I'm being harassed, and stalked, and that a journalist from a bigoted newspaper somehow managed to find my address using systems I'm pretty certain he had no authority to use. That could get you fired, couldn't it? Addresses, particularly where minors are concerned, would not be in the public domain.'

Asher jogged over. 'Who's that?' he said.

'Nobody, Ash. He's nobody,' Eli said.

'Just take my card and if you change your mind-' George said.

'I won't change my mind. Come on, Ash.'

Eli walked away, Ash and Specs following behind him. Out of the corner of his eye, he saw Asher glancing back at George. His skin crawled. He felt violated. George knew where he lived. A journalist from a scum of the earth newspaper knew where he lived.

'Are you okay?' Asher asked.

'Yes, I'm fine.' Eli schooled his face into a mask of indifference. 'I'm okay, buddy.'

'Was that an ex-boyfriend?' Asher said. Ash had never been allowed to meet Eli's boyfriends. There had been nobody serious enough that he wanted his family to meet them.

'No, it was somebody from a newspaper who wanted to know about the video.' Now that they were away from George, Eli felt safe enough to tell Asher the truth. He hadn't wanted to say anything in front of George because he hadn't wanted Asher to get sucked into any questioning.

'Oh,' Asher said, dejected.

They walked to the other side of the park. Specs eyed the ducks with suspicion before deciding they were as harmless as they'd always been and ignored them.

'How did he know where we would be?' Asher asked.

The question felt like a gut punch. Although Asher hadn't said it, and Eli suspected he hadn't meant it, he took the question to mean *'Why aren't you keeping me safe?'*

'Somebody in the police told him.' It hurt Eli's heart to look at Asher.

'Why would they do that?' he asked.

'Because some people will do anything for money,' Eli replied.

'That sucks,' Asher said.

'Yeah, it definitely does,' Eli agreed.

Asher was jolted from sleep by somebody beating their fist against the front door. Half-asleep, he made his way on wobbly legs to the top of the stairs and peered down them. Uncle Eli opened the door.

'Yes?' Uncle Eli said.

Asher squinted against the dark to try and see who was there. It was late. It had to be ten o'clock. It felt like he'd only just fallen asleep when he was woken up. He heard a man's voice but couldn't make out the words.

'Get the fuck off my property,' Uncle Eli demanded.

The man said something else. Asher could just about make out a pale face looming in the doorway.

'Leave. Now!' Uncle Eli's voice was panicked, frantic. It sent shivers up Asher's spine. It had been months since he'd heard his uncle sound like that.

'Be reasonable. We just want to talk to you,' the man said. 'Just a few questions.' The man stuck his neck through the open doorway. 'Ah, Asher is there too. We could have this whole thing over in a few minutes. I have a cheque ready to go.'

Uncle Eli turned to look up the stairs. His eyes were wide with fear. He went to slam the door, but the man stuck his boot-clad foot in the way. 'This is a big story, mate. I want this story. People around the world will read it. You'll be famous for the right reasons. Just think of what you could do with the fame… the money. You don't realise what you're fucking with. It's the story of my career.'

'Move your fucking foot,' Uncle Eli growled.

Specs shot from the bedroom, awoken by the raised voices. He was at the bottom of the stairs in an instant, his barking filling the space.

'Get it the fuck away from me!' Asher could just about make out the man's words above Specs's barks.

Uncle Eli said something, and the man must have removed his foot from the door because it was slammed shut in his face. After locking the door and sliding the chain lock, Uncle Eli rested his back against it.

'Are you okay, Ash?' he asked.

Asher nodded.

'We need to leave,' Uncle Eli said. 'They know where we live.'

'Who's *they?*' Asher asked.

'Everyone. That arsehole found our address online. We're not safe here. We need to go. Just until it all dies down. It has to, eventually. It has to.' Uncle Eli said the last part like he was trying to convince himself, rather than Asher.

'Where are we going to go?' Asher didn't really want to leave his home, but Uncle Eli was right. If their address was online, they weren't safe. His mind flashed with the comments from the YouTube videos. People actually hated them. And people online were terrifying. God only knew what they'd do if they discovered Asher's address, like the journalists had. It couldn't possibly be as bad as what Damont had done, but that didn't mean Asher wanted to live through it.

'I'll figure it out. Let's get some sleep. We'll leave first thing tomorrow.'

Asher watched Uncle Eli check that the door was locked. It was unsettling that his uncle was scared but trying not to show it.

Asher slunk back to bed and listened to the beeps of the burglar alarm that was never used. Tonight was the exception.

He closed his eyes and tried to sleep. All he could see was the fear on Uncle Eli's face. If Uncle Eli was scared, that meant there was a good reason to be scared. He gave up and pulled his dad's Gameboy out of the drawer next to his bed. He pressed the button to turn it on. The backlit screen came to life, casting the room in a blue glow.

The words flashed on the screen. Even before Asher read them, he knew what they'd say. He'd seen them before.

THEY'RE COMING FOR YOU.'

His fingers clamped tightly on the device. That wasn't what it was supposed to say.

'Who is this? Dad?' Asher whispered into the room. The screen went dark.

The screen flashed so brightly that Asher had to brace against it. As the light died away, the words, *THEY'RE ALMOST HERE,'* remained.

A lump the size of a football grew in his throat.

'Who?'

The words vanished. The *Pokémon Crystal* intro video started up as normal. The tinny soundtrack was as familiar as his own heartbeat, but it didn't ease the tension he felt in his muscles. He put the Gameboy down and tried to think back to what Simone had taught him during their therapy sessions. He didn't want to close his eyes. No, that wasn't true, he couldn't bring himself to close his eyes. He felt like he was being watched. Simone always said that you didn't have to close your eyes to meditate, although he usually did. He loved her guided meditations. Not that he'd tell anybody that. Boys at school could be cruel about anything that signalled you were different, and he didn't know many other almost thirteen-year-old boys who meditated. He was sure some of them were in therapy, especially the *bad* kids, but nobody spoke about it.

He stared at the ceiling and tried to relax. He focused on his feet, curling and uncurling his toes, and then slowly began to work his way up his body, clenching and unclenching each muscle in turn. When he'd finished, by scrunching up his face really tightly and then relaxing it, he thought about trying to go to sleep.

He closed his eyes.

The sense that something, *someone*, was in the room with him forced his eyes back open. There was no way he'd be sleeping that night. He decided it was stupid to try. He'd sleep in the car on the way to wherever they were going. Instead, he decided to pack his bags. He didn't know how long they'd be going for, so erred on the side of caution and packed most of his clothes and underwear and his favourite hoodie. The Gameboy stared up at him from the bed, the screen still glowing with invitation.

HOME SWEET HOME

Asher was passed out on his bed when Eli checked on him. He was on his back, arm sprawled across his forehead, hair stuck up in all directions. His face was slack. It was early; still dark. Each movement Eli made felt too loud. He shut the door as quietly as he could. He had a sneaking suspicion that Asher hadn't been able to sleep after what had happened to them the night before. The packed bags in his room confirmed that. Eli certainly hadn't slept. Sleep had come in spasmodic chunks. Padding back to his room, Eli dug his suitcase out of the wardrobe. The last time he'd used it, he'd been moving his clothes into Felix's house six months ago. Those six months felt like a lifetime. After packing a couple of weeks' worth of essentials, he zipped up the suitcase and carried it downstairs.

Coffee. He needed coffee. He clicked the kettle on and waited for it to boil, then spooned instant coffee into a mug.

Last night, while sleep evaded him, he'd found a long-term let Airbnb in the middle of the North Yorkshire Moors that was just about in budget. It would have to do. He'd been lucky to find somewhere that he could afford, and that would allow them to stay for a month. The owner said that she was flexible. She only did long-term lets, usually struggling writers or divorcees looking for space, she'd joked, so if Eli wanted to extend his stay, that likely wouldn't be a problem. The house had everything they'd need, and she would leave them to it. She didn't live anywhere nearby but was reachable by phone if they needed anything.

While waiting for the kettle to boil, Eli turned on the TV in the living room. Emmanuel's voice filled the room. The man was a hack. Smarmy. He wore exactly the kind of outfit you'd expect from somebody masquerading as a serious academic: a brown plaid suit over a white shirt, and small wire glasses perched on his nose. *The Breakfast Show* host, Amanda Every (*every*one's favourite TV host) leaned over the breakfast table as she listened, enraptured, by Emmanuel's story.

'What we have here is actual proof of the supernatural. While we do not yet know exactly what supernatural phenomena is causing the event in the video, we do know that it is something supernatural, and that is a huge step forwards in the field of parapsychology. We suspect, from the evidence we were presented with, that we are looking at a demon.'

Amanda Every gasped.

Eli walked away, leaving Emmanuel spewing his bullshit, to pick up his coffee. He returned to the living room as Emmanuel was saying, 'I suspect that the death of Lilith Lavelle, the primary suspect in the murder of Felix Eastwood, was as the result of this demon, or something related to it. Lilith had no prior history of suicidal tendencies or depression.'

'But surely you have to acknowledge that perhaps the suicidal ideation came from facing the reality of spending the rest of her life in prison?'

'Of course. That is certainly a possibility. However, the manner in which Mr Eastwood died suggests to me that the family suspected he was possessed by a demon and therefore murdered him in an attempt to kill the demon. One possible explanation for Ms Lavelle's death is that the demon did not die as a result of its host being murdered, and therefore there is a strong chance that it exacted revenge upon Ms Lavelle.'

Eli changed the channel. Today would be stressful enough without him self-sabotaging by watching that knobhead rip his family apart on live TV.

The road to the Airbnb could barely be called a road. It was a dirt path at best. It shook the hell out of Eli's old Honda Civic. The house itself didn't quite look like the photographs. The building stood proud atop a field of green heather. The photographs had been taken when the heather was in full bloom and had turned the landscape purple. In January, it was harsh, barren. The building was stone and looked more like a barn than a house. The Airbnb listing said that the barn was recently renovated. The photos of the inside had been modern and sleek.

'Plenty of space for you and Specs to go explore,' Eli said to Asher. 'It said on the listing that there was a natural swimming pool on the land somewhere.'

'I didn't pack my trunks. And it's January,' Asher replied, staring forlornly out of the window.

'We can get you some trunks,' Eli said. 'We're not on house arrest. We can go shopping. We're just staying away from home until everything dies down.' *If it dies down…*

Asher nodded and climbed out of the car, shutting the door behind him.

Eli sighed a bone-weary sigh and tipped his head back against the headrest.

'Did I do the right thing?' Eli said under his breath, knowing that an answer from his mum or brother wouldn't be forthcoming.

'Ready, Specs?' Eli asked the dog in the backseat.

Specs's ears pricked to attention.

'Come on then.' Eli got out of the car, the cold air was relentless. It took his breath away. He opened the back door for Specs and unbuckled the doggy seatbelt that was attached to his harness. Specs hopped out of the car and sniffed the sky before trotting over to Asher, who stood by the door.

'Ash, why don't you take Specs for a quick wander? See if you can get him to go to the toilet?'

'Sure,' Asher grunted.

'Just stay close to the house. We'll explore properly later.'

Ash didn't answer, but Eli knew he'd heard. There was no way he hadn't.

Asher took off at a slow pace, his head swivelling to take in the surroundings. Specs followed dutifully behind.

The air felt different. There was nothing for miles around them other than moorland. It was the last place anybody would have expected them to go. Eli, who preferred city breaks and would never willingly go on holiday to the *countryside*, had ended up in the exact kind of place he usually avoided like the plague. He turned his attention to the key safe, noting the small, lean-to shed propped against the side of the house. It looked older than the old barn, like it shouldn't even be standing.

The owner of the property had sent him the code for the key safe. 6-9-6-9. He chuckled to himself as he spun the numbers, revealing the key hidden inside. After opening the door, his first thought was, *Thank God it looks like the pictures.* It was all blonde wood, white walls, and stainless-steel accents. Open plan. At the centre of the room sat four three-seater sofas in a square around a coffee table. To the right was the kitchen and dining room, through an archway, rather than a door. *Nice.*

It took only three trips to empty the car. They'd packed light. They'd have to do a food shop later on, but that was fine.

Eli threw himself on one of the white linen sofas (which didn't scream *dog friendly*) as Asher trailed inside with Specs.

'You can choose which room you want,' Eli said. 'The bedrooms are upstairs.'

'Thanks,' Asher replied. He was quieter than he had been yesterday. The incident with the reporter(s) had shaken him as much as it had shaken Eli. It was a strange feeling, your privacy being violated like that, a sticky tar-like substance that clung to you and never quite went away.

Asher headed upstairs. Specs followed behind.

Eli had a small list of jobs to do. He had to tell Asher's therapist that their sessions would need to be online for the time being. And then there was Craig. Poor Craig who didn't deserve the way Eli had treated him. Something in Eli's brain nagged at him to make sure that somebody knew where he was, just in case something went wrong. Craig, who always had his phone in-hand, was their best bet, even given the rocky nature of his and Eli's relationship.

Eli typed out a message.

Hi Craig,

Sorry to do this but Asher and I have taken some time away. We had a pretty scary incident last night with a reporter showing up at our door after our address was leaked online. We're both fine, but we've gone away until this whole thing blows over. I just wanted to give you the address so that somebody knows where we are.

Eli typed out the address of the Airbnb and then re-read the message. It sounded dramatic, like a cry for attention. That was the last thing he wanted.

He deleted everything except for the address and started again.

'Hi Craig,

Just wanted to let you know that Asher and I have gone away for a while. We'll be back when this thing with Emmanuel blows over. I just wanted to let somebody know where we are. Hope you're doing well.'

He shook his head and pressed 'SEND' before he could change his mind.

As he pressed 'send', he remembered Mrs Birch. His neighbour from the old house. They still talked from time to time. She came over to visit with Asher and Specs too, every few weeks. He should probably let her know where they were. He sent her a very similar text to the one he'd sent Craig, but explained it as a holiday instead, and made no mention of Emmanuel. She texted back instantly.

Hello Eli,
Thank you for letting me know. Enjoy your holidays, my love.
Love from,
Mrs Birch xoxo

He smiled at her response. On impulse, as the phone was in his hand, he opened up his email. It was flooded with new messages, each with subjects featuring the words 'interview request'. Eli ignored each of them. He'd be speaking to exactly nobody about the video or anything video-adjacent. Asher came down the stairs. The *thump thump thump* of paws told Eli Specs was coming too. He'd always loved the way the ridiculous creature walked down the stairs. He hopped like a barrel with four stubby legs.

'Did you choose one?' Eli asked.

'Can I have the big one? The one with the huge bed and ensuite?' Asher asked, a glint of excitement in his eyes.

'Sure,' Eli said. 'You know Specs will still take up three-quarters of the bed anyway though.'

'Awesome. I'll take my stuff upstairs,' he said.

When Specs realised that Asher was going back upstairs, Specs sighed but followed obediently behind him. For the moment, instead of feeling like a fraud, Eli thought he'd done the right thing.

The feeling of success didn't last long.

His phone buzzed in the pocket of his jeans. He pulled it out and looked at the caller ID. A mobile number. He answered the phone.

'Hello?' he said.

'Is this Elijah Eastwood?' the voice said.

Déjà vu swept over him like a tidal wave.

'Yes,' he said.

'My name is Richie Dobson and I'm with the online newspaper-'

'How did you get my phone number?' Eli interjected. He didn't need to hear the rest of the guy's sentence.

'Oh, erm, I...' Richie Dobson stumbled over his words, trying and failing to pull an answer out of his arse that wouldn't make him sound corrupt.

'Where did you get my number?' Eli said.

'I got it from your website,' Richie hedged. They both knew this was a lie. His phone number wasn't online. New clients had to email him to discuss their projects before he'd give out his phone number. He hated the idea of new (or current) clients being able to call him on a whim at all times of the day, or night.

'It's not on my website.'

Richie sighed, 'I got it from Mr Wilson. You made his website for him... His website was in your portfolio, and I called to ask if he'd recommend you and he gave me your number.'

Eli almost admired that. It was clever. Something he hadn't anticipated.

'Mr Eastwood,' Richie continued, 'I'd love to ask you a few questions about your encounter with the ghost dimension.'

'What the fuck are you talking about?' Eli barked out a laugh. 'My encounter with the ghost dimension? Get over yourself!'

'I'm sorry, I don't understand,' Richie said.

'Clearly,' Eli replied, scoffing as he hung up the phone. 'Fucking Richie.'

The phone rang again almost immediately.

'How the hell do you block a phone number?' Eli said to himself.

'You-' Asher said.

'Jesus Ash! Make a noise or something.' Eli laughed, his heart beating out of his chest.

'I Googled it,' Asher said. He strode over on gangly teenager legs and perched on the back of the sofa. 'It says… Open the Phone app, tap *More*, then *Call History*, select a call from the number you want to block, and tap *Block/Report Spam.*'

'Thanks.' Eli followed the instructions and blocked Richie Dobson. 'You hungry?' Eli asked, turning his head to look at Asher.

'Always,' Asher said.

'McDonald's, and then we can do a food shop? You can wait in the car with Specs while I grab the shopping.'

ONE MISSED CALL

Asher sat in the back seat of Uncle Eli's car. It smelled of McDonald's even with the windows cracked. Although it was January and perfectly safe to leave Specs in the car, Uncle Eli never would. Asher supposed maybe he'd do it if he was just popping into the shop for a couple of things, but he was doing a full food shop and that took time. They'd left in such a rush that they hadn't even picked up toilet rolls, so it really was a big shop that Uncle Eli had to do. Asher didn't mind dog-sitting. The heaters had been left on, so he and Specs were nice and toasty. Specs was asleep with his head on Asher's lap after having eaten a box of chicken nuggets to himself, which he always did, while not once taking his eyes off Asher's burger.

Asher was on his tablet, playing a racing game that he'd downloaded for free. It was one of the only things he could do offline. Most of his friends had phones, but he didn't. If he had a phone, and data, he could play anything. He could go on YouTube or Facebook or play an online game. Now that they were on the run, he assumed that the chances of him getting a phone for his thirteenth birthday, which his dad had promised him, were pretty slim.

At first, he thought the noise was coming from his tablet. He paused the game, but the noise continued. It was Uncle Eli's phone. He'd left it in the cup holders between the front seats of the car, wedged between two McDonald's paper cups.

Asher slid the phone out from its hiding spot and looked at the screen. It was a number that wasn't saved in Uncle Eli's phone. He didn't answer it. He knew he shouldn't. Plus, like Uncle Eli, he hated talking on the phone to strangers. He let the call ring out.

Asher unpaused his game. Before he'd had the chance to make it around the track once, Uncle Eli's phone rang again.

'Oh my God,' Asher said.

He turned the phone to face him. It was a different number.

'This is weird,' Asher said to Specs. 'Should I answer it?'

Specs closed his eyes.

'Helpful, thanks.' Asher bit his lip, staring at the phone. The situation was strange. The phone had rung twice in a few minutes, with two different people calling him. It could be clients, but Asher suspected not. His uncle always told them that he preferred to be contacted by email.

While he was trying to decide what to do, the phone rang off.

'Problem solved,' Asher said to Specs.

He unpaused his game.

Barely a second passed before the phone started ringing again.

It was a different number.

'What's happening, Specs?' Asher had to answer the phone now. He didn't have a choice. What if it was an emergency and somebody was trying to get in touch with Uncle Eli? He wasn't sure why they'd be calling from different phones, but adults did weird shit all the time.

Asher tapped the screen to accept the call and said, 'Hello?'

'Is that Mr Elijah Eastwood?'

'No, it's Asher,' he said, cursing how awkward he was on the phone.

'Oh, lovely. Asher, my name is Cathleen Amstell and I'm a producer at Morning Glory TV. I wanted to speak to your uncle about asking you both to join us on the show.'

'How did you get this number?' Asher asked, remembering how annoyed Uncle Eli had sounded back at the house when somebody he didn't know had called him.

'Oh, erm, well, I'm sorry, I got it from a website,' she said.

'What website?' Asher asked. A producer of a TV talk show should be a confident person, as far as he was concerned. The fact that she'd stumbled over her words didn't fill Asher with confidence.

She exhaled. 'Reddit,' she said. 'I got the number from Reddit.'

Through some kind of divine intervention, Uncle Eli opened the car door. Asher stared back at him, feeling like a deer in the headlights.

'I forgot my phone. I need it to pay,' Uncle Eli said. He noticed the phone held to Asher's ear. 'Who are you talking to?'

'A producer from a TV show. She got your number off Reddit.' The words fell out of Asher's mouth in a jumble. Uncle Eli's face reddened.

'She got my number off Reddit?' He held out his hand to take the phone from Asher. 'This is Eli.' His words could cut glass.

Asher couldn't hear Cathleen's response, but the look on his uncle's face told him everything he needed to know. He was seething. Anger rolled off of him in waves. Uncle Eli was silent, the frown lines on his forehead deepening with each second that passed.

'Don't call this number again.' He hung up and shook his head. Looking to Asher, he said, 'That wanker Richie posted my mobile number online, and apparently our address too.'

Asher had heard about this kind of thing. 'He doxed us.'

'Doxed?'

'Released our info online. I don't know why they call it doxing, but…' Asher shrugged. Doxing could be really bad, but at least they weren't at home anymore so people couldn't just show up like the guy the other night.

'We're safe. Don't-'

Uncle Eli had been about to say 'worry', Asher suspected, but his phone had started ringing again. 'For fuck's sake!' He answered the call. Listened, and then said, 'Yes.' Uncle Eli was quiet for a second again, and then he hung up the phone. His eyes were wide. 'This is unbelievable. What the hell is happening?'

Asher shook his head. He didn't know how to answer that. *What the hell* was *happening to them?* It should all be over. The nightmare was supposed to be done. All he was supposed to be focusing on now was figuring out how to live without his dad, but it just felt like the nightmare was never-ending. It was surreal, though. His dad had died because of a demon. As had his nanna. As had the psychic cleansing charlatan, who happened to actually be a really good person. And, in some weird twist of fate, it had made them famous.

'I'm going to get this shopping,' Uncle Eli said. 'You okay for a few more minutes?'

'Yeah,' Asher said.

As Uncle Eli walked away, Asher heard his phone ring again.

'The world's gone mad, Specs,' Asher said. Specs yawned, as though he was exhausted by the thought of it all. Asher ruffled the space between Specs's ears.

The radio burst to life, so loud that Asher's hands moved to cover his ears instinctually. He grimaced against the noise. They never had the volume so high. He reached out to turn it down, his fingers spinning the knob to the left, but nothing changed. Specs's howl joined the cacophony. Asher turned the dial the other way, and then back on itself again. Nothing changed. He pressed the knob, which should turn the radio off. It didn't. The song changed and morphed into something else. A talk show. Still too loud for

Asher to concentrate on the words. It was garbled, like the radio was stuck between channels and hadn't quite found the station.

The words were distorted. *Ghost-like.* An involuntary shiver passed down Asher's spine.

Frantically trying to turn the radio off, Asher muttered to himself, 'Please, please, please.'

'They're coming for you.' The words felt like a knife grinding against bone. Tears fell down Asher's face.

The radio fell into silence.

Specs whined, crying.

'It's okay, Specs. It'll be okay.' Asher tried to keep the tremor from his voice, wiping his tears away with the back of his hand. 'It'll be okay.'

DROPPED THE BALL

Eli couldn't get a coherent story out of Asher. What he was saying didn't make any sense. The kid was visibly shaking when Eli made it back to the car. From what he could decipher, the radio had turned itself on, really loudly, and Asher hadn't been able to turn it down, or off. And then it had changed stations and had landed on a talk show. Asher had heard the words, *'They're coming for you,'* which had, obviously, shaken him up. They were under a lot of stress. There was no wonder Asher was on edge. Eli didn't know what to do to help. The drive back to their Airbnb was tense. Eli kept trying to distract Asher, but Asher wasn't biting. Eli wanted to cry. He wanted to scream. He wanted to slam his fists against the steering wheel. He was trying his best, but everything he did seemed to thrust him headfirst into another obstacle. It sucked. It fucking sucked.

Asher went straight to his room as soon as they walked in. Specs followed behind him. Eli wasn't sure he'd ever felt quite so alone. The silence was oppressive, deafening. He put Spotify on (choosing an old-school Pop Punk/Punk Rock playlist) and connected his phone to one of the house's many speakers. He attempted to ignore the fourteen missed calls and too many texts to count that filled his notification screen. He'd bought a new phone at the shop after realising his old number was a write-off.

After putting the shopping away in unfamiliar cupboards, Eli went to stand on the back porch. He needed the fresh air to pull him out of the oppressive funk he was in. Needing to get a new phone number, in the grand scheme of things, was a minor inconvenience. He stared out at the moorland surrounding the property. Somewhere out there was a natural swimming pool encompassed in acres and acres of natural landscape. It was beautiful. The icy blue sky stretched forever against the harsh green line of the rugged flat land. He could almost imagine Cathy running in billowing dresses in search of her sullen, handsome Heathcliff. The man she should have married.

Using his current phone (because the prospect of setting up a whole new phone made his skin crawl), he Googled, 'Can you report doxing to the police?' The answer was yes, yes you could. However, reading between the lines, it wouldn't be taken seriously. You could file a report to 101, the non-emergency line. Or to the platform where the doxing took place. Or to Action Fraud. It seemed like unless the doxing led to you being scammed, defrauded, or resulted in a cybercrime, you were screwed. Reporting it wouldn't have satisfied Eli anyway. The sorry excuse for a human being, Richie, would have been the one at the forefront, and he wasn't the one Eli blamed. He blamed Emmanuel. Emmanuel who was thriving off their pain. Emmanuel who had taken a difficult situation and made it impossible. The need to tell that prick exactly what he thought of him was overwhelming. Before he could question the usefulness of what he was about to do, Eli called Emmanuel's number. He answered on the second ring.

'Elijah?'

'It's Eli. Nobody calls me Elijah.' It was instinct to respond in that way.

'Eli. Have you changed your mind? Oh my God, your life will change so much! You wouldn't even believe what my life looks like right now, and you and Asher can have that too.'

'Is that what this was all about for you?' It wasn't the question Eli had been planning on asking. 'Fame? What happened to proving there was life after death? What happened to your journal articles and your professional career? You just wanted to be a fucking influencer, didn't you?'

'Eli,' Emmanuel said, in the overly calm voice that made Eli's teeth ache with frustration. 'You know that's not true. What I'm doing here, with the media appearances, is bringing attention to the cause. Just think of the funding opportunities that could come from this.'

Eli smiled, amazed at the extent of the cognitive dissonance Emmanuel was exhibiting. 'Jesus Christ, do you believe that? Have you managed to convince yourself that you're doing this for the research? The funding?'

'I haven't convinced myself of anything. It's the truth.'

'You're insane,' Eli laughed. 'Clinically insane! I called you to tell you that I'd been doxed because of you. We had to leave our fucking home because *journalists* were turning up at all hours, stalking us, and you're living it up on TV! Do you even realise the damage you've done? This is a boy's life you're playing with. His dad died. His grandma died. And you're making a career off of it.' Eli shook his head, allowing the January breeze to cool his heated cheeks. 'You're a fucking monster.'

'Eli, that's not true. You'd see that if you allowed him to be part of this. I've invited you both to be involved. You could make something good out of this, but you're burying your head in the sand and making the situation so much worse. It's almost like you don't want there to be a silver lining. Like you don't want Asher to benefit from this?'

'To benefit from his dad's death? To benefit from demonic fucking possession? Do you hear yourself? Oh my God, you're insane. You're actually insane, Jesus Christ.' Eli paced the room as he spoke.

'You called me,' Emmanuel said. 'Might I remind you of that.'

'I called you so that you could see the impact of what you'd done. We had to run away because of you. Asher was being bullied at school. We're getting ripped to shreds by strangers online. These are our real lives you're messing with. Can't you see that?'

'I'm not messing with anything. I don't owe you anything. This is for the greater good, for the furthering of our collective understanding of life after death. We've had this discussion, Eli. I feel like you're not listening to me.'

'*You* feel like I'm not listening to you.' Eli scoffed and then sighed. 'Look, I just want you to maybe consider somebody other than yourself while you're being chauffeured from appearance to appearance. He's a grieving kid who lost two of the most important people in his life at the hands of some evil that we can't understand. Just, for the love of God, remember that when you're counting your money.'

Eli hung up the phone before Emmanuel could counter. He slumped down onto the sofa. Calling Emmanuel had been a childish move, but he didn't care. He'd said his piece. It would make no difference, but he'd done it. He massaged his temples with shaking fingers. You couldn't make this stuff up. He felt better after his *discussion* with Emmanuel. It felt good to vent his frustrations; to focus his anger in an attempt to stop the acid from spilling over and burning somebody he loved.

The atmosphere in the house was as overcast as the weather. Asher had only come out of his bedroom thanks to Eli's coaxing. They ate their dinner, sausage and mash, off trays in front of the TV while they watched *The Inbetweeners*, something that Eli had only just allowed Asher to start watching. In the time 'before', Felix had always said no, but after what Asher had lived through, a few dicey jokes that bordered on offensive fifteen years after the show had been made didn't feel quite so *bad*. How could Eli tell Asher he couldn't watch a group of teenagers doing cringey things, when he'd witnessed the death of his father at the hand of a demon and a psychic?

Asher, who usually giggled along to the jokes, was silent, staring through the TV instead of watching it.

'Ash, you good?' Eli placed his tray on the floor so that Specs could lick it clean. It was a bad habit he had no intention of stopping.

'Yeah.' Asher didn't move his eyes from the TV.

'Asher,' Eli said, his word sounding like a plea.

'I'm fine. I promise. The thing with the radio scared me, that's all. I thought it was…'

'A demon?' Eli asked.

Asher nodded, smiling sheepishly.

'You're bound to think that. After what you've been through, there's no wonder your brain jumps straight to that explanation.'

Asher nodded, pursing his lips.

'There's something else?' Eli asked, leaning towards Asher.

'Sometimes Dad's Gameboy does weird things too,' he said.

'Like what?'

'It has messages on it.'

'Messages?' Eli wasn't following. Asher was talking about a Gameboy Color. It had no access to the internet. How could it be receiving messages?

'It said, "*They're coming for you.*" And, "*They're almost here.*" They flash up and then they go.'

'Which is what you heard on the radio?' Eli connected the dots slowly, trying to figure out what the hell that meant.

Asher nodded again, this time slightly bigger than before.

'Asher, I don't know what that means. How is that possible?'

'It's a demon. It has to be. What else could it be?'

'Let's think about this logically, okay?' Eli said. 'Just because demons exist and we know they do, doesn't mean this is demons. We can't just jump to that conclusion.'

'You're not listening to me!' Asher's voice sliced through the room.

'Whoa, Ash.' Eli stretched out his hand to comfort his nephew, but Asher jumped back. 'Asher,' Eli repeated, trying to hide his frustration.

'I don't get why you don't believe me.' Asher crossed his arms over his chest, making himself small.

'I do believe you, but we need to try to think clearly about this. You're going through a lot and -'

'It's a demon. I know it is.' Asher stared at the floor.

'Okay,' Eli said, acquiescing. 'So, if it is a demon, what do we do?'

'I don't know,' Asher said. He freed one of his hands and started scratching at the back of his neck.

'Okay, okay. I'll do some research. We'll figure it out.'

'What about Emmanuel?'

'What about Emmanuel?' Eli countered, hoping Asher wasn't suggesting what he thought he was.

'You should ask him to help us.'

Eli sucked his teeth. 'I don't think Emmanuel is a good idea. I don't think he knows a thing about anything. He's like Lilith was.'

'Not really,' Asher said. 'He's a doctor. He researches demons. He has to know something. And Lilith ended up being…' He sighed. 'Lilith was a good person.'

'I know she was, Ash. I do. But Emmanuel isn't.'

'We didn't think Lilith was either, at first,' Asher said. Eli wished he'd let it drop.

'I think what we should do is track it. Think about it scientifically. Whenever anything weird happens, write it down. Write where you were, the time, what happened, and we'll see if there's a pattern to anything. If there is, then we'll reach out to Emmanuel as a last resort, but I'm going to do my own research and see if there's anybody else.' There *had* to be somebody else who would help them. Or at least, who could appease Asher. Eli was certain that what Asher was experiencing was the culmination of grief and stress, he was looking for patterns where there weren't any. He'd heard a phrase a couple of times, or his game had glitched, and he'd found a pattern that wasn't really a pattern. He needed to get in contact with Simone. Asher needed to continue his counselling, now more than ever.

'I don't know,' Asher said. There was an all too familiar waver to his voice.

'I'm on it, Ash. Okay? I know I should have been doing this all along, after what happened to your dad and grandma. I'm sorry I didn't.' It dawned on Eli with crushing clarity that he knew that demons were real. He KNEW that demons were real. He KNEW what demons were capable of doing. Yet, he'd assumed that once Felix had died it was over, and they'd never have to worry about it again. The demon that was Nicolas Damont was gone, but Damont had told them flat out that there were other demons with different *preferences,* and what would he get out of lying about that? Eli should have been doing everything in his power to learn how to protect his family from them. Instead, he'd been worrying about how Asher was coping with the death of his father, which seemed to pale in comparison to preparing for a potential demonic attack. Grief was normal. People coped. What happened to people who were victims of demons? Eli was pretty certain the mortality rate was higher for demons than it was for grief. He'd majorly dropped the fucking ball. Panic rose in his chest, flooding his senses and covering his skin in prickling heat.

'I didn't either,' Asher said.

'You didn't what?'

'Research. A demon killed my dad, and I pretended it didn't happen.'

'It's not your job, Ash. It's mine. I should have… I didn't realise… I'll fix it, okay. I will, I promise. I think we should remember though that if demons exist, other things might too. Damont said spirits were demons that had been around for a long time and had become really powerful. Whatever you're experiencing, it might not be a demon. It might be something else. It might be something we've never heard of, so just don't get ahead of yourself.'

Asher nodded his head and turned his attention to the TV. That would have to do.

The threat of a panic attack clawed at his mind. In an attempt to distract himself, using his new phone, Eli started his journey into demonology, or whatever the hell the right word was, by Googling 'credible academic supernatural books'. He bought audiobooks of the five with the best reviews. A few on the list could only be found in battered old second-hand paperback form, so he bought those from eBay to have delivered to the Airbnb. He popped an earbud in and connected it to his phone (another annoying thing about having a new phone, setting up all the Bluetooth stuff), and started listening to the first book: *Beyond the Paranormal* by Dr. Willem Jones.

THEY'RE HERE

His dad is screaming so loud that it feels like Asher's head might split in two. Asher is cornered, his back against the wall. There is nowhere else to go. His dad takes laboured steps forwards, like the zombies in old horror movies, when zombies used to be slow. Specs tries to stop him. He bites chunks out of his dad's legs, spitting them out and going back for more. His muzzle drips with blood. Still, his dad continues screaming. Asher cannot move. He's frozen to the spot. He tries to move his legs, but they are not his own. His dad moves forward. His dad wants to kill him. He knows that. He knows that with every single cell in his body. He wants to kill him. Another step. Specs bites at the back of his dad's ankle, the part that really hurts if you kick it. The Achilles tendon. His dad falls. His leg crunches underneath him. It bends at an angle it shouldn't. He screams, not in pain, but frustration. Asher wants to scream. He tries to scream, but he can't. His voice doesn't work either. Specs looms over his dad.

Where is Uncle Eli? Asher thinks. He should be here.

Specs's jaws clamp on his dad's neck. There's a sickening snap. A fleshy noise.

This isn't how it happened. *The thought rushes into Asher's brain.* Where's Lilith?

'SHE CAN'T SAVE YOU THIS TIME.'

The voice is unfamiliar. It grates at Asher's mind, tearing at his reality.

'Dad!' Asher yells. His voice barely audible. 'DAD!'

Specs turns and looks up from the bloody mess. With wide eyes, the dog looks back down at his prey. Not prey, *Asher thinks.* Predator. His dad was the predator. Asher was the prey. Specs protected him. But it wasn't his dad. It was… something else. Something other.

'Asher.' Uncle Eli's voice.

But he isn't there. Asher can't see him.

'Asher, wake up!' Uncle Eli's voice is more urgent. Where is he?

Asher screams again, but no noise escapes him. It gets stuck in his throat. Weak and failing.

'Asher, you're dreaming. It's a nightmare. It's not real.'

It's not real. But it is real. It happened. Not quite like this, but it happened.

Asher felt like he'd swallowed razor blades. He was being held down. Two hands were clamped onto his shoulders, pushing him deeper into the bed.

'Get off,' Asher moaned.

'Hey, Ash, it's me. You're okay,' Uncle Eli said.

Asher's eyes blinked open. The familiar face hovering over him was filled with worry.

It didn't make sense. A second ago he was…

'You were having a nightmare,' Uncle Eli said. 'I heard you screaming. Specs was trying to wake you up, but you were…'

'I was screaming?' Asher said. It didn't make any sense. He'd been trying to scream, but he couldn't make his voice work.

'Yeah. Good job we're in the middle of nowhere, or the neighbours would have called the police. They'd think I was…' Uncle Eli stopped, not finishing the thought.

'Trying to kill me?' Asher finished for him.

Uncle Eli nodded his head once. 'Bad choice of words, Ash. Sorry.' He looked down at his hands, and then at Asher, releasing his grip. 'Sorry,' he repeated.

Uncle Eli sat back, and Asher attempted to manoeuvre himself into a sitting position. His throat hurt. It wasn't just sore, it *hurt*.

'Want to talk about it?' Uncle Eli asked.

'Dad,' Asher said.

'Dying?' Uncle Eli asked.

Asher appreciated that he didn't say, *being murdered*. He nodded.

'I'm sorry, mate. That's tough.'

Asher noticed the muscles in Uncle Eli's jaw tense and then release. He sighed, picked up the TV remote and pointed it at the small TV that sat on the dresser.

'What-' Asher started to ask.

'Film night,' Uncle Eli said. He nudged Asher over and climbed into the other side of the double bed. Specs took the opportunity to sit between them. Asher felt a flood of gratefulness wash over him. Uncle Eli hadn't made him ask. What self-respecting almost thirteen-year-old wanted to ask their uncle/surrogate dad to spend the night with them? But that *was* what Asher wanted. He didn't want to be alone, not when the waves of adrenaline were still working their way out of his body. He hadn't dreamed about his dad's death in a long time. And when he had *before,* he'd seen what had actually happened. Not something different. Somehow, this felt worse.

'I'm going to the toilet,' Asher said, getting out of bed. He'd woken up with a full bladder, on the verge of bursting. At least he hadn't wet the bed. His body had been so out of his control in the dream that it had been a very real possibility, and that would have been mortifying.

After using the bathroom, Asher stood in front of the mirror, watching himself as he washed his hands. There were bags under his eyes, deep black bags that looked like he hadn't slept in weeks. He gripped the edge of the porcelain sink so hard that his knuckles began to ache. It was a good feeling, a feeling that pulled him away from the fear that had pulsated through his body like a monster trying to break his bones from the inside.

'You're going through a lot,' he said to himself in a low voice. 'Nightmares are your brain's way of working through trauma.'

Since his dad's death, it had been *trauma this,* and *trauma that.* He didn't think any of the other boys his age would even begin to associate the word *trauma* with actual mental health unless it was to do with horror movies and video games. Trauma was real. He carried it around like a heavy black coat he couldn't shake off.

When he went back to the bedroom, Uncle Eli had put on another episode of *The Inbetweeners*. It was good. Distracting. Not even remotely associated with demons and murders.

'You okay?' Uncle Eli said as Asher climbed back into bed.

'Yeah.' Asher nodded. The look on Uncle Eli's face told Asher that he didn't believe him, but he didn't push it further.

Specs climbed between the two of them and laid his head on Asher's lap, almost as though in apology for what he'd done in the dream. Asher stroked the velvet of Specs's ear.

He wasn't sure who fell asleep first, but at some point, he'd fallen into a dreamless sleep with his uncle and Specs alongside him.

He peered through slitted eyes at the TV, still on in the background.

Instead of four boys running around in royal blue Rudge Park school jumpers, the TV was a mess of static. It looked like falling snow. The snow began to move out of focus. Asher opened his eyes wider, watching as the words formed.

'THEY'RE HERE.'

KILL YOURSELF

Asher had spent the day on the sofa, drifting in and out of sleep. Eli, in contrast, had spent the day trawling through various websites and books and journal articles, finding out as much as he could about the supernatural. He'd come to the useless conclusion that nobody knew anything, and even the *experts* were just speculating. There were many accounts of 'real-life' encounters with demons and the supernatural and ghosts and everything else that came along with that. It seemed, to Eli, that the paranormal forums and podcasts attracted people who were not of sound mind. In fact, when he tried to find credible sources, most of them were actually focused on the paranormal phenomena being a result of mental health conditions. Eli had to admit, many of the stories he read or listened to, did not seem feasible. They read like fiction - and that was coming from somebody who had first-hand experience of a demon. How was a person like Eli, attempting to protect his family, supposed to sort through what information was verifiable and what was a lot of shite? It was impossible. He needed fresh air. He felt like the walls were closing in on him.

'Asher, let's go find this swimming pool,' Eli said to a barely conscious Asher.

'What? Now?' Asher asked, rolling over onto his back and placing an arm over his head.

'Yeah, it'll be good for us to get some fresh air. Specs too. He's dying for a walk.'

'Okay.' Asher rubbed his neck.

'You slept funny?'

'Yeah, my neck hurts,' Asher cricked his neck to the side. Eli half expected to see a bruise or bloody handprint or something else destined to give him an aneurysm.

'All good?' Eli said.

'Yeah, just sore.'

'Fresh air will do you good. Come on,' he said. 'Walk, Specs?'

Specs shot up and trotted to the back door.

The natural swimming pool was a ten-minute walk away from the house. The photos hadn't done it justice. Specs, who usually avoided water at all costs, jumped straight in. Asher tested the temperature with his hand. It was freezing. There was no way he'd be doing any swimming in there, even if it was crystal clear. Asher thought '*swimming pool*' was a bit generous. It was, in essence, a big pond. Uncle Eli had read from the listing that the pool was fed from a natural spring, or something, and that's why it was so clean.

It was dotted with plants that he didn't know the names of, and some reeds stood tall on the edges. Specs swam to the middle of the pool. They'd never actually seen the little barrel swim. It was the funniest thing. The dog looked like he was built to sink, not float.

It was late in the day. Asher had slept for most of it, dozing in front of the TV, unable to keep his eyes open. He was exhausted. The fresh air had woken him up, but he'd wasted the whole day. The sun was setting over the moorland. He'd never actually seen a sunset in real life, he realised. It was beautiful. The sky turned blood red as the sun began to sink into the horizon.

'Should probably have brought a torch,' Uncle Eli said. 'It'll get fully dark soon.' He shook his head as though he thought he'd been really stupid.

'There're no streetlights,' Asher said. Last night, they'd not left the house after dark so it hadn't dawned on him that it would get really, really dark at night. He'd never been anywhere overnight without streetlights. Their house was the only thing for miles around too. It left him feeling uneasy. 'Why did you choose here?'

'What?' Uncle Eli said. He'd been trying to coax Specs out of the water.

'Why did you choose somewhere in the middle of nowhere, with no streetlights? It's going to get really dark.'

'We're safe here, Ash. This was the nicest place that was available on short notice and was in budget. There wasn't a lot of choice. I thought being in the countryside would be nice.'

'But we're all alone.'

'Just the three of us,' Uncle Eli said.

Asher thought about the words on the TV in the middle of the night: '*THEY'RE HERE.*' He wasn't so certain that they were alone.

'Can we go back now?' Asher asked.

'Sure,' Uncle Eli said.

Asher didn't wait for a response. He turned and walked back towards the house. It didn't take Specs long to catch up. Uncle Eli walked behind them. Asher could feel the disappointment radiating off his uncle. He felt terrible.

'He doesn't love you.'

Asher whipped his head around to the right, in the direction of the noise. There was nobody there.

It's just my mind playing tricks on me.

'He didn't want you.'

The voice came from the left.

Asher turned.

Nothing. Of course.

'Everything okay, Ash?' Uncle Eli said, jogging to catch up.

'Yeah. My neck's still sore, that's all. Slept weird on the sofa.'

Asher didn't look to see if Uncle Eli believed him or not.

Asher had gone to bed alone. He shut the door before Eli could ask him if he was okay alone, or if he wanted some company. And so Eli stood outside the closed door, listening to the muffled sound of voices on the TV. To knock, or not to knock? He ran his hands through his hair, pushing it away from his forehead.

'Looks like you're sleeping with me tonight, Specs,' Eli said. The dog sighed. 'Don't be like that.'

Eli walked away from Asher's door, wondering whether he was doing the right thing.

'Bedtime Specs,' Eli said. There was no point in them staying downstairs alone. He would let Specs do his final wee before bed and then head back upstairs.

Specs trotted to the back door, already used to the new house. The porch area was enclosed with a stone wall that looked fit to fall down at any moment. Asher was right. It really did get dark. Moonlight illuminated the moors, casting it in an eerie glow. The heather swayed in the breeze, making a sound like a mum shushing a baby. The moon was full. Eli couldn't begin to fathom the pitch black it would be on the night of a new moon. Specs trotted back in.

A figure.

It stood beyond the wall.

It was too dark to make out any features, but it was long, lean.

Eli squinted, cocking his head.

Specs turned back, facing outside, and snarled.

Eli shut the door, locking it. He jogged to make sure the front door was also locked. His heart hammered in his chest. He turned off all the lights so that he could see outside better, and so whatever was outside couldn't see him. He forced himself to walk slowly to the back patio doors. It was just his mind playing tricks in the darkness. He knew that.

He scanned the horizon. Nothing. No figure at all.

'You're under a lot of stress,' he whispered to himself, trying to placate his racing heart. It was just like he reminded Asher. When your mind was under stress, it did strange things to try and cope.

'Come on then, Specs,' Eli made his way upstairs.

At the landing, he paused outside Asher's room. Voices. Asher was talking to somebody. A school friend, maybe, from his tablet?

You're the parent, you have to know, Felix's voice said in Eli's mind.

Eli tapped on the door. 'Ash, I'm coming in.' He wanted to respect Asher's privacy, especially at that age, but he was also the parent in that situation, as his brother's voice had reminded him. If Asher was talking to someone, he needed to know who and how.

He pushed the door open and stuck his head in. Specs hurled himself past him and into the room, throwing himself on the bed and resting his head on his paws.

Asher was sitting on the bed, tablet in his hands. He looked up at Eli with wide, questioning eyes.

'You okay?' Eli said.

'Yeah,' Asher hedged.

'You were talking to somebody,' Eli said.

'It was the video I was watching.'

'I heard your voice.' Eli didn't want to argue with the kid. He'd been through enough, but he could tell Asher was lying.

'I was watching Lilith's video.' Asher held up the tablet so that Eli could see the screen.

'Oh,' Eli said. He racked his brain for what to say, and settled on, 'Why?'

'I don't know. It's the nightmares. Things don't happen like they do in the video.'

'Oh, Asher.' Eli had no idea what to do with what Asher had said. He couldn't fix the nightmares.

Asher shrugged.

'I don't think it's good for you to watch the video,' Eli said.

'It helps,' Asher said.

'Have you talked about it with Simone?' Eli asked.

'No, they've just started.'

Duh! Eli chastised himself. 'We'll get you an emergency appointment booked.'

Asher nodded.

'Do you want me to sleep in here?' Eli said.

'No, I'm fine. Can you take Specs?'

Eli blinked against the words. Not once had Asher ever asked for Specs to be taken away.

'Sure,' Eli said, anxiety fluttering in his stomach. He called Specs over. The dog reluctantly jumped from the bed and over to Eli. 'Goodnight, Ash. You know where I am if you want me.'

'Night,' Asher said.

Eli shut the door behind him. The slithering sense of dread crawled under his skin as he walked away.

Uncle Eli's laptop stood open in front of Asher. Upon it, Simone's face smiled back at him.

'You've had a busy few days,' she said. 'Tell me about it.'

Asher hadn't spoken to her since the video was released. There was a lot to catch up on. He spoke for a solid fifteen minutes about Emmanuel, the video, the journalists, the mean commenters online, the moving to a house in the middle of nowhere, and the nightmares. She nodded at various intervals, showing that she was actively listening. Asher liked her a lot. She was one of those people you could tell were kind.

'That's a lot to deal with,' she said.

It was a leading statement. Asher was supposed to treat it as a question, he'd learned.

'Yeah,' Asher replied, biting his lip.

'Is there a specific part you'd like to focus on?'

Asher shrugged.

She nodded, but didn't speak.

'It's just, I hate that *this* is my life. After Dad and Nanna died, I thought it was all over, but this thing with, with…' *Fucking demons*, he wanted to say. He could feel that something wasn't right. Something had followed them, maybe that *something* had been stalking them since that night.

'With what?' Simone said, and Asher knew that he'd been lost inside his mind for too long.

'With… everything.'

'I have to ask,' Simone said. 'The video. What's the story there?'

'It's fake.' The words were out of Asher's mouth in a second.

She nodded her head like she knew that all along. *She wanted to believe it was real,* Asher thought.

'Do you want to talk about how and why the video was made?'

'No.' Asher shook his head.

'Okay. What do you want to talk about?'

'I'm having nightmares about my dad dying, but it doesn't happen like it did in real life.'

Simone parroted the same thing as Uncle Eli: that our brains process real-life events while we're sleeping and that it's all natural.

'Let's think about your bedtime routine. Talk me through what you do in the run-up to going to bed.'

Asher did.

'So, you watch videos on your tablet or play a game before you fall asleep?'

'Yes.'

'Well, we know that the blue light from these screens can interrupt your sleep. It also isn't necessarily a relaxing thing to do, even if you feel like you might be relaxing. If you're able to relax before you go to bed, you're more likely to have a restful sleep. Shall we maybe have a little think about a routine you could try before bed?'

'Kill yourself.'

Asher wasn't sure whether the words were spoken aloud or whether they'd come from inside his mind. He'd fallen asleep after the therapy session, even though Simone had advised against napping as it could impact the *sleep quality* and therefore lead to nightmares. But Asher hadn't been able to keep his eyes open. He awoke feeling confused. It was one of those naps where he didn't know whether he'd been asleep for ten minutes or ten hours.

He rolled over, trying to get his bearings in the unfamiliar room. It was dark. No sunlight leaked from around the blinds. It had to be after five o'clock. Therapy finished at two. He tapped the unlock button on his tablet. 18:04.

Rats gnawed at the lining of his stomach. He felt nervous. Really nervous.

The screen of his tablet darkened. The room went dark. Asher laid his head back on his pillow. He should get out of bed, but the thought of moving made the rats in his stomach turn feral.

'You shouldn't have lived.'

'What?' Asher breathed, sitting up straight. He looked around the room for the source of the voice.

There it was. A shadow in the far corner of the room.

Asher sucked in a panicked breath. He couldn't move.

The figure stood still. The shape was familiar.

'Dad?'

There was no response. It couldn't be his dad. His dad wouldn't have said…

'Eli doesn't want you. You should be dead.'

Asher let out a low moan. His heart ached in his chest.

'Ash? You awake?' The door to the room creaked open, bathing it in light from the hallway. Uncle Eli stuck his head through the door.

'I'm awake,' Asher said. He swallowed back the tears that were building in his throat. He couldn't stop himself from glancing back towards where the shadow had been. There was nothing there.

'You hungry?' Uncle Eli asked.

'Yeah,' Asher said, climbing out of the bed. As he walked out of the room, he could feel eyes staring into his back. His neck prickled with goosebumps.

RADIO SILENCE

'Have you noticed Emmanuel hasn't posted anything on social media today?' Eli said to Asher. They were sitting at the dining table; empty plates that had previously been filled with pizza sat before them.

Asher opened his mouth to formulate an answer, but Eli cut him off.

'I know you have Facebook, probably an Instagram too?' Eli said.

Asher bobbed his head, pursing his lips. He looked like he was waiting to be told off.

'I don't care. I know you're not stupid. You're smarter than most of the kids your age. But did you notice about Emmanuel?' Eli didn't give a shit if Asher had social media accounts. There were far worse things he could be doing than spending time looking at nerdy stuff online. What Eli was bothered about was the fact that Emmanuel's Facebook, Instagram, and his blog, had gone from multiple posts a day to absolutely nothing at all. Complete radio silence.

'Yeah,' Asher admitted. 'I did.'

'It doesn't look like he's been on any podcast or TV shows either, as far as I could tell.' Emmanuel had been everywhere. Literally everywhere. Every TV show that recorded the day of, or a day in advance, every podcast, YouTuber, TikToker that dealt with anything vaguely supernatural - Emmanuel had been there, front and centre, loving the limelight. Today, he wasn't anywhere at all.

'Yeah, it's weird.' Asher seemed quieter than normal, but he was always tired after the therapy sessions. He'd slept for hours. Eli hadn't dared to wake him. If he was sleeping, then that was what his body had needed.

'Yeah, weird…' Eli said, sensing that the topic of conversation was over.

'I've been thinking about school,' Asher said. 'I don't think I want to go back.'

'You want to go to a different school?' Eli asked.

'I want to home school. I looked it up. All you have to do is tell my school and then send a letter to the council saying that you're home schooling me.'

'Asher, I don't know if that's-' Eli's heart sank. Asher's school had been very understanding when he'd called and told them that they were going away for a few weeks because of the issues that stemmed from the video circling. The teachers were emailing work for Asher to do, which they hadn't started to tackle yet. He knew that many schools wouldn't be so understanding.

'Please,' Asher said.

Eli nodded. 'We'll look into it. For now, you've got the work that school is sending you. You can start with that?'

'Don't make me go back to school.' Asher's eyes were ringed in red.

'Where's this come from?' Eli asked.

'I was thinking about it when I woke up,' Asher said. 'I don't think anybody will forget the video.'

'Hey, you don't know that. Things go viral and then vanish into thin air.'

'Not when it's people you know. If you know somebody who went viral, you don't forget that.' Asher's cheeks were flushed a deep mottled red.

'Fair enough,' Eli said. 'But we don't have to rush into anything just yet. I'll look into it. We could always look at a different school-'

'Don't you want me at home?' Asher's voice snapped like a broken string.

'What? No, of course I do. Why would you say that?' Eli shuffled his chair closer to Asher so that their knees were almost touching.

'Because you won't let me home school. If you don't want me at home-'

'I want you at home,' Eli said, definitively. 'But it's not that simple. I have to work, and I want you to have a normal life. To be around kids your own age. To do all the things you're supposed to be doing. I don't want this video to ruin your life.'

'Maybe it already has,' Asher said.

'Don't say that.' Eli's voice was harsher than he'd meant it to be. 'I know it feels like that now, Ash, but-'

'I knew you wouldn't understand.' Asher pushed his chair away from the table and went to stand. Eli grabbed his arm.

'Asher. I do understand. It's happening to me too, remember. I know it's worse for you, with school and the other kids, and that you lost your dad.' Eli stumbled over the last part of the sentence, tears falling down his cheeks. 'But I lost your dad too. He was my brother. And Nanna was my mum. I understand what you're going through better than anyone. You can talk to me.'

'It's not fair,' Asher said. His own eyes brimmed with tears. 'It's not fair. Why is this my life?'

'I know, Ash. I know.' Eli pulled Asher against him. 'It's not fair,' he said into Asher's hair. 'But we're in this together. We have to get through this, we don't have a choice.'

Three figures stood in the corner of Asher's room.

Although he couldn't know for sure. One was taller than the others. He'd started thinking of it as *Dad.* There was no logical explanation other than the fact that it reminded Asher of his dad. It had the same body shape. The same posture. The one next to him was smaller, thinner. *Lilith.* He decided. It had to be. The third, *Nanna.* Dad had always said that the spirits he saw looked just like real people. When his dad first realised he could see the dead, he couldn't tell who was alive and who had passed, but the spirits Asher was seeing were not like that. They looked to be made of shadow, or fog. They were all black, with no distinguishing features, other than their shapes. They made Asher nervous. He'd never been able to see spirits before, not in the way that his dad had. But *this* wasn't what his dad had described. Maybe he had a slightly different gift to his dad. Or maybe he was a late bloomer after all, and he was just now developing the ability to see the spirits of the dead.

'You're here,' Asher whispered. 'I knew you wouldn't have passed on without saying goodbye.'

His dad reached out to him from the corner of the room. Asher watched from his bed as a long arm slowly meandered out towards him, grasping at the air.

'I've missed you,' Asher said.

The spirits didn't speak. His dad withdrew his hand. They stood in the corner, translucent but dense, substantial. Asher could feel them looking at him, studying him. They were checking that he was okay.

'Why can I see you now and not before?'

The spirits didn't answer.

Asher wondered if maybe, like Damont had said, the spirits of his dad, Lilith, and Nanna had grown in strength since their deaths and only now were they strong enough to make themselves visible to him. It made sense, he supposed. It explained why they hadn't shown themselves before.

'Will you stay with me?' Asher asked, desperation filling his words.

'*Until the end.*' The voice was unfamiliar. It didn't belong to Dad, Lilith, or Nanna.

An electric current rolled over his skin. It prickled. Maybe people's voices were different once they'd died. Yes, that had to be the explanation.

Asher fell to sleep with the figures watching over him.

He dreamed of his Nanna's body, swinging from the light fitting in her flat. A small part of him was aware that he hadn't seen it in real life. Uncle Eli had kept him away, but it felt so real. The way her neck was bent at an impossible angle. The way her mouth was hung open. The way her eyes bulged from the sockets.

His eyes shot open, staring at the ceiling. Specs wasn't there, but the figures were. They weren't in the corner. They were looming over him, peering at him. They had no faces. Asher tried to reach out, to touch one; they looked like they were made of a nearly solid mist. Their bodies ebbed and flowed, but it didn't seem like his hand would pass through them. They looked *hard*.

His hand wouldn't move.

The figures leaned closer, their heads twisting and turning, snake-like.

THEY'RE HERE FOR YOU!' The voice was deafening. It didn't come from the figures. It came from everywhere, all at once. Asher's instinct was to fling his hands up to cover his ears, but they still wouldn't move.

'Please, no!' he tried to say. No voice came from his mouth.

The figures' faces began to split open where their mouths would be. It looked like they were screaming. There was an old painting that Asher remembered of a weird face that looked just the same. Then it clicked in his mind: his mum in the wedding video. Her face had distorted in the same way.

'What's happening?' he tried to say.

Tears fell from his eyes, dripping to the pillow beneath him.

The figures swam closer to him, their faces descending until they were only a breath away.

Their mouths yawned open wider than he thought was possible, like they wanted to swallow him whole.

MOVE. Asher commanded his body. Nothing happened.

'Oh God, no. Please stop! Please don't!' He heard the words only in his head.

'It's your turn now.' The three mouths didn't move, but Asher *knew* that the sound came from them.

Then they screamed. A piercing, nerve-shattering scream.

Asher closed his eyes. His hands found his ears. He didn't realise right away that his hands had moved, only that the screaming was muffled. He opened one eye a slit, as much as he dared. The shadow people were gone, and it was morning.

Eli looked up from the laptop resting on his lap towards the patio doors, watching as Specs ran rings around Asher. Asher had volunteered to take Specs out, and Eli had understood that Asher meant to go alone. That was fine. Eli had gone down a Google Scholar rabbit hole after searching 'demonic possession + parapsychology'. He still felt at a complete loss about where to find credible information about the paranormal. The majority of academics and scientists blamed paranormal events on mental illnesses or naturally occurring phenomena: a draft, a gas leak, a brain tumour. He'd found an article written by a psychiatrist who claimed that many of the patients he'd cared for throughout his career had, in fact, been possessed by *entities,* which was why their conditions had been *untreatable.* Eli found himself in a strange no-man's-land. He didn't believe the psychiatrist for a single second, but he did believe in demonic possessions. Everything seemed so false. The journals that approached demonic possession and paranormal experiences from the perspective that they were real, tended to lean towards not being particularly highly regarded or peer-reviewed, but that didn't mean that some of their articles were not legit. He was reaching a point where he wanted to pull his hair out. Every article that provided *helpful hints and tips* on protecting yourself from demons, spouted exactly the same things that Lilith had tried, things that had been proven not to work. The only thing they hadn't tried the last time around, was an exorcism. Although the literature on exorcisms was just as difficult to stomach as everything else Eli had read. Exorcisms were even more controversial than the study of parapsychology in general. Parapsychology attempted to be scientific in nature, Eli found - investigating mental or seemingly paranormal phenomena - while people studying exorcisms simply wanted to either prove or disprove the existence of God. Even while skipping the articles intent on disproving demons (and other demon-adjacent beings), and only reading the abstracts on many others, Eli hadn't even scratched the surface of the mass of information out there.

He closed his laptop in frustration and turned his attention back to Asher and Specs. It was 4.30 PM, and the sky was just beginning to darken. Asher was standing completely still. Although Eli could barely make out his features, Asher looked like he was talking. He stared off into the distance, so Eli could only see his profile. Specs was pointed the same way. He was barking, Eli realised, but there was nothing in front of them.

Oh God, Eli thought. *It's happening again.* It couldn't be, though. It just couldn't. *This* was a manifestation of grief. This was mental illness, or something explainable. It had to be. It had to be because if it wasn't...

Eli resisted the urge to run out there and find out what was happening. Instead, he picked up his phone and called Simone. Asher's therapist answered on the second ring. Eli introduced himself.

'I just wanted to ask your opinion on something,' he said.

'Of course. Go on.'

'I've noticed Asher talking to himself.'

'In what kind of way?' Simone asked.

'I'm not sure how to explain it. A weird kind of way. I walked past his room and heard him talking. He didn't sound upset or anything, more conversational. And now I'm standing watching him. He's stood outside with Specs, our dog, and talking to somebody that isn't there.'

'Like a proper conversation?' She sounded worried. There was a sharp edge to her voice that hadn't been there when the phone call had started.

'Yeah.'

'He's pausing for somebody to answer him?'

'Yeah. It looks like it. I'm in the house, so I can't hear what he's saying but...'

'Is he unwell? Does he have a temperature?' The urgency in her voice felt white hot.

'Not that I know of.'

'You need to check.' Although he was ninety-nine percent certain she hadn't meant it that way, Eli took it as a dig at his parenting skills. He fought back the urge to get defensive and tell her that he never intended to be a parent.

'I will.'

'If he has a temperature, you go straight to A and E.'

'And if he doesn't?'

'Well, hearing voices is a hallucination. It could be just auditory, or there could be a visual element too. Either way, it's indicative of a few different things. Stress, trauma, and grief can all cause hallucinations. Hearing voices in some people is a normal thing. We don't know why it happens, but as long as it isn't intrusive or upsetting, it's not usually an issue.' She paused. Eli knew there was more. 'In Asher's case, as he's never heard voices before, as far as we know, it's something to keep an eye on and it is concerning me. It could be the result of his grief, which we're working through, of course, but it also could be a sign of something else.'

'Schizophrenia?' Eli held his breath. He'd had an ex with schizophrenia and although his ex lived a normal life and had the condition under control, it was still a terrifying thing to be diagnosed with.

'No need to panic. I'm not concerned about schizophrenia, and you don't need to be either. It's something to monitor. Children hearing voices often terrifies parents, and it's understandable, but in and of itself, it isn't something to panic about. You will know if you should be concerned. Trust your instinct. If in doubt, you can call me or book an emergency appointment with your GP or ring one one one.'

'Yeah, okay.' Eli knew his voice didn't sound convincing.

'Eli, you're doing a good job. I know that you're in a difficult situation, but Asher adores you and you've stepped into the role of primary caregiver incredibly well, especially under such difficult circumstances. You're going through that new parent phase but with a teenager, not a baby. All new parents panic about everything. It's normal.'

Eli wanted to tell Simone the whole story. If Asher was talking to himself after the death of his father and that was the only concern, he felt he could deal with it. Right now, he was juggling the, *'Is this a demon problem or a mental health problem?'* scenario, and that was what made it immeasurably more difficult. Simone had put his mind at ease (a little) about the whole talking to himself thing, at least.

'Eli? Just keep an eye on him. If you think the voices are having a negative effect, do what I told you, okay? Trust your instinct.'

'Thank you,' he said.

Asher had turned his back to the house, so Eli could no longer tell if he was talking. Specs had stopped barking, at least. He trotted around the heather, sniffing and scratching at the earth.

The movement was so quick, if Eli had blinked at the wrong moment, he would have missed it. Asher's head snapped back over his shoulder. He stared at Eli. His facial expression was unmoving. It was like somebody had told him he was being watched.

AN UNWELCOME VISITOR

Eli was half awake when a noise jolted him from his bed. As his surroundings came into focus, he heard the noise again. Knocking. Someone was at the door. He pulled himself from the bed, stuffed his feet into his slippers, and made his way downstairs. It didn't occur to him until he faced the door that he was in a house that was miles away from anything. There was no reason for anybody to be there. He cursed the owner for not putting a peephole in the door.

There was another knock. This time, if Eli wasn't imagining it, it was more aggressive. He turned the lock and yanked open the door, annoyance prickling at his skin.

'Elijah.' Emmanuel stood in front of the open door, wearing jeans and a hoodie, with a five o'clock shadow dusting his chin.

'What the fuck are you doing here?' Eli said, his body tensing in shock.

'I need to talk to you.'

'How did you know where we were?' Panic flooded through Eli. 'Did you tell anybody we were here?'

'No, of course not!' Emmanuel looked genuinely offended by the question. 'I'd prefer not to tell you how I-'

'You convinced Craig to tell you?' Eli asked. Craig was the only person with the address, other than Mrs Birch, and Mrs Birch had no online presence at all. She was practically untraceable.

'He didn't want to tell me, but…'

'You can be very convincing, I'd imagine.' It was not a compliment.

'I didn't have a choice. I tracked him down based on your social media activity. He was the only person it looked like you talked to in real life. Although you hadn't interacted with him in a while…'

Eli didn't answer the question that was evident in Emmanuel's words.

'I need to talk to you,' Emmanuel said.

'You need to leave,' Eli countered.

'It's an emergency. I have something to show you.' Eli registered the letter in Emmanuel's hand. 'Can I come in?'

'No.'

'Eli, don't be like that. This is important. It's about Asher, and you, and…' Emmanuel's hands raised themselves in a way that read *everything else*.

'You shouldn't have come here,' Eli said. 'You had no right to just show up!' He was losing the battle with his temper.

'It's a letter from Lilith's cellmate.' Emmanuel's usually perfect face was blotchy from the cold. Worry crinkled his forehead.

Eli felt like the wind had been knocked out of him.

'What are you talking about?' Each word felt like a chore.

'Lilith's cellmate sent this to me. I think you need to see it.' Emmanuel held out the envelope. Eli snatched it from him. He stood there, letter in hand, trying to figure out what to do next.

'If I could come-'

Eli shut the door and walked away.

'Who was that?' Asher padded down the stairs, Specs at his heel.

'Emmanuel,' Eli said.

'What? Why?' Asher stuttered.

'He gave me a letter from Lilith's cellmate,' Eli explained.

'Where is Emmanuel now?'

'Probably still out there.' Eli shrugged. The letter felt like it was burning a hole in his hand.

'You shut him out?' Asher gave him a questioning look.

'Well, I wasn't going to invite the bastard in.'

Asher pursed his lips. 'It's cold. It has to be like two degrees.'

'Well, he made the decision to come here. That's his problem. He might have gone anyway.'

Asher walked to the door and opened it.

'Asher, hi!' Emmanuel's voice said. Specs growled from behind Asher's legs.

'Nope, still there,' Asher said. He shut the door again. Looking at Eli he said, 'Maybe we should just let him in.'

'If he wanted to, he could wait in his car. Nobody's forcing him to stand outside.'

Asher considered that for a moment and then nodded.

'Let's look at the letter then,' Asher said.

After a brief internal struggle about whether to show Asher the letter before he'd read it himself, Eli gave up and opened the already pre-opened envelope. It was written in blue ballpoint pen.

Dear Mr Emmanuel Stark,

My name is Olivia Miller, and I was Lilith Lavelle's cellmate. I was the one who found her hanging in our cell. She'd done it in the night while I was asleep. I woke up and saw what she'd done. I don't know how she did it without me hearing her. But that's what got me thinking that maybe she was telling the truth. Maybe all those stories she told me were real, you know? She told me that you didn't help her, but that you were the only one to take her seriously. I saw you on TV, talking about that video. I got the address of your agent from the internet and posted this letter there, so I hope this found you.

In the week before Lilith died, she told me what was going to happen. She said that a demon was angry, and it wanted a sacrifice. She said that it was going to kill her. People say stuff like that all the time here. You can imagine that the women here aren't all sane. I humoured her, but I didn't for a second think it was real. I have a master's degree in biochemistry, for God's sake. I don't believe in all that stuff. I didn't believe in all that stuff. What I mean to say is that I'm educated. I'm not what a 'normal' person would associate with somebody awaiting trial for stalking, I can assure you, but my story is not relevant here. What is relevant is that I am an educated woman, and you should take me seriously. I saw Lilith talking to herself. I thought she was talking to herself, but now I know otherwise. She was talking to something I couldn't see. She said that it wasn't Damont, the demon/spirit, whatever you want to call it from before. It was something else. In her final week, Lilith barely slept. She didn't eat. She panicked. She was jumpy and always looking over her shoulder. She told me that if something happened, I had to reach out to you and Eli Eastwood (I posted a letter to his house too, she had his address in a notepad by her bed). You might be wondering how I know she was being haunted (again, I have no idea what the correct terminology is), and that she wasn't crazy. Well, when I woke up, Lilith wasn't hanged. I mean, she was, but she was hanging - like she was propped up in the air. The blanket wasn't taut. It was kind of hanging bunched up, loose. She said, 'WARN THEM! THEY'RE NEXT!' and then she dropped. The sound of her neck snapping will forever be ingrained in my mind. I'll never forget that. So I'm doing as she asked. I'm warning you. I'm warning Eli and Asher.

What I saw in that cell wasn't right. It was evil. It was dangerous. If I believed in a god, I would pray for you all.

Olivia Miller

(New Manor)

Eli read the letter twice. The second time was more painful than the first. Each word felt like a fist to his gut.

Asher was drip white.

'What does this mean?' Asher asked. Eli, the adult, wanted to tell him that it would all be okay, but he couldn't. *'WARN THEM. THEY'RE NEXT',* the letter had said.

'We need to let him in,' Asher said. He was right.

'Shit,' Eli said through gritted teeth as he stomped over to the front door. He held it open but didn't say anything. Emmanuel, who was still standing directly in front of it, looked surprised but obviously knew better than to question Eli's offer. He walked through into the hallway, visibly shivering.

'What do we do now?' Eli asked. He went into the living area and sat on the sofa. Emmanuel followed behind him and sat down. He looked comical in his puffy coat and woollen hat. He wore no gloves, Eli noted. His fingers were magenta from the cold.

'We need to do something to stop it,' Emmanuel said.

'You're the expert,' Eli said. 'What do we do?'

Emmanuel looked pained. 'I don't know.'

'You don't know!' Eli slammed his hand on the coffee table. 'You're a world expert! You're supposed to know, Emmanuel. You're supposed to know what to do. If you don't, then who does?'

'That's fair.' Emmanuel's voice was irritatingly calm.

'Emmanuel,' Eli said. It took everything in him to dull his temper to a manageable state. He leaned over his knees. 'For fuck's sake, I need you to help us, or find us somebody who can.'

Emmanuel nodded. 'Have you ever heard of the podcast *Possessed!?*'

'You have got to be fucking kidding me,' Eli said, his blood beginning to boil.

'Believe it or not, the host is a very skilled and respected paranormal investigator. She's a leading voice in the field, despite not coming from an academic background.' There was snark in the final clause of the sentence.

'You're telling me that you don't know anybody with a professional background, who can figure out whatever the fuck this is, who can help us?' Eli asked.

'I'm saying that nobody in academia, who is worth their salt, has any proof of demons existing, and therefore has no proven way to combat them. Those who claim to, are frauds. Parapsychology, or anomalistic psychology, is rife with academics desperate to prove that their field is valid. It's near impossible to sort the credible from the chaff. Which is why the video Lilith sent to me is-'

'We're past that,' Eli said.

'Well, Mona, from *Possessed!* is absolutely credible and has more proof than any academic I've ever known. On her podcast, she proves or disproves paranormal activity. Many fellow academics are huge fans of hers.'

'Do it,' Asher said. 'Contact her.'

'I'm glad you said that,' Emmanuel said, 'because I already did. She's on her way.'

Eli bit his tongue to prevent him from snarling in frustration. At least Emmanuel was trying to help this time, as far as Eli could tell. 'Why are you here?'

'Because I want to help,' Emmanuel said.

'And?' Eli pushed. There was more with Emmanuel. There was always more.

'Because there's a chance to get more evidence.'

'There it is!' Eli shook his head. The audacity of Emmanuel never ceased to amaze him.

'Look, two good things could come out of this. One, we could protect you and Asher from whatever is coming for you. Two, I could further my research which would have practical applications to help others suffering similar experiences.'

Eli shook his head, resigned to the fact that he needed Emmanuel's help.

'Also, and I don't suggest this lightly, I think it's time we contacted a Catholic priest,' Emmanuel said.

A DEAD END

'We're not Catholic,' Eli said.

'I know that,' Emmanuel said, 'but we're grasping at straws here. We need to nip things in the bud. If something really did kill Lilith, and if it's coming for you, we can't allow it to reach the point of possession because then we're fucked. In theory, and I *do* stress this is theory, there are four degrees of demonic manifestation. First, is infestation.'

'I know all this,' Eli said. He'd done the research. Read the articles.

'But just to make sure we're on the same page?' Emmanuel stuffed his pinkened fingers in his pockets.

'Okay.' Eli glanced at Asher, who was staring back at Emmanuel enraptured.

'Infestation is your typical haunted house stuff. Footsteps, figures, moving objects, that kind of stuff. The second step is oppression, physical attacks, nightmares…'

Eli noticed Asher flinch.

'... depression, anxiety attacks, basically, a significant impact on your life, and emotional/physical health. Then is obsession. You fail to be able to function. You can't sleep, don't eat, you may become suicidal. You become, as the name suggests, obsessed with the demonic activity. It consumes your life. Until this point, according to current literature, and I should stress that I am not Catholic either, these issues can be addressed by a deliverance minister and don't require a fully qualified exorcist.'

'Fully qualified exorcist,' Eli repeated, shaking his head at the absurdity. Although, if he was completely honest, a qualified exorcist was no more unbelievable than demonic possession.

'Yes, a fully qualified exorcist. You saw the impact a demon could have. Would you really want to mess around with somebody not qualified?'

'You said you weren't Catholic. But you believe in *qualified exorcists?*'

'I believe that the laws of demonology transcend religion and that the Catholics have pretty much led the charge in that department in recent history. Even if I don't believe in Catholicism or God, or whatever else, it would be stupid of me not to acknowledge their knowledge base, even if it is skewed toward a specific religion.' Emmanuel made his point well, Eli had to admit.

'My mum said that exorcisms only work if you believe in God,' Eli said.

'With all due respect, what makes your mother an authority figure on this?' Emmanuel said. A valid question, but it rubbed Eli the wrong way.

'The fact that she had first-hand experience with demons. The fact that she could see spirits like Felix could…'

The look on Emmanuel's face told Eli he'd said too much. Emmanuel hadn't known about any of that.

Eli dipped his head in acknowledgement.

'From my perspective,' Emmanuel said, 'we need to throw everything at this we can in order to prevent a repeat of what happened last time. Calling in an expert, even if they are part of a religion you don't believe in, would be pertinent.' Emmanuel bit his lip. 'I want to know more about this seeing spirits thing too, and whatever your mother experienced. The more information I have, the better equipped we are to deal with this.'

'What was the fourth step?' Asher asked. 'Possession?'

'Yes,' Emmanuel said. 'The fourth step is possession. Although, possession isn't what people typically think it is. The demon doesn't consume the person's consciousness and use their body. Both consciousnesses are vying for control. It's a battle of wills.'

'You're saying that if my dad had fought harder, he wouldn't have tried to hurt me?'

'Not at all!' Emmanuel looked genuinely upset by Asher's words. 'I'm saying that your dad would have been doing everything in his power to stop the possession.'

Mollified, Asher shrugged.

'Right, I need you to tell me everything,' Emmanuel said.

Eli still didn't trust Emmanuel. There was a small part of Eli that thought Emmanuel could have faked the letter just to come to the house and get Eli to *tell him everything*.

'I want to ring the prison. I want to talk to Olivia.'

Eli knew enough about the prison system to know he wasn't going to be able to talk to Olivia that day, more than likely. He could give his phone number to the prison staff and ask them to pass it on to Olivia. Hopefully, she'd call him, but who knew how long that would take.

'Can you ask about Lilith's body?' Asher said.

'Of course,' Eli said. He dialled the number.

The conversation with the prison lasted a few minutes. On Asher's behest, he asked about Lilith's body first. He was told that the body was in the morgue and that they were waiting for family to claim it. Eli asked if he could claim it - she'd put him down as her emergency contact after all - and the officer had laughed. *Friends couldn't claim bodies*, she said. When he asked about Lilith's cellmate, and whether his phone number could be passed on to her, the woman on the phone went quiet.

'I'm sorry, sir, but Olivia passed away a couple of days ago.'

'What? How?' Eli choked out.

'I cannot disclose the details of her death.'

'Did she kill herself?' Eli pushed. He was too aware of Asher and Emmanuel's expressions. Shock. Terror. Disappointment.

'I'm sorry, I can't…'

Eli hung up the phone.

'Fuck,' he said.

'She's dead?' Emmanuel asked.

Eli nodded. *That* would have to do. He'd have to trust Emmanuel had the best intentions. What else could he do?

Asher laid in bed listening to *Possession!* Mona Koestler, the sole presenter/podcaster, told the story of Kristy Bamu, a fifteen-year-old who was killed in London in 2010 by his sister and her partner in an *exorcism gone wrong.* He died in his older sister's bathtub after days of being abused and tortured.

'The couple accused him of witchcraft, or *kindoki* - as it is referred to in their native Democratic Republic of Congo. There is some debate around whether Magalie Bamu and Craig Bikubi genuinely believed Kristy to have been utilising *sorcery* or *witchcraft.* But, as the judge said, *'The belief in witchcraft, however genuine, cannot excuse an assault to another person, let alone the killing of another human being.'*

Asher swallowed at those words. He'd watched Lilith murder his father who they all believed to be possessed. What would a judge have said had they known the truth? He'd listened to Uncle Eli telling Emmanuel everything, in so much detail that it made Asher's skin crawl. It felt like a betrayal, but a necessary one. Emmanuel was the only person who had the means to help them. He'd failed them the last time around and had caused them no end of pain by releasing the video, but he seemed remorseful. And Asher believed that people could change.

Asher felt like he'd been plunged into an ice bath. His skin pricked with goosebumps. He knew *they'd* be there before he looked. The three figures returned whenever there was darkness. Asher had tested his theory by turning the light off in the bathroom, and the *things* had emerged. He hadn't told Uncle Eli or Emmanuel about them yet. He wanted to know for sure what they were first. There was a chance that it was his dad, Nanna, and Lilith, and he didn't want Emmanuel to try and banish them or exorcise them or whatever.

But what if they're something else?

The thought was unnerving. He'd tried to ask the figures who they were but never had a response. They whispered things to him: bad things, things that he hoped weren't true, which tipped the scales towards them not being his dead family, but that also didn't mean they were demons. If they were demons, Asher would *know*. He'd be able to tell. It would feel like it did last time, and it didn't. Nicolas Damont had felt oppressive, ever since Lilith had first walked into their house, it was like a thick cloud of fog had descended on them. Asher didn't get that feeling now. They could be spirits, stuck here and trying to move on. That was the most likely theory, but if there was a chance…

'*Emmanuel is going to kill you.*' The voice was a sibilant whisper.

'*He isn't here to help you.*' A different voice. Asher wasn't sure which of the figures it came from.

'He's here to bury you.' Another voice.

Asher shook his head. 'Who are you?'

'You'll never survive this.' It sounded like the voice was behind him.

'You'll pay for what you did.' This time it came from in front of him.

'This time, you won't win.'

That did it. Any hope that the creatures made from darkness were not *bad* (he purposefully didn't want to think of the word *demonic),* had evaporated. A chorus of cackling laughter erupted out of them. It filled Asher's brain, consuming his senses. He covered his ears, but it didn't dampen the noise. He stood, stumbling, the noise knocking him off balance. He ran to the door, slamming it shut behind him. The hallway was light. The creatures were gone. He could hear Uncle Eli's voice downstairs talking with Emmanuel.

They looked up from the kitchen table when Asher walked into the room. Before Emmanuel was a laptop. Before Uncle Eli was his phone.

'I have to tell you something,' Asher said.

Uncle Eli nodded.

'It's definitely started again,' Asher said.

'Ash, what do you mean?' Uncle Eli looked exhausted.

Asher told them everything. Neither interrupted. They waited for him to finish.

Emmanuel looked to Uncle Eli and waited for him to say something. But Uncle Eli didn't look like he could talk. He patted the seat next to him. Asher sat down.

'Thank you for telling us,' Uncle Eli said. Asher had braced himself for an attack of *why didn't you tell me sooner?* It was what his dad would have probably said. He felt overwhelming relief. He also realised that he was warm again.

'I'm going to do everything in my power to help you,' Emmanuel said.

Asher believed him.

'But I do have one condition. I've already explained this to your uncle, and he agreed, somewhat reluctantly, but still…'

'What's the condition?' Asher asked.

'I want to record what's happening. I want to treat this as an experiment. I want more proof.'

'You're letting him treat us like lab rats?' Asher asked his uncle.

'Ash, I don't have another choice. What else can I do?' He bit out, 'We need him.'

'What, you wouldn't help us if we don't let you record what's happening? That's fucked up!' Asher snapped at Emmanuel, who jumped back. It gave Asher a wave of satisfaction.

'You think I haven't already said all that?' Uncle Eli asked.

'Then why are you letting him do this to us? It's blackmail.' Asher was fuming.

'It will be using scientific instruments, okay? A legit experiment. It might help us as much as it helps him.' Uncle Eli massaged his temples. He did that whenever he had a headache.

'What do you mean?' Asher asked.

Uncle Eli opened his mouth but closed it again.

'He means in case anything goes wrong, we'll have proof of what actually happened,' Emmanuel said.

'You mean if somebody gets killed?' Asher felt faint.

'Or hurt, or if somebody accuses somebody of doing something they didn't.' Uncle Eli gave a pointed look at Emmanuel. 'Emmanuel has promised that no footage will be released without our consent.'

'And you believe him?' Asher was appalled.

'I have to,' Uncle Eli said. 'I have to.'

A HUMAN EXPERIMENT

Eli lay in bed. Asher snored beside him. Specs grunted and rolled in his sleep from the foot of the bed. Emmanuel had taken the third bedroom, across the hall from Asher's room. Asher hadn't wanted to go back to bed on his own, which suited Eli just fine. Asher had come to the conclusion that the *things* he was seeing *were* demons, and not his dad, Nanna, and Lilith, as he'd hoped. Eli was in awe that Asher's desire for the *things* to be his family had overridden all of the evidence against that explanation. Asleep, Asher looked so young. The last six months had changed him, forcing him to grow up too quickly.

Eli had kept the lamp on while Asher had fallen asleep, as requested, but it was too bright. There was no way Eli would be able to drop to sleep with it on. What Asher had said about the demons only being there in the dark, Eli wasn't sure about. He wondered if, maybe, the demons were only *visible* in the dark, but they were there all the time. He tested the theory.

With the lamp off, Eli scanned the room. There was nothing out of place. No demonic black figures. No cold spots. No weird smells. Nothing that would imply paranormal activity. There was still a chance that nothing was happening to them, Eli reminded himself. It could all have been a bunch of coincidences. Lilith could have been suicidal. Her friend could have been crazy. Asher was grieving. There was a logical explanation to all of it, an explanation not founded in the supernatural. He couldn't jump straight to demons because of what had happened before. Just because it had been a demon then, didn't mean it was one now.

A scratching noise came at the window.

Eli held his breath, listening.

Scratch. The sound of a fingernail against glass.

And then a tap.

Tap. Tap. Tap.

Eli pulled himself, reluctantly, out of bed.

He didn't want to open the blinds, but he had to. It was probably just a tree branch or something. But there were no trees at the side of the house.

'Shit,' he said under his breath.

He stood before the blinds, his hand on the cord.

Tap. Tap. Tap.

The light sound of a fingertip.

Please God, don't be a fingertip.

He slowly manipulated the cord, and the blind began to raise. The bottom of the window was frosted with condensation. As the blind rose, Eli could see nothing at all, the slick window disguising what lay outside.

Using the sleeve of his shirt, Eli wiped the window. He leaned close to peer outside.

Below stood three figures.

Human-like.

Just as Asher had described.

His breath caught, panic rising in his chest.

They stood about fifty yards away. Outside the confines of the garden, but close enough that Eli could make out their shapes.

They took a step forwards in unison, moving as though one entity.

And then another step.

They approached the house with bitter slowness, savouring each sinister step. Their bodies were rigid, all except for their heads, which tilted.

Eli couldn't tell for sure, but they looked like they were smiling.

'THEY'RE HERE FOR YOU!'

Eli spun around. The words had come from behind him.

Asher slept soundly. Specs grumbled, hackles raised. The room was, otherwise, empty.

Eli's heart pounded aggressively inside his chest. He could hear the drum beat of his pulse in his ears. He turned his attention back to the window. The figures had vanished. On the window was a childlike drawing of a hanging stick figure. Eli placed his palm against it, attempting to wipe it away. The drawing remained untouched.

It was on the other side of the window.

Eli, Asher, and Specs watched Emmanuel turn the house into an experiment.

'We have to use a scientific method to approach this, or the data we gain will be invalid and unreliable.' He was in the process of sticking motion detector sensors around the living area. 'The issue with paranormal investigations is that they're not replicable. They're uniquely individual phenomena, so you're not going to be able to replicate the study and get the same data. The difficulty applying the scientific method to paranormal investigations is part of the reason we're not taken seriously.'

Emmanuel was in full lecture mode. Eli had managed to bite back his comment about how Emmanuel had brought all the equipment he needed for his 'big experiment' before Eli and Asher had even agreed to let him stay with them.

'Whatever happens, we'll have multiple different sources of data to look back on.' He stuck another motion detector to the front of the TV cabinet. 'Would the two of you be opposed to keeping a diary? I often feel like humans sense things that aren't there so if you could keep a note of-'

'Sure, whatever,' Eli said. He tried to ignore the look of disappointment on Asher's face.

'It doesn't have to be anything fancy. Just, for example, "Sixteen forty-eight - I felt like somebody was watching me," and we can cross-reference that with the data from the equipment,' Emmanuel explained.

'Remind me again what the equipment is?' Eli asked.

'We have motion sensors, temperature sensors, humidity sensors, cameras and voice recorders, and EMF and EVP meters. I assume you know what they are?' Emmanuel gave him a pointed look.

'Electromagnetic field detectors, and electronic voice phenomena,' Asher interjected. Eli shot him a questioning glance. In response, Asher shrugged.

'Correct,' Emmanuel continued. 'All of these are being tracked and monitored by a computer programme one of my graduate students came up with. I'll get an alert to my phone if anything goes outside of set parameters.'

'Cool stuff,' Eli said. He thought back to Felix setting up the cameras in his house, hoping to prove that he was being haunted.

'I'll grab a notepad for each of you, and a pen, and if you can make notes like we said, that would really help.'

'You're hoping that something happens,' Asher said.

Eli's head turned in Asher's direction. He was curled up on the sofa, his legs tucked under him, Gameboy in hand.

Emmanuel didn't answer, which was also an answer in itself.

'My dad died. My Nanna died. Lilith died. Her cellmate did too. You shouldn't want this to happen.' Asher's voice was quiet, but steady, mature. Eli felt a twinge of pride at the way he was holding himself.

'I know that,' Emmanuel said. 'I do. I don't want anybody to get hurt. Genuinely, Ash-'

'Asher,' Asher corrected. Only family called him Ash.

'Asher,' Emmanuel said, pursing his lips. 'I don't want anybody to get hurt, but it seems that there is some presence here, and if we were able to get proof of that…'

'Yeah, I know, it would change the way we see the world, life after death, and everything else,' Asher said.

'I think we'll leave you to it,' Eli said. 'It's Asher's birthday tomorrow, and a haunting isn't going to stop me from buying him some presents.'

Asher's birthday had come around with a ridiculous force. It was the first birthday since Felix had died, and if Eli was completely honest with himself, he was dreading it, but he would never let Asher know that. Between fleeing in the middle of the night, and the weird stuff happening at the Airbnb, the plan to take Asher to choose presents had been left by the wayside.

'Now?' Asher said.

'No time like the present.' Eli shrugged.

'Was that pun intentional?' Asher rolled his eyes.

'Yes, yes it was,' Eli said. 'Emmanuel, are you going to be okay with Specs?'

Specs peeled open one eye. He'd been asleep in the chair next to the radiator, like a cat.

'I think we'll be fine,' Emmanuel said.

Specs closed his eye and resumed snoring. It was a good sign. Specs had become an unofficial paranormal radar. If he was chill, the house was safe, in theory. It was only 1 pm. They had a few hours before it got dark, which was when things usually took a turn for the sinister.

Asher didn't know what he wanted for his birthday. In the years gone by, his birthday was his favourite day of the year, but this was his first one without his dad. He could tell Uncle Eli was struggling with it too, but he hadn't said anything. They'd driven to a shopping centre about half an hour away from their Airbnb and Asher was being escorted around the shops, Uncle Eli repeating, 'Just tell me what you want, and we'll get it,' every now and again. He was trying his hardest, and Asher didn't want to be ungrateful, but…

'Does it feel good to get out of the house a bit?' Uncle Eli asked. They traversed the aisles in Game.

'Yeah, maybe. I don't know.'

'I get that,' Uncle Eli said. 'Ash, if you're not sure what you want, you don't have to get something now. I just thought it might be nice to choose something, you know? Something a bit positive.'

'I know.' Asher made the effort to smile.

'Want to just go home? I want to at least get you a cake, and we need some more shopping if Emmanuel is planning on staying.'

'And Mona,' Asher said.

'Oh God yeah, and Mona,' Eli said.

'Let's just go get the shopping. If that's okay?' Asher said.

'Of course. Whatever you want,' Uncle Eli said. His shoulders slumped, leaving Asher feeling guilty. 'I know it's hard for you right now,' Uncle Eli continued. 'This birthday isn't going to be much fun, but we'll do our best with it. Why don't you choose some food and snacks, and we'll watch some films and eat our weight in chocolate?'

Asher smiled a real smile. 'Yeah, thanks.'

'Your wish is my command.'

Eli dropped the shopping bags in the kitchen. Asher followed suit.

'Emmanuel? Specs?' Eli shouted.

A faint rumbling noise caught Eli's attention.

'Is that Specs?' Asher said, confusion evident on his face.

'Oh God,' Eli said. 'Specs!'

A snapping bark came from upstairs. Eli ran, taking the stairs as quickly as he could.

Specs was standing outside the closed door of Asher's bedroom, snarling, foam dripping from his exposed teeth.

'Specs, what is it?' Eli asked. He bent down to stroke the dog, to try and pull him out of whatever had got him locked on. Eli's hand tapped Specs on the back. 'Specs, what's up boy?'

Asher approached the bedroom door with caution. His fingers closed around the knob. He looked back at Eli, who nodded. Asher twisted and pushed open the door.

Emmanuel stood behind it. Drip white. His eyes were wide but unseeing.

'Emmanuel,' Asher said.

Specs lunged. He moved before Eli could grab him and hold him back. 'No! Specs!' Eli shouted.

Specs didn't bite Emmanuel. He dodged around him and toward the corner of the room; where the figures were standing. Their limbs were long and contorted, stretched out and fucked up.

Emmanuel began to babble. 'They're real. They're real.'

'What happened?' Eli said to Emmanuel.

'They're real. They're real. I couldn't get out. The door wouldn't… I was trapped.'

'The door opened fine for me,' Asher said, not taking his eyes away from the shadow creatures.

'It wouldn't move.' Emmanuel's chest juddered as he tried to inhale. He began to turn slowly. His hand raised. His finger pointed. 'They're real.'

A BAG OF ROCKS

Emmanuel's hands ringed the steaming mug of tea in front of him.

'You need to tell us what happened,' Asher said. It wasn't fair, he knew, but he was feeling impatient. After everything Emmanuel had done to them, all the shit he'd caused, the paranormal expert was freaking out because he'd had his first real-life supernatural experience. For somebody who studied the supernatural for a living, you'd think he'd have been more prepared.

With a shaking breath, Emmanuel said, 'I saw them. The shadow people.'

'And?' Asher pushed. Uncle Eli reached out and placed a hand on his, a silent way of telling him to cool it.

'They told me things. Terrible, awful things.' Emmanuel slowly brought the mug to his lips and sipped.

Frustration grew within Asher. 'Like what?' he snapped.

'Asher,' Uncle Eli warned.

'What?' Asher said, his annoyance bubbling over. 'We're supposed to tell him everything that happened to us. He uses us to further his career, like what happened to us was absolutely nothing, and now he's acting like a baby!'

'People handle things in different ways. Sometimes people don't react like they'd expect to,' Uncle Eli said. His voice was too calm.

'He's an adult!' Asher's skin flushed with anger. The red-hot heat prickled at his cheeks.

'They said they're here for you,' Emmanuel said. He looked up through his lashes at Asher.

'They're here for me?' Asher said. 'I'm not being funny, but *duh.'* Asher shook his head. Of course, they were here for him. Whoever they were. They were targeting him. All the signs pointed to that.

'We need an exorcist here. Now.' Emmanuel raked his nails through his hair.

'What else did they say?' Eli asked.

'Nothing that concerns you.'

'Did they know things about you?' Asher questioned. Damont had *known* things. He'd been able to make Asher and his family see things, things that nobody knew about. He'd known things about Lilith too.

Emmanuel dipped his head. Asher took that as a 'yes'.

'Damont knew things too,' Asher said. 'It's happening again.' He turned to his uncle. 'Let him get an exorcist here. What we did last time didn't work. Emmanuel said Mona Koestler will be here tomorrow. He also said that she'd have ideas on other things to do.'

'I still don't like the podcaster being here,' Uncle Eli said. 'The rest of the world already knows too much about our lives.' He glared piercing daggers at Emmanuel.

'She knows what she's doing. She knows more than anybody about this.' Emmanuel attempted to reassure them.

'Then why couldn't she tell you what to do over the phone? Why does she have to come here?' Uncle Eli's face was stone-cold. Asher rarely saw him like that.

'She needs to be here to figure out what we're fighting. You can't fight something if you don't know what it is,' Emmanuel explained.

'But we do know what it is. It's a demon, but I don't think it's Damont. I don't think it could be. When Lilith killed my dad, she killed Damont too. I could feel it. I felt him die.'

'Maybe demons can't die. Maybe he's back. Maybe killing the host doesn't kill the demon, just injures it. These are all things we have to consider.' Emmanuel was growing more animated after his weird turn.

'Emmanuel, what exactly did you see in Asher's room?'

Emmanuel gulped. 'Three of them. Like Asher said. Three *things*. They were tall, black, huddled in the corner of the room. Their mouths stretched open like they were trying to swallow me. They leaned closer.' He shook his head. 'And then they began to tell me things.'

'You wanted us to be honest with you,' Asher said, losing any ounce of patience. 'We need you to be honest with us. What did they say?'

'They showed me my husband's death. Over and over again. I could hear the machine flatline when he died.'

'Why did he die?' Asher asked. Uncle Eli, again, shot a look at him. The time for politeness had gone. Plus, loads of people had asked how his dad had died.

'Brain tumour.'

'I'm sorry,' Uncle Eli said.

'Yeah, sorry,' Asher chorused.

'It's okay,' Emmanuel said. 'It was a long time ago. I'd just forgotten how the hospital room had smelled.' He wiped a tear away. 'I'm going to go and catalogue the experience. Excuse me.'

Mona was the same height as Asher. Her jet-black hair was cut into a blunt bob that sat just above her shoulders. She had a thick fringe that rested on top of her heavy glasses. If Asher was being honest, she looked just like Edna Mode from *The Incredibles*. He did not tell her that. She came with more luggage than Asher thought a person could take on a plane.

The taxi driver, a bald man with a bulldog face, grunted as he unloaded the boot of his car. He drove off before Mona could ask him to take the bags to the door. She stood beside her bags in the middle of the driveway. Asher stared at her from the door.

'You must be Asher,' she said. Her American accent sounded foreign to his ears, even more so than Emmanuel's (which was Canadian, he supposed).

'I am.'

'Want to help me with my bags?'

The feeling of déjà vu felt like a weighted blanket over him.

'Okay.' Asher shuffled forwards.

Uncle Eli and Emmanuel came to the door. Emmanuel hugged her tightly and thanked her for being there.

Uncle Eli shook her hand. 'Thank you for coming.' He sounded almost sincere.

'Thank you for allowing me to be here. I hope I can help you figure this shit out and get you guys back to normal.'

'I hope so too,' Uncle Eli said. He picked up two of Mona's cases without being asked and walked them inside. Asher dragged another case behind him. It felt like it was full of rocks.

It turned out, the case was full of rocks.

Once inside, Mona unzipped it and began pulling out stone carvings. Some looked like monsters. Others looked like bulls, lions, birds, and a whole host of other animal-like things. Most of them were made out of black stone. There were a few that looked to be made out of sand.

Asher's sense of déjà vu grew.

'These are various protection statues that I've collected during my travels. Many different cultures rely on these to ward off evil, amongst other things. Better safe than sorry, I think.' She placed a figure outside the front door. Another on each windowsill downstairs.

'Asher, can you go and put these upstairs for me? One on each windowsill, please?'

Asher did as he was asked, taking as many of the statues as he could carry. With loaded arms, he climbed up the stairs. The stairs curved back on themselves and deposited him on a landing. There were two bedrooms to the left (Asher's and Emmanuel's) and one to the right (previously Eli's, and now Mona's). Asher turned his head, deciding where to start.

Specs's growl caught him off guard. In his shock, he almost dropped the statues.

Specs paused beside him in the now all-too-familiar stance; hackles raised, chest puffed out, lip curled, ears standing to attention. He was looking towards the end of the landing. There was a window, enough to let in plenty of light, had it not been a dull day.

'What is it, Specs?'

He was answered with a bark, and then a whine aimed towards the end of the corridor. Where Asher's bedroom was. 'We have to put these out,' Asher said.

He approached the window with caution, Specs remaining glued to his side. He placed a figure with horns down on the windowsill.

'One down,' he said to Specs, who was still grumbling to himself.

The air had shifted. Asher could feel it too.

'Bedroom now, Specs,' he said. Talking aloud helped him to feel safe. Nothing had ever happened in the daytime. He had nothing to worry about.

He opened his bedroom door, quickly scanning the room. Everything was where he'd left it, as far as he could tell. A feeling like an ice cube on his spine spurred him forwards. He thrust another statue onto the window, not bothering to check which one he'd put down and walked into the little ensuite attached. There was a small window, up high. He had to stand on the toilet lid to reach it. He gently placed the statues on the floor in front of the shower and climbed onto the toilet holding just one. It was small enough to fit in the palm of his hand. He didn't bother to look at it. Reaching up on tiptoes, Asher placed the statue on the windowsill.

The *thing* in the window hit him like a physical blow. A face, pushed up against the glass. Hands with long, spindly fingers pressing and stretching. Something was trying to peer in. Asher stumbled backwards, losing his footing. The snap as his right foot hit the floor was loud enough to shake the room. Tears sprang to his eyes as blinding pain erupted from the joint.

Specs's barking turned into crying. Uncle Eli flung himself into the room.

'What happened?' he asked frantically. He knelt down next to Asher.

'I fell. I think I broke my ankle,' Asher managed to say through shaking sobs. 'Something was in the window.'

Uncle Eli tentatively pulled up Asher's trouser leg.

Asher winced. 'Don't touch it.'

'We've got to go to the hospital.' Uncle Eli turned to the door; Emmanuel and Mona were there, hovering. 'Help me get him to the car.'

Emmanuel placed a hand under one of his arms, Uncle Eli got the other. Together they yanked him up so that he didn't have to put his foot to the floor.

Panic flooded through Asher. He'd broken his ankle. It was broken. He'd felt it bend back on itself.

'Breathe, Asher,' Uncle Eli said. 'Slow and steady.'

He tried. He really did. Each movement caused shockwaves of agony up his leg. By the time they reached the car, he was ready to collapse. He heard Uncle Eli say to Emmanuel, 'Stay here. Look after Specs.' And then a car door slammed, and they drove away.

YOU KILLED ME

As they suspected, Asher's ankle was broken. Not badly, but badly enough. It was wrapped in a red plaster cast. He was given crutches and a plastic boot and told to go back to the fracture clinic in six weeks. Asher had fallen asleep on the sofa almost as soon as they got home. Specs curled up next to him.

Emmanuel made coffee for everyone. They sat at the kitchen table as Mona explained her set-up and what would happen next.

'My first point of call is to figure out what is happening here,' she said. 'There's a chance, however small, that this isn't actually supernatural in origin.'

Eli opened his mouth to speak, but she shushed him.

'I have to rule that out first, while also being careful. Hence the protection statues. Hence the symbols I've written on the doors and windows.'

'Hence what?' A throbbing headache broke out through Eli's skull. 'This isn't my house!'

'They're in pencil. They'll rub right off. If your family is in danger, you'll be thankful I did that. Emmanuel got in touch with his contact at the Catholic Church. We're waiting to hear back from them. I've washed the doors in holy water while you were gone, and I've said the prayers of Saint Michael. I've also placed crucifixes in each room. Not crosses. People get the two confused. A cross without Christ is pointless. It's the sacrifice you're trying to summon with the crucifix. And now, we wait.'

'Now we wait?' Eli sighed. He turned to Emmanuel. 'You told her what happened to Felix and my mum, right? And Lilith?'

'I did,' Emmanuel confirmed.

'The thing is, I can't do anything without proof. Without proof, my conclusion would be that this is either the result of mental illness or something in the physical environment. A gas leak, for example. Emmanuel has placed all of his gadgets around, and he's given me access to the recordings. I've also added a few of my own too. We need proof. Especially if we're going to ask for an exorcism. The Catholic Church will not perform an exorcism without extensive proof. They've already got a bad reputation to contend with.'

Eli wanted to cry. He felt the tears welling behind his eyes and swallowed them back.

'Emmanuel filled me in on what's been happening here. He told me what he believes he saw.'

'Believes he saw?' Eli felt himself becoming hot with anger.

'Yes, believes he saw. Nothing is proven yet. He hadn't yet set up the camera in that room, so we don't have proof of anything.'

'What about the other devices? The temperature thing? The EMF reader? The EVP?'

Emmanuel's face blanched.

'What?' Eli said.

'I couldn't…'

'Let's do it now.' Eli left no room for argument.

Emmanuel turned on his laptop. He opened a program called, 'GHOST MONITOR 2.3', and the screen filled with graphs and measures. He selected the menu and pulled up, 'Historical Data'. After scrolling to the right time and date, Emmanuel pressed 'PLAY'.

In one corner was a blank screen that said, 'VIDEO FEED'. There was a box with an EMF scale, which looked like a rainbow with a dial. Another one had the EVP data. Mona came to stand behind the two of them. They watched the screen. The EMF dial flickered, but didn't move drastically. Nothing else happened. At the bottom of the screen was the time. The seconds passed. The EMF dial shot to the far end of the scale, landing in the red column. It vibrated there. The laptop began to emit a beep. A steady beep, like a heart monitor. The sound of a hospital room.

'That's coming from the EVP, but it shouldn't… It should only pick up words.' Emmanuel's voice was heavy with confusion.

'*YOU.*' The word sounded like a gunshot.

'*KILLED.*'

Eli stopped breathing.

'ME.'

The laptop emitted a scream, loud and piercing.

And then it ended as abruptly as it started.

It was replaced by Specs's terrified barks.

Asher was sitting up, staring at them.

'What was that?'

The beeping ended.

Emmanuel stuttered, 'That's not how I remember it happening. That's different.' He pointed at the computer screen.

'How's that for proof?' Eli looked at Mona.

'You could have doctored that,' she said, although her voice was quiet.

'For fuck's sake. It's the first time we've listened to it! How did we doctor it? Why would we?'

'For the fame?' Mona threw up her hands. 'The only reason I'm here is because of the hype around the three of you.' She gestured towards Emmanuel. 'He's all over the news, and he's dragged you with him. This case is massive. It'll be huge. You've got a lot to gain by faking stuff.'

Eli was lost for words. It was happening again. He wasn't being believed.

Eli sat with Asher in bed. Specs was between the two of them. His ears were standing to attention. He'd been on edge since Asher had fallen. Asher snored. It was good. After the day he'd had, he needed sleep. It was easy to forget how significant breaking an ankle was. In the context of what Asher had been through, it didn't seem like such a big deal, but it was. Mona's arrival meant that Eli would be sharing Asher's room for the time being. He wasn't complaining. He didn't want to let his nephew out of his sight.

The sound of glass breaking pulled Eli from his thoughts.

Asher remained asleep.

Specs sat upright.

'What the hell was that?' Eli said under his breath. His watch told him it was 11.34 PM. He left the room and stood at the top of the hallway, listening. Emmanuel and Mona's muffled voices came from down the hall. He followed them. They were in Mona's bedroom.

'I don't know what happened,' Mona said.

'I told you something was happening here,' Emmanuel replied.

Eli crept closer.

'I never said there wasn't. I said I needed proof. I have a reputation to protect.' Mona's terse whispers sounded desperate.

'What's going on?' Eli said, announcing himself as he walked through the door. Mona was dressed in a Metallica shirt that reached to her knees. Emmanuel in a pair of tartan pyjama bottoms.

'The mirror smashed. It looks like something threw one of the statues at it. And then…'

Eli stopped listening. He approached the mirror for himself. It hung above the dressing table. The top right corner held a spider web crack from where the statue had hit it. But that wasn't what caught Eli's attention. Written on the mirror in block capitals were the words, '*YOU NEED TO LEAVE.*'

'How?' Eli asked. The words looked like they'd been written in condensation, like somebody had breathed on the mirror. Eli reached out and wiped his fingertips against the words. His fingers left trails through them.

'Maybe you should listen?' Eli said. 'Do we really want to piss them off more?'

'You keep saying *them* like it's separate entities,' Mona said. 'That's rare. It's more likely one entity projecting three figures.'

'You believe us now?' Eli groaned.

'It's hard not to,' Mona said. 'We need to check the camera, Emmanuel.'

Emmanuel left the room, returning moments later with his laptop.

He set it up on the dressing table in front of the mirror and opened up the program. After selecting the camera feed that read, 'ELI'S BEDROOM', the screen populated with different measures like before. Emmanuel dragged the cursor back five minutes and pressed 'PLAY'.

Mona was in bed, scrolling on her phone. Her face was illuminated by the screen's glow.

The mirror smashed. Mona shot up.

A bloom of breath grew on the mirror.

An invisible finger began to trace the words; each letter was made with painstaking slowness.

'YOU NEED TO LEAVE.'

'There's your evidence,' Eli said.

'Rewind it,' Mona demanded.

Emmanuel did.

'Watch the statue,' she said.

Emmanuel pressed 'PLAY'.

Eli focused his attention on the statue. He couldn't make out what it was from the video, but it was palm-sized.

It began to float, an invisible hand picking it up.

Emmanuel blinked, and the statue made contact with the mirror. It had been thrown too quickly for him to see it on the video.

'Can you slow it down?' Mona asked.

Emmanuel did.

Eli leaned closer to the screen. This time, you could clearly see the statue flying through the air and smashing into the mirror, the cracks ballooning outwards.

'The EMF reader is going insane when that happens,' Mona said.

'Do you need more proof?' Eli said, turning to look at her.

'Honest answer: yes, I do. The more proof, the better. If we want more eyes on this, we need more proof.'

'We don't need more eyes on it, we want it to stop.' Eli looked to Emmanuel for support. Emmanuel looked to the floor.

'Get this thing out of the house. I'll do your fucking podcast. I'll do whatever you want, but no more *proof.* I want this to be over.'

Eli stormed out of the room. He had to check on Asher.

The bed was empty.

'Asher?' Eli shouted.

That was when he saw him. Asher was standing in front of the window. No crutches supported him. Thankfully, his broken ankle was encased in the plastic boot.

'What are you doing?' Eli said. He ran around the bed. Asher stood on his broken ankle. 'The doctor said you shouldn't-'

'They said it's our fault.' Asher's voice was void of any emotion; flat and blank. 'They said that we caused this. We killed him. It's our fault.'

Asher collapsed to the floor. Eli reached him in time to break his fall.

'What did you mean?' Eli said.

Asher's eyes were closed. He didn't answer. He was sleeping.

Eli heaved Asher's dead weight into the bed and shouted for Mona and Emmanuel.

LORD, BLESS THIS HOUSE

Mona leaned close to her laptop, her nose almost touching the screen. She was watching last night's video recordings, from each camera. Every so often, she paused the video and jotted something down in a notepad with a Ouija board cover, which Eli thought was in bad taste.

'I'm compiling data to share with the Church,' she said when Eli asked what she was doing. 'The more data we have, the more likely they are to consent to an exorcism. They don't just hand them out anymore, there are hoops you have to jump through.'

'And the priest is coming today?' Eli asked.

'Yes,' Emmanuel answered. 'After lunch. He's going to perform a blessing on the house, and on each of us.'

'What does that involve?'

'Prayers, basically. Probably some holy water,' Mona said without looking up from the screen.

'That's it?'

'They always do that first. The Catholic Church has a policy of *do the least and see if it works*,' Mona said.

'They have a bad reputation with exorcisms,' Emmanuel said, 'as you know, so the less-is-more approach is their new priority. It isn't great, I suppose, if you're actually dealing with a demonic infestation, but for the most part that's not the case.'

Eli nodded. 'You hear that, Ash?' he called into the living area.

'Yeah!' Asher yelled back. He was sitting on the sofa playing on Felix's Gameboy. Eli hadn't brought up what happened last night, and Asher hadn't either, so Eli was taking that as a good sign. Asher seemed well-rested. He was smiley. Happy. It was unnerving.

Tendrils of panic clawed at Eli's mind. He dropped onto the sofa next to Asher. He opened up his laptop and continued his search for any semblance of useful information in the sea of useless shite. An attempt to distract himself, and also to feel somewhat useful.

The priest arrived, as promised, after lunch. He was painfully stereotypical: a middle-aged man with greying hair at his temples and a small paunch at his stomach. He introduced himself as Father Edwards. His hand was clammy when Eli shook it.

Emmanuel had filled him in on everything, it seemed. It was obvious that Father Edwards was on edge from the second he walked into the house. Specs completely ignored him, which Eli took as a good sign.

'What I'll do is say a prayer of protection in each room and then we'll pray together for the people here.' Father Edwards refused offers of tea and coffee and got straight down to business.

He started at the doorway. 'Dear God, please bless this entryway in Jesus's name. Please guard all who enter and leave.' He splashed holy water from a small bottle into the doorway. He then moved to the kitchen and repeated the action, saying a different prayer. 'Lord, send down your mercy and your blessing upon us here and upon this house. May your angel of mercy watch over it and keep all who live here safe from anything that is evil. May he guide us into the fulfilment of your holy will, teaching us to observe what Christ has taught us.' He splashed holy water again, first on the floor, then the window, and then the cupboard. He turned into the living area, where Asher sat on the sofa, observing. The priest repeated his previous prayer.

Eli stood alongside Mona and Emmanuel, trying not to look too uncomfortable. Attempting to put his feelings about the Catholic Church aside, he was determined to keep an open mind. They did have a track record with dealing with demonic activity, more so than any other major religion, but that didn't mean he liked it. His mum's words kept coming back to him. *Exorcisms don't work on non-believers.* Lilith had said the same thing too, but he pushed that aside. He was willing to try anything at this point. And if demons were real, who's to say that gods weren't real too?

At the patio door, the priest visibly blanched, but said his prayer, 'Dear God, please bless this entryway in Jesus's name. Please guard all who enter and leave.'

The priest began to make his way to the stairs.

'Do you want us to come with you?' Eli asked.

'No, young man. I'll be fine,' he said.

With a groan, Father Edwards made his way upstairs.

They waited in silence, listening as he opened doors, spoke unintelligible words, and then moved on to different rooms.

He re-emerged ten minutes later.

'I'd like to say a final prayer with all of you.' Father Edwards walked into the living space. It was clear he expected everyone to follow him. He stood beside Asher. 'I do hope that leg isn't causing you too much trouble, young man,' he said.

Asher shook his head. 'It's fine.'

'Good, good. Now, let's all join hands,' Father Edwards instructed.

Asher didn't move his hand into Father Edwards's waiting hand.

'Sorry,' Eli said. 'It's just, this feels very similar to something we did last time.'

'With the psychic?' Father Edwards asked.

Eli nodded.

'Ah, young man, you see, the difference is that I am a man of God. I have the authority to bless this home. This time, it is different. You have my assurance of that.'

Asher, reluctantly, reached out his hand and placed it in Father Edwards's.

Eli held Asher's in one, and Emmanuel's in the other. Mona completed the circle.

'Hear us, Lord,' Father Edwards spoke solemnly, with closed eyes. 'And send your angel from heaven to visit and protect, to comfort and defend all who live in this house. You taught us, through your holy words, that *"The Lord will guard you from evil, he will guard your soul."* I ask, in the name of your son, that you protect your children from the evil they have faced. Keep them safe from harm. Amen.'

'Amen,' everyone repeated.

The hands were dropped. Asher continued to look sullen.

'May I speak with the adults in the kitchen?' Father Edwards said.

Asher's brows furrowed.

'Anything you want to say, you can say in front of Asher,' Eli said. Hiding things from Asher was pointless. The kid had been through enough. He needed to know the truth.

'I really don't think that's wise.' Father Edwards smiled sheepishly.

'With all due respect, Asher's been through more than most children his age. He's seen…' *his father become possessed and then murdered* '…a lot. He needs to be here for conversations that involve him.'

Father Edwards scrunched up his lips and then said, 'Okay. That's your choice and I respect that. I am concerned about you. About those around you. I feel that you are in danger, and I am escalating your case to the bishop and recommending that we perform a minor deliverance prayer, which is sometimes referred to as a minor exorcism.'

'Minor?' Emmanuel said. 'You think this only warrants *minor?* After what happened last time?'

'Yes,' Father Edwards said. 'There's a way to do things. You have to bear that in mind. And minor deliverances aren't a small or common thing. The Church performs a handful each year in the UK, and perhaps one major exorcism every few years. It's not like the movies, you know that.'

'I thought, given the circumstances, it would be escalated more quickly,' Emmanuel said.

'This is the correct way of doing things, and in the vast majority of cases, a minor deliverance will suffice. Please don't read into the word *minor.* It is very misleading.'

'What happens next?'

'The bishop of your diocese will consider my request and if accepted, he'll send the most appropriate person to complete the task. It will not be me. There are others in the Church far more suited to the role.'

'Thank you, Father,' Emmanuel said.

'When should we expect to hear from you?' Eli asked.

'Soon. Very soon, I would have thought.' Father Edwards nodded his head gravely. 'I wish you all the best. I'll be on my way.'

Eli didn't miss the fact that he made the sign of the cross as he left the building.

'Well, fuck…' Asher said.

The adults turned to look at him. Eli cracked a smile.

'Fuck indeed,' Eli agreed.

THE WORLD ISN'T READY TO BELIEVE IN DEMONS

'I'd like to interview you now,' Mona said. 'I would like to get the background content for the podcast done and dusted.' She'd spent the last few hours *protecting* the house, and the occupants inside it, based on the guidance of her contacts. At this point, it felt like she was throwing shit at the wall and seeing what stuck. They each now wore evil eye pendants, protection runes had been traced onto their skin in felt tip pen, and all of the windows and mirrors had been covered with sheets or newspapers, amongst other things that Eli suspected did nothing at all. Emmanuel said that Mona was one of the most knowledgeable people out there when it came to demons, and he had to trust that. In exchange for her *expertise,* he offered his soul. That was dramatic, but that was how it felt. Telling the story of what happened *last time* hurt. Every bone in his body told him not to do it. It felt wrong. So wrong.

'Mona, can I ask you something?' Eli picked at his nail bed.

'Sure,' she said, bustling around, setting up the podcast equipment on the kitchen table.

'Have you ever actually helped people or just documented/debunked it?' It was the question Eli had been trying to avoid asking.

'Honest answer?' Mona looked up from the microphone she was clamping to the table. 'I'm usually debunking things or documenting how other people *fix* them. Usually, I look at poltergeists, ghosts, apparitions. On the rare occasions I see something bigger than that, it tends to be a case of documenting. Exorcisms work. They do. I've seen it many times, whether it's the power of suggestion or down to faith, I couldn't tell you. That doesn't make it any less scary. It makes it one thousand percent worse.'

'How many people have died in the stories you've covered?'

'Where I believe it to be demonic possession or infestation?' She bit her lip and shook her head. 'Too many. But it gets written off as a medical issue – they're suffering from epilepsy, or a brain tumour, or mental health issues – even when there's no proof. The world isn't ready to believe that demons exist. That's what my podcast is for. I want to show that *sometimes*, it is a demon. Not always, but sometimes, and that we have to be open to the idea of that.'

'That doesn't make me feel better, but thank you for telling the truth.'

'I will do everything I can to help you. Documenting it and identifying how to *treat* the infestation is key. Just like an illness. We need a diagnosis before we can move on to treatment. Emmanuel said that you were told that killing the host works for demonic possession and that's why your brother was killed. I agree with him, but there are many other things we can do before we get to that stage.'

'Like what?' he asked.

'I'll keep that to myself for now. Just in case. Sometimes the element of surprise helps. Now, are you ready?'

'As I'll ever be,' Eli said.

'Cool, let's get started then.'

It took hours for Eli to tell the story of Felix, Lilith, and Damont. Every time he thought it was over, Mona would ask further questions. Reliving the worst week of his life, in graphic detail, with the threat of it happening again looming over him, had been near impossible. When it was finally over, he excused himself and went to the bathroom. He sat on the closed toilet seat and put his head in his hands. He couldn't prevent the tears from falling. He allowed himself the moment of weakness. He wouldn't allow Asher to see him like that. He was Asher's protector. Asher had to trust him.

A knock came on the door. Three sharp raps, and then Emmanuel's voice, 'We need you to see this, Eli. Can you come downstairs?'

'Two minutes,' Eli answered, trying to steady his shaking voice.

'Be quick.'

Eli wiped his eyes with the heels of his hands. The mirror above the sink had been covered with a sheet.

Probably for the best, Eli thought. He wouldn't be looking too great after the day he'd had. It was probably better not to know for sure.

He walked downstairs to find Emmanuel, Mona, and Asher waiting for him by the dining table in the kitchen. Asher was sitting on a dining chair, his broken ankle propped up on another.

'What's wrong?' Eli said, his eyes searching the group for an answer.

'Listen to this.' Mona tapped the screen on her laptop. It made a warbling noise that sounded almost human. She let it play for a few seconds and then tapped the screen again.

'What was that?' Eli asked.

'You,' Mona said.

'What do you mean?' Mona had listened back to bits of the recordings during the short breaks. Eli had heard her. It hadn't sounded like that.

'Did something go wrong with the equipment?'

She shook her head. 'The equipment's fine. The recording should be perfect, but this is how it sounds…'

'You're asking me to do it again?' Eli felt tears threatening to fall again. Recording it once had been hard enough.

'Not today,' she said, 'but I will need it again. I'm sorry.'

Eli nodded. 'What's to say it won't happen again?'

'I want to do it in chunks and upload it to the Cloud in between. Emmanuel has volunteered to go next, to give you a break. I know today was awful for you,' Mona said. 'And Asher will go after him.'

Eli inhaled sharply. 'Can't we do this without Asher?'

'I want to do it,' Asher said. He sat up straighter.

'Why?' Eli couldn't fathom why on Earth he'd want to relive his dad's death.

'Because it will help. We know this stuff is real, and Mona is trying to prove to other people that it is too. If my story helps to prove that, then maybe it will mean other people take it seriously, and we can stop them from losing their families.'

'Oh, Ash,' Eli said. The lump in his throat prevented him from saying anything else. He squeezed his nephew's shoulder.

'What do you think caused that?' Eli asked. He knew the answer, but he wanted somebody to say it.

'I think we all know what caused it,' Emmanuel said.

'You're the guy who wants proof.'

'We can't prove what caused the audio files to corrupt like this,' Mona said, trying to keep the peace. 'But I promise you, my equipment works perfectly. And, there's this…'

She pressed some buttons, and her own voice emerged from the laptop's speakers, clear as a bell.

'Can you go over that one more time for me?' The recording of Mona said. 'Explain exactly what happened when Felix brought Lilith back to your house.'

Then was the part that should have been Eli, but instead of his voice, the distorted, underwater gargle emerged.

'Shit,' Eli exhaled.

'Yep,' Emmanuel said. '*Shit* is right.'

The voice that should have been Eli's sent a shiver through his body. It made him itch. 'Can you stop it, please?'

Mona did as she was asked.

'There's something else too,' she said. 'The video cameras have picked up something weird in the bedrooms.'

'Weirder than somebody writing on the mirror?' Eli asked.

Mona looked to Emmanuel, who tilted his head in agreement.

'I'd say so. Yeah, definitely weirder.'

INFESTATION

Mona was right. What the cameras had picked up was definitely weirder.

'The video cameras record sound too. It's not perfect sound quality, but it's good enough. I first caught the noise in Emmanuel's bedroom,' Mona explained.

'That's what you're calling it? A noise?' Eli shook his head.

'What would you like to call it?' Mona asked.

'Laughter,' Eli said. 'It's laughter.'

'I try to avoid definites wherever possible, we're dealing with the unknown and falling into the habit of definites-'

'That's laughter,' Emmanuel interrupted. 'I'm sorry, I have to agree with Eli. That is definitely laughter. And, forgive me if I'm wrong, but it sounds like a child.'

'I agree,' Eli said.

Asher nodded. He'd shrunken into himself somewhat since Mona had played the noise.

'So, that was at three forty-five AM this morning. Now, if you listen very carefully, you'll hear something else.'

From the laptop came a gentle pattering noise.

'Is that footsteps?' Asher said. His face was ghost white.

'It sounded like it, although it could be many things,' Mona said.

'Like what?' Asher asked. He was looking for reassurance.

'It could maybe have picked up Specs moving in a different room, or-'

'Specs doesn't wake up and wander around in the night. He's a Staffy. They don't budge,' Asher said, parroting something Eli had said many times.

'But that would be a logical explanation,' Mona said.

'None of this is logical,' Asher replied.

'No, you're right. Asher,' Mona said, looking older than her twenty-odd years. 'If you don't want to be here for these conversations, you just have to say so.'

'Why wouldn't I want to?' Obviously affronted, Asher sat up straight.

'It's just scary stuff we're talking about, potentially,' Mona said.

It was a nice gesture, Eli thought, but sorely misplaced.

'I watched my dad die, and then I found my Nanna hanging in her old people's home.' He raised his eyebrows.

'Fair enough!' Mona said, 'You make an excellent point. Anyway, on that note, Emmanuel noticed some things too...'

'Yes,' Emmanuel said. 'The EVP keeps throwing out certain words: crash, fire, dead, mum, possessed, killed, murderer, devil, demon.'

'Aren't they wildly invalid?' Asher asked. Eli's mouth hung open in shock at Asher's question.

'Yes, they are. However, this is a top-of-the-line, newly-'

'But still, there's no proof that the words coming out of it are anything but random?' Asher said. Eli suppressed a smile.

'That is true, but these words are all related to your previous infestation,' Emmanuel argued.

'Previous infestation?' Eli said. 'We didn't have bed bugs, we had a fucking demon.' Eli shook his head.

'There's no need to be aggressive,' Emmanuel warned.

'I don't think he was being aggressive,' Mona said, at the same time as Eli said, 'I wasn't being aggressive.'

Eli continued, 'It's just, if this wasn't all so fucking scary, this would be laughable, you know? You lot don't make it easy to trust you, that's all. *Infestation.* Jesus Christ.'

'The cameras also picked up screams,' Mona said. 'Women's screams. They happen sporadically throughout the day and night.'

'I haven't heard any screams,' Eli said.

'No, neither have I,' Mona said. 'Which suggests that something is manipulating our recording equipment, or it is happening on a plane of existence, or dimension, other than our own.'

'A plane of existence, another dimension?' Eli used his thumb and forefinger to grip the bridge of his nose.

'Again, I remind you that we know relatively little about paranormal activity or the supernatural. There is research to suggest that there are many different dimensions or planes of existence. In fact, many world-renowned physicists believe in the multiverse theory, and quantum physics says-'

'Okay, I'll take your word for it, for now,' Eli said.

'So, something is affecting the electronic equipment,' Emmanuel suggested.

Asher cleared his throat. 'It's been happening to Dad's Gameboy too.'

Mona nodded. She'd obviously already been filled in about that. 'We need to figure out what to do next. Obviously, I'm tracking the data and noting everything down. It's important to keep things as scientific as possible, but these kinds of things don't always adhere to scientific protocol.'

'You can say that again,' Emmanuel muttered.

'What do we do next?' Eli asked.

'We try to communicate,' she said.

'If you pull out a fucking Ouija board…' Eli warned.

'Don't be ridiculous. Although, it's worth pointing out that there's nothing nefarious about Ouija boards. If you use them properly, they're harmless. If you treat them like toys, that's when you're,' Mona glanced at Asher, 'fucked.'

'What do you propose?' Emmanuel asked. It was funny to see him hanging off Mona's every word. Emmanuel was the *respected academic*. Mona was a twenty-something podcaster.

'We'll use the spirit box and ask questions. We'll also try a few different things. I have some tricks up my sleeve. We have to make it as easy as possible for the spirits to communicate with us. Spirit boxes are usually the best bet. However, people say they're unreliable, which is true to an extent. It all depends on the person using them, and the manufacturer of the spirit box.'

'What tricks?' Asher spoke. His voice was sullen.

'Pardon?' Mona turned to look at him.

'You said you had tricks up your sleeve. What tricks?' he asked.

'There are things that can help to make a spirit more active,' Mona said. 'A room crowded with electrical devices, for example, has been found to amplify spirit activity. Providing various objects with which the spirits can interact, that's another good tool. A dark room with candles - spirits often find it easy to manipulate the flames.'

'You keep saying *spirits*,' Emmanuel said.

Eli's eyes snapped in Emmanuel's direction.

'I don't think any of us believe for a second this is a run-of-the-mill spirit,' Emmanuel continued.

'No, you're right,' Mona said, 'but *spirit* encompasses a myriad of different things. I could have just as easily said *entity*. A spirit is simply, by paranormal definitions, energy originating from an individual who has died. The energy can manifest in different ways: orbs, residual haunting-'

'I know all that,' Emmanuel said. His tone was knife sharp.

'Then what's the problem?' Mona's shoulders squared.

'This is a demon. What the Eastwoods dealt with before was a demon too,' he answered.

'We don't know that categorically,' Mona said.

Emmanuel looked at her with pity.

'We do know that,' Eli said. 'We do. If you go antagonising it, you'll end up putting us all in more danger. What happened to Felix proved that demons exist, and that they can kill. We need to figure out how to get it to stop, not make it worse. You have proof now, right? We can stop this.'

Emmanuel nodded his head. 'I agree with Eli.'

'That's what I'm trying to do,' Mona said. 'You brought me here to help. You know I'm the best at what I do. I might not have your fancy degrees, but I know my shit. I've seen things you would never believe. I know what I'm doing. The demons, if that's what they are, want something. That's why they're here. My job is to figure out what they want, while also trying to make a living. I need proof. The more proof I have, the better the podcast episode goes over with listeners, and the more I can help other people.' Mona bit her lip and puffed out her cheeks. 'Look, I've seen this before. If a demon doesn't possess you, it wants something else. Otherwise, it would be in your body and taking over. It doesn't want that, it wants something else. Let me try to figure out what. Please.'

'Tell us,' Emmanuel demanded.

'It's not a nice story, and it doesn't end well,' Mona said.

'What happened?' Asher asked.

'Fine, okay,' Mona agreed. Her expression was unreadable. 'It was about five years ago. I was in the US. I'd just started the podcast, and everything was going well. I was invited to a house by the family that lived there. They were hearing noises, seeing shadow people, objects were moving, strange smells, you know the drill. The second I stepped foot into that house, I knew something was very very wrong. The air felt like static. It was a mum, dad, and two young boys. After a few days investigating, getting data and trying to either prove or debunk, one of the boys told me that they had an imaginary friend. His name was Mr Smiley, and he lived under the bed. I didn't think too much into it, kids have imaginary friends. But one night, I was watching the video feed I set up in their room and I saw Tony, the younger boy, sit up straight in bed, turn to the camera, and smile. It was the creepiest thing I'd ever seen. A proper Cheshire Cat grin, but his eyes were closed. The video feed cut out after that. I tried to call the parents but there was no answer. I was staying in a hotel nearby. When I finally got hold of them, they were hysterical. Tony was missing. His brother, Lucas, said that Mr Smiley had taken him. That Mr Smiley had no children of his own and took children whose parents didn't love them. Lucas said that Mr Smiley could only take one child at a time, but that he was going to come back for him the next night.

'We set a trap. The parents still thought it was a kidnapping of the human kind, or that Tony had run away from home and Lucas was trying to explain it in a way that made sense in his little kid mind. I stayed at the house that night, watched on the monitors all night as Lucas slept in his bed. Nothing happened. He didn't stir. He slept through. Except when his parents went to wake him up the next morning he wasn't there. I didn't take my eyes away from the screen for a second, and neither did they. I watched them walk into his room. He was in the bed when they did. I swear it, but they said he wasn't, and when I checked the video feed, he wasn't there at all that night.'

Mona released a shaky exhale. 'Mr Smiley left a note. A calling card. The boys had an etch-e-sketch. On it was written, *"They're mine now."* The demon hadn't possessed the boys. He wanted them for himself. That's why we need to know what this demon wants.'

'You're calling it a demon now, you realise? You also alternate between a singular entity and plural.' Emmanuel stared at Mona, studying her.

'Humans apply names to things. It's what we do in order to attempt to understand the world. I have no idea if this *thing* is one or two or multiple. I also don't know if it's the same type of thing that killed Felix. If you're referring to it as a demon, for argument's sake, we'll call it… them… a demon or demons.'

'Did they ever find the kids?' Eli asked.

Mona shook her head. 'No, the parents were suspected of murder, but nothing could be proven beyond reasonable doubt. As far as I know, they changed their names and moved away.'

'Did you air the podcast?' Asher said. Eli watched Specs nudge his large head against Asher's dangling hand. Asher absentmindedly scratched the dog's ears.

'I did. I take it you're not fans?' Mona smiled awkwardly.

'It was where I first heard of Mona,' Emmanuel said. 'It was the story that catapulted her into the limelight.'

'Hmmm,' Asher sighed wearily.

'What is it?' Mona raised an eyebrow in question.

'It's just, well, maybe you shouldn't have aired the episode. You're profiting off grief just like Lilith was,' Asher said.

'I have to make a living somehow. This is what I'm good at. What I do proves that the supernatural exists. It also proves that we need to be sceptical and scientific about how we approach it. Things aren't necessarily ghosts and ghouls, but they *could* be. So many times, I see people imprisoned or sectioned for mental illnesses that aren't mental illnesses. Proving that something could be real would help to open people's eyes.' Mona's voice raised in pitch. Her words tumbled out of her. 'So that they don't just write people off and send them to an asylum.'

'I'm not sure people are just *sent to asylums* anymore,' Emmanuel interjected.

'Yeah, well, if you want my help, we need to find out what the demons want.' Mona's tone reminded Eli of his mother when he

192

and Felix were naughty as kids. A spasm of unexpected sadness gripped his heart.

'It's not like we have any other choice, is it?' Eli said.

'No, no it's not,' Emmanuel said in agreement.

COMMUNICATING WITH THE DEAD

Asher sat straight-legged in front of the coffee table, his broken ankle splayed out to the side. Uncle Eli sat opposite him. To his right was Mona. To his left was Emmanuel. Specs lay in the space between Asher's legs. On the table between them was the spirit box. It looked like a walkie-talkie.

'Now, remember, we might not hear a response straight away. It might only show up on the audio recordings the box takes later. It's a combined EVP and spirit box, and the data goes-'

'Straight to your laptop, yes, we know.' Asher was impatient. His stomach churned and his skin tingled. He just wanted to get this over with. Mona had insisted that they do it together. She'd also insisted on turning off the lights and lighting a bunch of IKEA candles around the room. If she was aiming for a creepy atmosphere, she'd definitely achieved that.

'I'm going to ask questions, and we'll wait ten seconds for a response each time. I will continue with the questions even if we don't gain an audible response.' Mona paused, looking around the room. 'All of the other sensors are set up too, so we'll have a full picture.'

Just get on with it! Asher wanted to yell. Every alarm bell in his body was telling him this was a bad idea.

'Ready?' Mona asked.

Everyone nodded. Uncle Eli pursed his lips and stared straight at Asher.

'Is somebody else here with us?' Mona enunciated each word, speaking slowly and loudly.

Ten seconds.

The air felt heavy.

'Can you tell us your name?'

Ten seconds.

The candles cast eerie shadows around the room. They moved with the flickering of the flames.

'What do you want from us?'

Ten seconds.

Specs began to growl. Asher stroked the dense fur on the back of his neck.

'We can help you. Tell us how we can help you.'

Ten seconds.

Uncle Eli turned around, casting a glance toward the patio doors. A frown line knitted its way across his forehead.

'Why are you here?'

Ten seconds.

The room was warm. Suddenly and overwhelmingly warm.

'Where do you come from?'

Ten seconds.

A scream. Or was it the wind? Nobody else reacted.

'Were you once a human being?'

Ten seconds.

Ice trailed around Asher's ribcage. He shivered. Looked down. The shadowed outline of a finger traced against him. He couldn't move, frozen to the spot.

'How long have you been deceased?'

Ten seconds.

A deafening shriek peeled across the room. Drawers flung open, contents clattering to the floor. Candles blew out. They were plunged into darkness.

'Turn the light on,' Uncle Eli said.

'No, don't, they're trying to tell us something.' Mona was frantic, the hitch in her voice sliced her words short.

'Fuck that,' Uncle Eli said.

Asher rubbed his hands over his stomach, his ribs. There was nothing there. There was nothing…

A hand.

Long, spindly fingers.

The scream barked out of him.

He stood, heaving himself up and wobbling on his broken ankle.

Specs snarled. Asher couldn't see him. He couldn't see anything.

The hand dug into his skin. He could feel the nails piercing the flesh.

'It's got me!' Asher yelled.

'Where are you?' Uncle Eli's voice.

A bang. A thud.

'Asher?' Emmanuel spoke. The word was close. Emmanuel's hand clasped his arm. 'I have him, Eli. I have him.'

'Who are you? What do you want?' Mona said.

'Can somebody turn on the fucking light?' Emmanuel growled.

'It's not working,' Uncle Eli said. 'I need a different switch. Shit.'

'Are you hurt?' Emmanuel asked. His breath was hot on Asher's skin.

'Its fingers. My belly.' Asher cried, fat tears rolling down his cheeks.

Specs continued to whine, biting at the air.

Asher was vaguely aware of Mona continuing to ask questions into the air.

The room was so dark.

'NO!' The voice was his dad's.

Everything went still. Silent.

'I'm so sorry.' Lilith's voice.

The smell of blood and bile and shit lay heavy on the air. With every breath, Asher tried not to choke on it.

'What's happening?' Who's there?' Emmanuel's breath was ragged. Asher could feel the dampness of it on his face.

'It's my dad dying,' Asher said.

You bitch! his dad said. No, not his dad, Damont. His dad had been possessed.

Run. Leave. Now.' Lilith's words echoed around the room. Dread pooled in Asher's stomach. The fingers were no longer slicing into him.

'I'm sorry, Felix, I'm sorry.' The desperation in Lilith's voice sounded like nails on a blackboard.

'Oh my God, no.' Uncle Eli. Asher couldn't tell if he'd spoken now, or if they were words from a memory.

'He needs to die,' Lilith said.

'He's my brother.' Definitely Past Uncle Eli.

'That wasn't your brother. Kill the host, kill the demon,' Lilith said. Her words were empty. Stoic.

'Daddy?' That was Asher's voice, but he hadn't spoken. The words sounded like a desperate baby calling out for safety.

The lights flashed back on. Blinding.

Uncle Eli stood by the light switch, stooped and shaking. Tears ran down his cheeks. He didn't wipe them away.

Mona was in the same position, legs tucked under her on the floor.

Emmanuel had hold of Asher's arm, the fingers wound tightly around his wrist. He examined Asher, open-mouthed. 'What the fuck was that?'

Specs howled, jumping up against Asher.

'We need to listen to those tapes.' Mona stood, dusting herself off. Her hand vibrated wildly as she moved her finger against the mousepad of her laptop.

Uncle Eli ran to Asher, circling his arms around him. Emmanuel released Asher's hand and stepped away.

'Are you okay?' Uncle Eli asked.

'No,' Asher whispered into his uncle's shirt. 'I don't understand what happened.'

Uncle Eli didn't say anything. He pulled Asher tighter against him. 'We'll be okay,' he said.

Asher wasn't sure who he was trying to convince.

'Oh my God!' Mona's voice tore Asher away from his uncle. She knelt before the laptop. 'We have something.'

Asher watched Emmanuel and Uncle Eli share a look.

'The stats went crazy. The temperature rose. The vibrations in the room. The motion sensors. The EMF! It's all off the charts. We need to watch it back. Thank God we set up video as well as audio.' The grin on her face was wild, feral. Asher didn't like it one bit.

Mona angled the laptop towards Asher and started the video playback.

'The EVP recorded in real-time with the video, so we should get answers to the questions…'

Nothing.

There was no response to any of her questions.

Asher watched himself jump as the cold finger had touched his rib cage.

Mona's grin began to vanish. 'At least we still have the data from the-'

The room went dark. The thermal imaging camera kicked in, altering the video feed so it showed them all as orange blobs against a blue background.

Their own panicked voices could be heard.

Asher held his breath, waiting for his dad to speak. For Lilith.

'Shouldn't we be hearing Felix by now?' Uncle Eli asked. Asher noticed his bottom lip trembling as he spoke.

'We should.' Emmanuel confirmed.

'Damn,' Mona said. 'It didn't pick up their voices. I'm going to need you all to record exactly what you heard in your journals right now.'

'Want.' The spirit box spat out the world.

Heat flushed through Asher's body. He stared down at the small black device.

'The. Boy.' There was a long gap. Nobody breathed. *'He. Stole. Now. He. Pays.'*

'Jesus,' Uncle Eli exhaled.

'Jesus.' The spirit box repeated the word. *'Cannot. Help.'*

They remained in silence, staring at the spirit box like it was alive.

'You figured out what the demon wants. Now what?' Emmanuel demanded.

'I…' Mona said. 'I've never had one interact so…' She shook her head back and forth, her messy black hair flying around her face. 'I suppose we find out why it wants him.'

OCCAM'S RAZOR

'Who do you want?' Mona asked.

The question was redundant, as far as Eli was concerned.

The spirit box was annoyingly quiet. The demon had succeeded in freaking them out. It didn't need to answer any more questions on demand.

'Why do you want them?' Mona said, directing the words at the spirit box.

Eli squeezed Asher's shoulder. Asher didn't remove his eyes from the coffee table and the contraption sitting on it.

'If it is Asher you want, give us a sign.'

Eli shot Mona a warning glare. She didn't react.

'Any sign will do,' Mona continued.

'I think that's enough of that,' Eli said.

'We need to know why it wants Asher, Eli. How else are we going to protect him?' A judgemental tone infiltrated Mona's voice.

'How are you going to protect him? Even if you know why they want him, what are you going to do? Be realistic!' Emmanuel's words took on weight.

'I need you to call the priest back,' Eli said to Emmanuel. 'We need to tell him what happened. We need to get an exorcism or something right now. The blessing clearly did naff all.'

'I'll call him now,' Emmanuel said. He left the living room.

'I think your family is marked,' Mona said, looking up at Eli from her crouched position.

'Marked?' Eli rubbed his forehead with one hand, keeping the other firmly clamped onto Asher.

'Yes, marked. I've read about it before but never witnessed it firsthand. Most people go their entire lives without encountering an intelligent entity, be that demon, spirit, or whatever else. Some people, through means we don't quite understand, become *marked* and experience entities more regularly. The theory is that once a person has experienced a haunting and they believe what they witnessed, they are more susceptible to attacks from entities because they have something that signifies they're an easy target. They're already believers. What happened with the demon Nicolas Damont marked you and your family.'

'Oh, good,' Eli said, sarcasm oozing from his words.

'In my experience, families who've had negative paranormal experiences - hauntings, possessions, poltergeist activity - the vast majority of them will experience something similar in the future,' Mona said.

'And you're just telling us this now?' Eli asked. He could feel his heartbeat pounding in his temples.

'It's just a theory, we're not working with absolutes here,' Mona said. 'The thing is, it might help us to understand what the demons want with you. We have no knowledge of what demons technically are. I'm sure Emmanuel has said all this before, but the theory that they're spirits that have hung around on our plane of existence for too long, and in doing so have gained the strength to manipulate our environments, and our bodies in some cases, has no proof, other than anecdotal evidence. We can't write off anecdotal evidence, though. People are quick to say it isn't scientific, but there's nothing more scientific than anecdotal evidence. Every scientific theory we accept as fact today started as an anecdote. You said that Nicolas Damont was a murderer who raped and killed children back in France hundreds of years ago, yes?'

'Yes.' Asher spoke before Eli could.

Mona's cheek twitched. 'Either that's true, or the demon was using it as a cover for what it really was. We only have the demon's word for it, but you're not the only ones to have experienced something like this. Many other people, from all over the world, have given written or verbal accounts of spirits claiming to be powerful because of their age and the fact they haven't *crossed over* to wherever we're supposed to go next. We have no scientific support for this argument; in fact, physics, in theory, disproves it.

However, there are many things that physics doesn't explain, and it doesn't mean they're not true.'

'What are you getting at?' Eli didn't need a lecture. He already knew everything from Mona's monologue.

'If this is the same thing that happened last time, then we have to assume we're working with demons. It is the logical explanation. Occam's Razor, and all that. But if that's true, then these demons used to be people. They died a long time ago. They're strong, and they want Asher, but why?' Mona uncrossed her legs and leaned back against the sofa.

'Damont wanted Asher too. Felix died because he was trying to stop him from getting Asher. He wanted Asher because…' (the words tasted like acid in Eli's mouth), '… because he wanted to do to Asher what he did to the other kids.'

'So, these demons want to abuse and kill me too?' Asher stuttered.

'No. No. No. No.' The word repeated from the spirit box over and over again.

'If you don't want to abuse him, then why do you want him?' Eli yelled. His chest ached, trying to swallow down tears. The panic attack that had been brewing all day threatened to crown.

'No. No. No.'

'Fuck you!' Eli snarled. Anger engulfed him. He released Asher's shoulder, grabbed the spirit box and threw it across the room with all the strength he could muster.

Panting heavily, he watched as it stopped a foot in front of the wall and hung there.

Mona scrambled to pick up her phone and take a photo.

'What the hell?' Emmanuel gasped.

The spirit box flew back across the room toward Eli. He shoved Asher out of the way and ducked. The device clattered onto the floor and smashed into little pieces.

'Oh my God!' Mona exclaimed. Eli half expected her to clap her hands like an excited seal.

'This can't be happening,' Emmanuel said. 'It's impossible.'

'But it did. It happened! I need to check the video feed,' Mona said.

'I'm going to get some fresh air,' Eli said. 'Coming Specs?'

Specs barked once. Eli pulled on his shoes and noticed Asher standing up, grabbing his crutches, and following behind.

They left through the patio doors and into the damp, dank air.

Once away from the house, Eli turned to look at Asher. They were almost the same height, only a few inches between the two of them. When had that happened?

'I don't know where we go from here, Ash,' Eli said. The dam of emotion had reached bursting point. He released a shaking breath.

'There's no point leaving, is there? Going somewhere else?' Asher asked, eyes pleading for answers.

'I don't think so. Damont followed us from your house to mine.' Eli placed his fists in the small of his back and stretched.

'Father Edwards said he was going to ask for a minor exorcism though. That might fix things.' The hope in Asher's voice as he spoke felt like shards of glass piercing Eli's heart.

'Yeah. If anybody can get rid of a demon, it's the Church.'

'Even though Nanna said an exorcism was pointless if you didn't believe?' Asher spun, so he was facing Eli. 'Nanna said it wouldn't work.'

'Nanna didn't know everything,' Eli said.

'Which is why she's dead,' Asher said, forlorn.

'I suppose so, yes, but she died trying to protect the people she loved.'

Asher thought about that and then nodded.

'We have to give the exorcism a try. If it doesn't work, then we'll be one of the lucky few who get a full-blown exorcism, not just a minor one.' The fresh air had calmed Eli's nerves. He was back in the headspace of being a protector for Asher. He had to be optimistic. He had to believe the exorcism would work. If not, they were well and truly fucked.

MIDNIGHT FIGHT

'What did you do?'

Eli blinked away sleep, trying desperately to regain consciousness. Raised voices. Downstairs.

'What were you thinking?' Emmanuel roared.

Eli looked across the bed to Asher. He was sleeping soundly with Specs's head across his legs. Eli listened carefully. He could hear Mona talking but couldn't make out her words. Torn between staying in bed with Asher, or going down to investigate, Eli decided on the latter. He crept out of the room, leaving the door ajar, and made his way downstairs.

Mona and Emmanuel stood across the dining table from one another. Emmanuel's face was red, blotchy. He leaned heavily on the table. Mona stood back, arms crossed protectively across her chest.

'What's going on?' Eli sighed, looking at his watch. 'It's two in the morning.'

'She uploaded the videos and data to her socials. She did a fucking TikTok about it!' Emmanuel slammed his fist on the table.

'You did what?' Eli raked his fingers through his hair, trying to calm his temper.

'Everything we have. The data from the devices. The video that shows you throwing the spirit box. The spirit box talking. The internet's all over it like a rash.'

Eli couldn't bring himself to appreciate the irony of what Emmanuel was saying.

'You didn't,' Eli challenged, shaking his head at Mona.

'This is concrete proof, and a good taster for the podcast. Plus, there's the bonus that if somebody knows how to help us-'

'Why the fuck would you do that?' Eli's skin prickled. It was happening again. His family would get raked over hot coals by a bunch of armchair warriors on the internet.

'I just said-'

'Why didn't you ask? I thought we were collecting data to prove what's happening here, and then you'd put together something cohesive with Emmanuel. Wasn't that the whole point?' The muscles of Eli's jaw tensed.

'Well, yes,' Mona said, 'but then I was laid in bed replaying it over and over and I thought, *why wait?*'

'Show me what you did,' Eli commanded.

'Sure,' Mona said. She handed her phone to him. 'It's the last video.'

The TikTok cover photo was Mona's scared face overlaid with the words '*EASTWOOD HAUNTING. NEW PROOF.*'

Eli tapped the screen and watched in horror as Mona's face, superimposed over the top of the video of their living room, explained what the viewers were seeing. The recorded video ends with the spirit box smashing on the floor and the group staring at it. It then reverts to a full screen of Mona. She briefly summarises what's happening at the house and the fact that they're waiting for approval for a minor exorcism. She launches into a quick backstory about *the Eastwoods*. While she does that, she displays a still from Emmanuel's video of Asher floating in the air, his arms and legs broken. She teases that the full podcast, and more proof, will be coming soon.

The phone felt like fire in Eli's hand. He dropped it to the table, sighing in defeat.

'I'm sorry,' Emmanuel said, placing a hand on Eli's arm. 'I thought we could trust Mona to-'

Eli shrugged away from Emmanuel. 'You're one to fucking talk. Both of you are only in this for the money. You always have been. This is my family. My nephew is being hunted by-' the word was bitter, hard to choke out, 'demons. This is our lives. Don't you get that? I thought you were better than that. I thought,' he spun to face Emmanuel, squaring up to him. 'I thought you were genuinely sorry.'

'I am,' Emmanuel pleaded. 'I didn't...'

'You have no right to get on your high horse. You did the same thing she did.' He stepped towards Mona. 'It's gotten worse since you got here.' He didn't want to believe she was purposefully making it worse, but…

'I know,' Mona said. 'That's why I posted the video.'

'She posted to all her socials, not just TikTok,' Emmanuel said.

'Stop!' Eli seethed. 'This isn't helpful. Mona, you should have asked before you did that. You know you should. I needed your help, and you…' He turned his attention to Emmanuel. 'Fuck, I don't even want to look at you.' He stormed out of the room and back upstairs to Asher.

Eli crept back into the bedroom. Specs stood on the bed, glaring at the TV mounted to the wall. The screen was filled with static, illuminating the room. Hunched forwards, Specs was ready to pounce. Asher sat slowly, rising from his slumber. 'Did you hear that?' he said. 'They're laughing at me.'

Eli stayed awake all night, sitting beside Asher like a sentinel while he slept. Emmanuel poked his head around the door the next morning, after the sun had risen, and asked if Eli wanted coffee. Eli took it as an apology and nodded his head.

'I'll bring you one up,' he said.

A few minutes later, Emmanuel placed the mug of coffee in Eli's hand.

'Thank you.'

'About Mona,' Emmanuel said. 'She means well. I think, like me, she got ahead of herself. In our world, proof of the supernatural is the greatest discovery.' His voice was low so as not to disturb Asher. 'Well, I mean, if we can definitively prove life after death, or demons, it's the greatest discovery of mankind. We all get a bit trigger happy when we have what we deem irrefutable proof.'

'I take it she's being told she's faked the video,' Eli said, despite his tiredness, and fear, he smirked.

'Yeah. Mona's respected in the field, and it's rare she ever posts *proof*. She usually just shares stories and provides the odd bit of proof. She's being ripped apart.'

'Good,' Eli said.

'Not good,' Asher mumbled, unravelling himself from the covers.

Eli and Emmanuel looked down at him.

'We need people to believe her so they can help us,' he elaborated.

'The Church is sending Bishop Williams to perform the minor exorcism. Father Edwards said that the Church is taking it very seriously. They said our evidence was convincing, and that's high praise indeed from the clergy,' Emmanuel explained.

'Good. When will he get here?' Eli asked.

'Or she,' Asher interjected.

'Exorcisms are still mostly performed by men.' Emmanuel laughed. 'It's a very archaic profession. He'll be here tomorrow evening. He's coming from Italy.'

'The Vatican?' Eli asked, shocked that they were actually being taken seriously, and The Church was sending the big guns.

'God no, he was on vacation,' Emmanuel said. 'But still, he's one of the UK's best, apparently, so… I'm hopeful about it.'

Eli dipped his chin, slowly nodding his head.

'Do me a favour,' Emmanuel said. 'Don't give Mona too hard of a time. She's a professional, but she got over-excited.'

'Emmanuel,' Eli warned. 'This is my family we're talking about.'

'I know,' Emmanuel said, as Asher said, 'What did she do?'

'She uploaded the video from yesterday as a teaser for the podcast. It's on her socials,' Eli answered.

Asher scoffed, rolling over and reaching for his tablet. From over his shoulder, Eli watched him open TikTok and type in Mona's name.

The video Eli had watched last night was the latest upload. 800k views. 50k likes. Too many comments to count. Asher scrolled down through the comments, stopping every now and again to read one aloud.

'This is so fake.'

'I thought you had more integrity than that.'

'You can see the strings.'

Occasionally, there was a comment in support of the video.

'Wow, this is amazing!'

'I can't believe you caught that on camera.'

'God have mercy on your souls.'

'Where is Mona now?' Eli asked.

'In her room,' Emmanuel said. 'She hasn't been out yet this morning. I think she's hiding.'

'Good,' Eli said.

In the morning light, the house didn't feel as oppressive. Sunlight washed away some of the looming dread he'd felt last night. In moments like that, Eli understood how people could write off hauntings as nightmares.

Eli, Asher, and Specs remained close together, only separating when one ventured to the toilet. Eli napped on and off throughout the morning. It wasn't that he wanted to, but he knew he'd be useless if he didn't, and the daytime felt like the safest moment to snatch sleep. Emmanuel's face was buried in a laptop, analysing the data from yesterday, and scrutinising last night's findings. It was 2 PM by the time they decided they should go and check on Mona, who still hadn't emerged from her room.

They went together, the four of them, travelling in a pack. Eli gave Asher a piggy-back up the stairs.

Emmanuel knocked on Mona's door. There was no answer.

'I don't think she's there,' Asher said. Eli had the same thought. He sensed that she was missing.

'Mona, can we come in?' Emmanuel asked the closed door. Still no answer.

Emmanuel turned back to Eli, who shrugged. 'Go for it.'

Emmanuel turned the doorknob and pushed the door open. As though one entity, they peered into the room. It was empty. The room was a cluttered mess of *stuff*. Make-up, books, tech equipment, were all strewn in a layer of detritus.

'She must have gone out,' Eli said.

'When? Where?' Emmanuel asked. 'I was up at six thirty this morning, and I didn't hear her go.'

'I was up all night,' Eli said. 'I didn't hear her either. You should call her.' It wasn't as much a suggestion as it was a demand.

'Yeah, you're right. Hang on.' Emmanuel released his phone from his pocket, selected Mona's contact, and placed the phone to his ear. It rang and rang and rang.

'This is the voicemail of…' a robotic voice spoke. 'Mona Koestler,' Mona's own voice said, before the phone reverted back to the robotic voice. 'Please leave a message after the tone.' *Beep*.

'Mona, this is Emmanuel Stark. Can you let us know where you are and that you're okay? Thanks.' He hung up the phone.

'What do we do now?' Asher asked.

'Now we wait,' Emmanuel said.

They went back downstairs and resumed their previous positions. The atmosphere had shifted in the room. It felt *off*. Wrong.

'I have a bad feeling,' Asher whispered to Eli.

'Me too,' Eli agreed.

'Oh shit,' Emmanuel said. His wide, fearful eyes stared at the laptop screen. 'You need to see this.'

'What is it?' Eli was already on his feet.

'The video feed from last night,' Emmanuel answered. His face had paled. He looked like he was about to be sick.

Eli and Asher crowded behind him. Asher was getting quick on his crutches. So quick that he almost beat Eli to the table.

Emmanuel tapped the 'PLAY' button. It was a video of Mona's room, labelled 'BEDROOM THREE'.

Eli's heart pounded out of his chest as he watched the demons take Mona.

MONA'S INTERLUDE

The sound of children's laughter shook Mona from her sleep. She lay in the mess of covers, unfamiliar surroundings swimming into focus. The room was pitch black. She was sure she'd left the lamp on when she went to sleep.

She didn't actually remember falling asleep. She'd tossed and turned for hours, fretting about the decision she'd made. *It's better to ask for forgiveness than to ask for permission,* her mom had always said. She shouldn't have uploaded the content without asking permission, that was painfully obvious, but she also knew she'd never have been given permission. Also, if she was being honest with herself, it *was* her content. She filmed it. She analysed the data. She owned the videos and stills, all except the one of Asher hanging from the ceiling. Until yesterday, she'd suspected that it was fake. Deep down at least. But what happened with the spirit box, the way the demons were able to manipulate matter, it was unbelievable. In her whole career, she'd never seen something so convincing.

It was a good idea to release the content. It would help with ratings and maybe even bring in additional help, because she was in way over her head. Mona was usually late to the party. Stepping in after the haunting had happened and debunking, or proving, the *evidence.* This time, she was in the thick of it. No experience could have prepared her for this. Most of the time, the suggestion of getting a priest to do a blessing did the trick, provided the priest knew what he was doing. Occasionally, a minor exorcism, or calling on the protection saints, would be required. Very rarely, the use of protection *spells* and symbology did the trick. There was no recipe for getting rid of a demon. You had to throw shit at the wall and see what stuck.

The giggle pulled her from her thoughts. It was childlike, high-pitched, not a noise that Asher would have made.

She listened intently, not daring to move a muscle.

There was no doubt in Mona's mind that something supernatural was causing this *haunting.* There were too many coincidences for it to be something with a rational explanation. That being said, she believed with both her heart and her brain that human beings have the power to manipulate their environments in ways they cannot understand, in ways that can be incredibly dangerous and manifest as *hauntings.* Another, slightly less logical, explanation was that spirits, demons, and ghosts, are energy left over when a living thing passes away. Sometimes these masses of energy are sentient, sometimes not. What was happening to the Eastwoods was either a sentient spirit, demon, *et al.,* or Eli/Asher manipulating their surroundings and causing the hauntings. She didn't want to tell them that yet. Telling a person that you thought demonic activity was the result of the unlocked potential of their brain didn't tend to garner great results.

'Come play with us.'

Mona's blood froze in her veins.

A small hand stretched from the blackness of the room in front of her, somehow darker than the pitch black. The smoky tendrils caressed her cheeks, trailing long fingers down her neck, her right arm, and then clasping firmly around her hand.

'I can feel you,' Mona stuttered, through her shaking jaw and chattering teeth. 'That's not possible…'

Physics says…

'Some things are beyond human comprehension.' The voice was silky, smooth, as though spoken through a smile. *'You should have left when you were told.'*

'We're hungry,' a different voice said. Still childlike.

'It's been so long since we fed,' a third voice.

'Who are you?' Mona forced the words from her aching throat. She'd never felt fear like it.

'Come with us, and we'll show you.'

The hand weaved its fingers through hers, tugging her from the bed. An impatient child on Christmas morning.

'Okay,' Mona assented. What other choice did she have? This was the culmination of her life's work. Her career had built to this. With her free hand, she snapped her phone into the monopod's clasp, a fancy selfie stick that allowed her to film on the go. Even though she was terrified, there was no way she wasn't capturing it. Her phone was set to upload all videos and photos to the Cloud.

She pressed record, pointing her phone's camera toward the demonic hand; only then did she realise there wasn't enough light to film.

'Come with us,' a voice said.

Stumbling out of bed, Mona tiptoed to the bedroom door. The hand dragged her along. The force of it was unsettling. It felt so solid. So real. It *pulled* her.

She snuck out of the bedroom. She was escorted down the stairs and out of the back door, moving so swiftly she felt like she was floating. Outside, the ground was slick, ice cold under her feet. There was no way she was going back for her shoes. This was history in the making. She'd waited her whole life to experience something like this. Something first-hand. An intelligent being not only communicating with her but *touching* her. Excitement overrode her fear.

The demon's hand felt *neutral,* if that was the right word. It was neither hot nor cold, but it was dense. Solid. Mona swung the camera around to her face, and then down to the hand. Through the viewfinder, she could see the hand. At the elbow, it wisped away into nothing, melting into the night sky. The only source of light was the moon.

'Where are we going?' Mona asked aloud, saying a silent prayer for the demon to answer. The proof she was getting was off the charts life changing.

Nothing. The fingers tightened, and the hand pulled harder.

It was uncomfortable, the nails dug into her skin, piercing and drawing blood.

She checked the viewfinder again.

Worth it.

The video she was recording would change everything.

Discomfort turned to pain. The nails sliced, digging into the flesh of her hand.

She cried out but found herself unable to make a noise.

Digging her feet into the soft earth, Mona tried to stop. She tried to ask why they were hurting her. They'd spoken to her. They'd invited her to follow them. Mud and grass seeped through her toes. Agony erupted from her hand as the demons tore forwards, dragging her staggering behind.

The corpses of heather sliced like knives at her legs through her tracksuit bottoms.

The demon's fingernails pushed through to the underside of her hand. The pain was blinding. Tears streamed down from her eyes. She tried to scream. She tried to utter any sound. Despite the torture, she kept her left hand gripped around the monopod. The footage she was capturing was too important for her to let go. To let go, would be to fail humanity.

She fell to the floor, knees striking rock.

An instinctual cry of pain escaped.

'Why are you doing this?' she managed to stutter. Her voice was back. A semblance of relief titrated through her body.

We're hungry.' The high-pitched voice came from in front of her. She tilted her head upwards. With only the stars and a sliver of moon lighting the moorland, she saw the shadow figures. Except they weren't shadows. They were silhouettes, solid silhouettes. Three of them. One tall, two smaller.

'Who are you?'

Names have power. We learned that from him.' The words came from three invisible mouths.

'Who?' Mona trembled, cupping her bleeding, torn hand.

Nicolas Damont.'

It didn't make sense. None of it made sense.

'Who are you?' she pleaded for an answer. This was proof of sentience. Proof of something outside of our realm of understanding. But what was the connection? Did spirits communicate in the afterlife? If that was the case, how would that knowledge change humanity?

Her throat closed, an invisible fist wrapping around it and squeezing it like a vice.

She tried to suck in a breath.

Panic flooded every cell of her body.

The pressure in her head, her neck, her chest, was unbearable.

How long could she take it?

The sensation vanished.

'Consider that a warning, friend,' the demons said.

Mona fell forwards, dropping the monopod. Her mangled hand screamed with white-hot intensity. She coughed, great hacking coughs, and gulped as much air as she could. Bile burst from her mouth and onto the rocky floor.

She looked up, wiping residue from her face.

'*What* are you?' she asked.

'That's a much better question.' The giggling laughter cocooned her. It darkened into a low rumble.

'You might call us demons. Others might call us devils.' The shadow figures stretched tall, looming over her.

'Were you human once?' Mona braced herself for the answer.

Where the shadow figures' mouths should be, split into wide smirks

Mona's pulse pounded inside her ears. She could no longer feel her hand. The pain there had vanished. The fear she felt was palpable. A solid entity of dread.

Adrenaline forced her body to shake uncontrollably.

This was what she'd wanted. She'd wanted proof of an afterlife.

'What do you want with me?' Mona said, when she realised an answer wasn't forthcoming.

'We already told you.' The figures snapped back to their original shape, appearing only a few feet in front of Mona. *'We're hungry. We need to feed. And we have no other use for you.'*

They were going to eat her.

The understanding came with a wave of calm acceptance.

Something like this had been bound to happen. She'd put herself in dangerous situations with the sole purpose of proving the afterlife. The guise of scientific impartialness was long since forgotten. She'd needed there to be an afterlife so badly that she'd ended up ending her own life.

'Why do you need to feed? Why me? Why not one of the others?'

'Because we are not here for you. We do not want you.'

Mona focused her attention on the middle figure, despite the voices coming from each of them.

'We've seen your memories. We've seen your childhood. What your father did to you. What your mother allowed him to do. Those memories will taste delicious.'

Mona shook her head. 'My father didn't...'

'You can't lie to us. We see all. You were right, all demons have their own tastes.'

'You eat memories?' Mona knew she was about to be killed. She accepted that, but the camera was also recording everything, uploading it to the Cloud as it happened, provided there was signal. *Please God, let there be a signal.* She could still make her mark from beyond the grave.

'Some memories shape us in such a profound way that they become part of our souls. There, they fester and moulder. What your father did to you is a bruise covering your entire body. Your entire soul. We can see it. We can smell it. It's why we chose you.'

'The others have trauma too,' Mona said, beyond the point of caring about people's perception of her. She'd throw anyone else under the bus to stay alive, to ride the wave of these findings, to be the one to prove the afterlife.

'Your trauma is just the type we're looking for.'

What started as a rumble of laughter, exploded into deafening giggles.

Children. Definitely children, Mona thought.

They descended on her. Their fingers penetrated her skin. She felt it all. She felt them rip her body apart. She felt them feast on her soul. There would be nothing left of her when they'd finished. No afterlife for her. Between the flashes of blissful blankness, Mona saw the demons. Truly saw them. Their small frames. Their sad eyes. Children. They were only children.

SHIT'S CREEK WITHOUT A PADDLE

Eli, Asher, and Emmanuel watched Mona walk with an outstretched hand, grasping something shadow-like. They watched her walk out of the backdoor. They watched her vanish from sight.

'Fuck,' Eli said.

'We need to go and try to find her,' Asher said. 'She could have fallen and hurt herself.'

Or the demons could have got her, Eli thought. 'Yeah, I'll go now. Emmanuel, you stay here in case she comes back. Look after Asher.'

'I want to come with you,' Asher said.

'I'll be quicker on my own,' Eli said. He shook his head in apology and walked to the back door, his shoulders slumped dangerously. Specs looked torn.

'Go with him,' Asher said to the dog.

Specs whined but did as he was told.

Uncle Eli shut the door behind him, and Asher observed from his seat at the table as they vanished from sight, following the same route Mona had.

'There has to be something else we could do,' Asher said. 'I don't want to sit here and wait. I need to do something.'

'You watch the rest of the footage from last night, maybe you can catch something else,' Emmanuel instructed.

'What are you going to do?' Asher asked.

'I'm going to look through her stuff and see if anything is missing,' he said. 'You okay down here alone?'

Asher nodded his head. 'I'll be fine,' he muttered.

'Shout if you need anything,' Emmanuel said.

Asher clicked the space bar, playing the video from the point where they left off.

The room was dead and remained dead for the hour he stared at the screen.

Emmanuel emerged from upstairs and said, 'Her mono is gone.'

'Her what?' Asher cocked an eyebrow.

'Her monopod, she uses it for filming. Her phone isn't there either, so I assume she's taken both.' Emmanuel's eyes widened, a flash of understanding permeating his features. 'Give me the laptop.' He snatched it from in front of Asher and opened the Cloud server.

'What are you doing?' Asher leaned closer to see the screen.

'She uploads everything directly to the Cloud as a backup. Part of our *agreement* was that we had a shared folder with everything in it. Hang on…' He clicked through different folders. 'Oh, shit. Look.'

'A new upload,' Asher breathed.

'From five-thirty this morning,' Emmanuel said. 'Should we play it?'

'We have to.' Asher watched Mona's face blink to life. 'Turn up the volume.'

'There's no sound,' Emmanuel replied.

Eli returned back to the house halfway through the first viewing. The room had been silent. Asher and Emmanuel hadn't even glanced up from the screen when he went and stood behind them. He fought for breath as he watched Mona be led onto the moors by demons. Fought for breath as they tore at her, ripping her apart.

The video went black.

'Play it again,' Eli insisted. Instinct told Eli to shield Asher's eyes. Watching the video once was bad, watching it a second time… But experience told him that shielding Asher from what was on the video was pointless. The kid had already seen it once. But he'd also seen far worse.

They watched the video in silence once more. Mona had recorded her own death.

'Is that real? It can't be real,' Eli said. His head felt like it was being pressurised. 'What the demons did…'

'It doesn't make sense.' Emmanuel paced, exasperated. 'Why would they let themselves be filmed like that? She recorded them on an iPhone for God's sake! Humans have spent their entire existence trying to prove and disprove demons, and somehow Mona Koestler managed to film something like this on a fucking iPhone.'

'Damont did too,' Asher said. 'I mean, we never saw him as clearly as…' He gestured to the screen. The demons had looked almost human. He could nearly make out the features in the creases of their shadowed faces. 'They were children. They looked like children.'

'Yeah,' Eli said, sighing. He rubbed at his temples, trying to get rid of the headache and failing. 'I went there, where she died. There was no sign of her. I'm sure. I'll go and check again but…'

'It's getting dark soon. I'd rather you not go out there alone,' Emmanuel said.

'I'll have Specs,' Eli countered.

'Please don't,' Asher said. 'We'll check tomorrow. The exorcist will be here tomorrow as well. We just have to wait for one more night.'

'They killed her.' Eli couldn't believe that he'd had to say that aloud. He needed to go and check again. There had to be some sign of what had happened to her. 'We have to ring the police or…'

'And say what? Say that demons killed a podcaster who was staying with you?' Emmanuel swallowed. His Adam's apple bobbed in his throat, surrounded by cords of stressed tendons.

'I don't know what to do. What should we do?' Eli groaned.

'We should tell the police,' Asher said. 'Show them the video. Say we don't know what's happened, but we found it. They probably won't take it seriously anyway.'

'Yeah. Yeah, I think you're right. We have to do something,' Eli said, and dialled 101.

'Wait,' Emmanuel said. 'She's just uploaded a video on TikTok.'

'She's what?' He locked his phone and shoved it back in his pocket.

'Yeah. Just now. The video… Damn, it's the video we just watched.' Emmanuel looked up from the screen.

'How?' Eli stuttered. 'How is that possible?'

'It isn't,' Emmanuel said. 'Unless she scheduled the video herself. You can do that now, but she'd have to be alive to do it.'

'The video's fake?' Asher asked.

'I mean,' Emmanuel puffed out his cheeks, releasing the air, 'it must be. Either that or the demons are messing with us.'

'It isn't fake though, is it?' Eli rasped. 'What happened to her…' He swallowed a shaking breath. 'That was real. You could tell. Can demons do that? Why would they?'

'Visual effects can be pretty sophisticated,' Emmanuel shrugged, clearly attempting to delude himself. 'But I don't know why they'd…'

'I don't think it's fake either,' Asher interjected. 'She wouldn't leave all of her stuff here. She left thousands of pounds worth of equipment and faked her death? She had no reason to. We already had plenty of proof that the demons were real, she didn't need to fake it. And if she died, what would she get out of it?'

'Maybe somebody found her phone, and they uploaded it?' Eli suggested. It occurred to him that he believed the video was real. He believed Mona was dead. The only thing that he couldn't fathom was how the video had just been uploaded to TikTok.

'And figured out her password, found the video and decided to upload it to Mona's TikTok? That doesn't make any sense,' Asher said.

'It makes about as much sense as demons uploading the video,' Eli said.

They stared in silence at the laptop screen, the video of Mona playing mutely.

'The demons manipulated my voice on the podcast recording,' Eli whispered. He was missing vital pieces of the puzzle. He just couldn't make sense of it. They were trying to solve a maths equation without enough information. The demons were easily capable of interacting with technology. That much was obvious. It wasn't a question of *if* they could upload a video to social media, but *why*.

'We don't know that for sure,' Emmanuel said.

'Oh, for fuck's sake, Emmanuel. Of course we fucking do!'

Emmanuel raised his hands in surrender.

'I don't know,' Eli said under his breath, shaking his head. He tried to steady his breathing. 'None of this makes any fucking sense. Tomorrow, first thing, I'm going to go back and look. Maybe she left her phone out there and some kids picked it up and…' he trailed off.

'What if she is out there, on the moors, alone?' The low tone of Asher's words told Eli the kid knew that was a long shot. 'I think we should call the police now.'

'Maybe don't mention the video?' Emmanuel suggested.

'Fuck,' Eli said. 'I'm just going to tell them what's happened, minus the paranormal stuff.' Telling the police anything demon-related was a one-way ticket to finding himself sectioned and Asher taken away from him.

'Your call,' Emmanuel said.

After giving himself a second to allow his heart rate to calm, Eli phoned the police. He explained, in a roundabout way, that Mona and Emmanuel were friends from overseas who were staying with them for a while. He mentioned that there was a video posted online that gave them cause for concern about Mona's welfare. It wasn't a lie, but it also wasn't technically the truth. Either way, it would have to do.

The call operator didn't sound concerned. He said that somebody would be out as soon as possible. When Eli asked when that would be, he replied, 'As it isn't an emergency, it may be awhile.'

'You did the right thing,' Emmanuel declared when Eli hung up the phone.

Eli shot him a confused look.

'You had to do it,' Emmanuel elaborated. 'It was the right thing. I was worried how it would look, but your story sounded plausible.'

'Yeah, I've got some experience with that,' Eli said.

Although he'd only known Mona a few days, her loss was visceral, gut-wrenching. Panic began to course through him. He caught Asher's eye and smiled, trying to silently tell him that he was fine. He took a deep breath, in through his nose and out through his mouth, breathing purposefully until the potential panic attack abated.

Eli didn't sleep. They left the lights on downstairs as a beacon for Mona, just in case. Although no one was optimistic. The house felt quiet, dead. When Eli heard scrambling and scratching from Mona's room, he sighed and went to find out what it was. There was no sensation of dread. Nothing crawled on his skin or sent ice into his stomach. It was a flat feeling. A safe feeling.

Emmanuel was on his hands and knees, rifling through Mona's suitcase. He turned when Eli walked in. 'I don't think she'd mind,' Emmanuel said, by way of explanation.

'What are you looking for?' Eli sat on the bed.

'I don't know,' Emmanuel said. 'I just get the feeling that there's something we're missing. Mona's a professional, I know I keep saying that, but something about this doesn't feel right. She had proof of demons, Eli, actual proof.' He sighed and knelt back onto his feet. 'I can't even begin to explain how *big* something like that is. And now she's dead. They ripped her apart, but why? Why not you, why not Asher?'

Eli couldn't answer.

'It doesn't make sense. The demons were here before her. They've said over and over that they're here for you and Asher, so why lead Mona out there and…' With his hands, he mimed pulling apart. 'And you said there was no blood. No nothing.'

'I didn't see anything,' Eli said, although he was beginning to second guess that. He'd stood in the exact spot the video had been filmed, but he hadn't noticed anything.

You hadn't been looking for blood, he thought.

'There's something we're missing.' Emmanuel returned to pulling out contents from Mona's bag in a frenzy.

Eli sat back and watched as Emmanuel flung a variety of objects across the room: tarot cards, sage, candles, a torch, spare batteries… Things that Eli didn't recognise.

It went on for an hour. The contents of Mona's already messy room were spread to every corner.

Emmanuel unfurled his legs from under him and sat cross-legged. His breath was heaving. Tears ran down his face.

'Emmanuel,' Eli said, making no move to touch him.

'I'm sorry.' Emmanuel sniffed and wiped his eyes. 'She was young. And was doing so much good for the community. And I killed her.'

'You're blaming yourself?' Eli questioned.

'I invited her here, didn't I?' he said.

'By that logic, it's my family's fault, we're the ones being targeted.' Eli tried to gather his thoughts. Emmanuel looked down at the floor.

'I'm sorry,' Emmanuel whispered. 'I'm sorry for all of this. I should never have posted your video. I was stupid, and desperate, and floundering. My career was fucked. I used you, and I shouldn't have done that. And now…'

Emmanuel's shoulders heaved as he sobbed quietly. He placed the palms of his hands flat against his face, splaying his fingers widely. 'I don't know what to do.' The words were barely audible. 'I don't know how to help you.'

'It's not your fault.' Eli surprised himself.

Emmanuel didn't move. He continued to cry silently.

'Emmanuel.' Eli reached out his hand and placed it on Emmanuel's shoulder. 'This would have happened with or without you. You need to pull yourself together, though. You can't fall apart right now. You can't.'

Emmanuel sniffed. He exhaled forcefully. 'You're right. We need a plan. It's gone way beyond proving the supernatural. We need to end this.'

'What do we do?' Eli asked. His voice was small, almost infantile. 'The exorcist will be here later, but… But what if that doesn't work?'

'I need to think. I don't know. This is unprecedented. Until this point, everything has been theoretical. We're in unchartered waters,' Emmanuel said.

'Shit's Creek without a paddle.'

'You can say that again,' Emmanuel replied. 'Okay, right, let me think. We need to figure out if anything works. I think we need to be looking at historic stuff. Since the Scientific Revolution, nobody has taken parapsychology seriously.'

'Nobody?' Eli laughed uncomfortably.

'The only people who take it seriously are parapsychologists. Everyone else thinks we're insane. And because we've never had any concrete proof that spirits, demons, ghosts exist, we don't have anything concrete to banish them. Like I said, this is new. Mona could have…'

'Don't,' Eli warned. 'Don't do that. You said it yourself, Mona knew entities better than anyone and even she didn't have *proof* until now. What's worked for her in the past? All those people she interviewed who she believed were genuinely infested by demons, what did they do to get rid of them?'

Emmanuel blanched. 'In most cases, they died, and Mona came in after the death. But you're right, there has to be something. I'm going to try to log into her laptop and see what she's got saved in her personal folders. There might be something there. Do you want to listen to her past episodes? Zone in on any that reference demonic activity?'

'Yeah, okay, I can do that,' Eli said, relieved to have a task.

Emmanuel heaved himself off the floor and picked up Mona's sleek silver laptop. 'Any ideas what you think her password would be?'

'No idea. You knew her better than I did.'

'Damn,' Emmanuel said. He opened the laptop. 'Okay, let's see…' He began typing.

Eli searched through Mona's podcast and found an episode entitled *The Demon of the Upper East Side*. He pressed 'PLAY'.

MONA'S RETURN

Asher couldn't move.

He lay on his back. The *thing* was staring down at him from the ceiling. His arms were pinned to the mattress at his side. No matter how hard he flexed, he couldn't move his body. Specs stood at the bottom of the bed. He was silent.

Asher wanted to cry out to him to help, but he couldn't form the words. He couldn't make his mouth move. Why wasn't he helping? Why wasn't Specs doing anything?

Asher's body was snapped in half, forcing him upright. The TV was full of static snow.

'We want you to watch what we did to her.' The voice came from above him. It was followed by laughter, peeling across the room in waves. Hysterical, howling laughter.

Mona's face filled the TV screen. A different angle to the video he'd seen.

Tears fell down her face in sheets. Snot bubbled from her nose. Her dark hair fell in saturated clumps over her forehead. Her mouth contorted into a silent scream, chin jutting out. Through chipped, spider-webbed glasses, she screwed her eyes shut. The camera zoomed out. It showed Mona's full body, lying prone on the ground. Inside her stomach, something writhed. Turning over and over. It undulated inside her skin. Shadows descended on her, tugging at her shirt, her arms, legs, her hair. Fingers groped and yanked, pulling harder and harder until she began to tear. Arms came free from the shoulders, blood oozing and bubbling from the joints, almost black in the darkness of the night. Then her legs. The hands grabbed at her hair, balling it in fists, which turned and tightened. And then they pulled.

Mona's eyes remained tightly shut. Her mouth was lax.

Asher closed his eyes, predicting what would happen next.

Black fingers caressed his cheeks. They found his eyelids and pulled them open.

Mona's neck began to tear. The skin stretched and snapped, long slits growing and expanding, like ladders in tights.

The hands in Mona's hair gave a violent yank and twist.

Asher's brain told him there would have been a loud crack as Mona's skull was separated from her spine.

Ice-cold terror dripped through Asher's veins as he watched the camera zoom out further. A demon, shadowed in black, almost the shape of a human, picked up Mona's head from the ground and held it aloft with its too-long limbs. It smiled into the camera.

No. No. No. No. Asher repeated the word like a prayer.

'We want the world to know who we are,' the demon's voice came from above him. Asher couldn't move his head to look up. His body wouldn't listen. The demon's hands held his head in place. *'The world will know what you did to him.'*

Laughter. Not just one voice, but a chorus of voices spread around the room, infiltrating all of Asher's senses. He wanted to scream. He tried to scream.

'You'll be next. The world will watch you suffer at our hands.'

More laughter. It grated against Asher's senses, setting the cells of his body alight.

'Sleep now. We cannot wait to play with you.'

Asher fell into a deep sleep.

Eli woke to the sound of knocking at the front door. He'd fallen asleep on the sofa; drool caked his chin. His watch told him that he'd only slept for two hours. Specs barked and barrelled down the stairs.

'Stay there,' Eli said to Specs.

He opened the door and was greeted by a policewoman. Thirty years old, at most, blonde hair pulled back in a slick bun.

'You called last night about a missing person?' the policewoman said curtly.

Eli nodded. 'Yes, we did.'

'And they've still not returned?' the policewoman asked. She sounded bored.

'No,' Eli confirmed.

'Hmm,' she said. 'May I come in?'

'Sure, erm, Officer?'

'Emmerson,' she said.

Eli stepped aside and allowed her in. Specs eyed her from the sofa but didn't move. 'Would you like a drink, or…?'

'No, I'm good, thank you. I wanted to talk to you because we looked into Mona Koestler, and we noticed a very strange video circulating online.'

'Ah.' Eli nodded his head and pursed his lips.

'You've seen it?' Officer Emmerson raised an eyebrow.

'Yes, we did,' Eli said.

'And it was uploaded after she went missing,' Officer Emmerson said. It wasn't a question.

Eli nodded. 'Yeah, it looks that way.'

'Well, given Miss Koestler's online presence and the fact that she said she was here debunking some kind of *supernatural event*, we feel like it's most likely that the video and her disappearance is some kind of publicity stunt.'

'I don't-' Eli tried to interject.

Officer Emmerson raised a hand. 'That being said, we're going to search the area around the house. Given that Miss Koestler isn't local, and the moorland can be harsh and difficult to navigate, protocol dictates we take a look.'

'Thank you,' Eli said. It was better than nothing.

'I have bodies on their way here now. I'll let you know if we find anything. In the meantime, keep an eye on Miss Koestler's socials. It seems she's quite active. And keep calling her. You never know. I'm not worried, so you shouldn't be.'

You don't know the half of it, Eli thought.

Emmanuel came downstairs with Asher on his back, carrying his crutches.

'You are?' Officer Emmerson asked.

'Emmanuel Stark, a friend and colleague of Mona's. This is Asher, Eli's nephew.'

'I was just explaining that we're going to do a sweep of the moorland directly surrounding the house, but that we're not worried. Given the video online, it's worth taking a look, but we're sure the video is a hoax for the podcast's publicity.'

Emmanuel glanced at Eli, and then back at Officer Emmerson. 'We appreciate you checking,' he said.

Officer Emmerson turned on her heel and walked back out of the front door. It was so unceremonious. So nonchalant. Eli was half-tempted to call her back and ask her to take the whole thing more seriously.

'Well,' Eli turned to Emmanuel and Asher. 'That was that.'

'She didn't ask about the demons? Or the content of the video?' Emmanuel asked, having placed Asher on the floor and handed him his crutches.

'Nope. Other than to say that they'd found it, obviously. I suppose they think Mona's a bit…' Eli twirled his fingers in a circle at his ear. 'I would have too, before.' Even with a mother and brother who could see spirits, Eli would still have rolled his eyes at the idea of demons. As far as he was concerned (and his mum and brother, for that matter), 99% of supernatural claims were false. People who could talk to the dead, experienced paranormal activity, or claimed to be *psychic,* were usually liars looking for fame, money, or attention.

'The police probably deal with a lot of weird shit on a daily basis,' Emmanuel agreed. 'And they're overstretched as it is. It's a miracle they've even come to look for her.'

Asher made his way to the sofa on his crutches and sat down, shoulders hunched. Specs trotted beside him, whining.

'Everything okay?' Eli asked.

Asher shook his head. 'Last night, I had a dream.'

Eli sat beside him. Emmanuel hung back, awkwardly.

'I watched Mona die.'

'That's to be expected; maybe we should get in contact with Simone and…'

'No,' Asher said. 'It wasn't really a dream. I don't think it was, anyway.'

'Tell me,' Eli said.

Asher told him about the TV. About the demon touching his face and holding his eyes open. About watching Mona be ripped apart. About how the demons on the TV said they wanted the world to see what they were.

'They uploaded the video,' Emmanuel said, as though he was talking to himself. He looked ill.

'Are you hurt?' Eli asked, scanning Asher's body for signs of injury.

'No, but it was awful. I couldn't move. And Specs…' Asher began to cry. He leaned into Eli, who wrapped his arms around Asher's head and held him close.

'Specs is okay,' Eli assured him. 'He's a tough cookie.'

'They're using the electronics a lot,' Emmanuel said. The way he said it made Eli suspect he was still talking to himself. 'And the mirror. The windows. The *touching*. They're old. They have to be.' He looked at Eli, who still held Asher against him. 'You said that what we're calling demons are old spirits that have gained strength instead of moving on.'

'Yes,' Eli said, unsure where Emmanuel was going. Asher remained pressed closely to him.

'There's something we're missing… There has to be. The electronics… The fact that they want the world to see who they are. They're not camera-shy or trying to hide away like these things typically do.' He bit his lip and then continued. 'For years, people have been trying to catch credible paranormal activity on camera and here we have demons throwing themselves at us. Why?'

Eli shrugged. 'They want the world to know who they are,' he said.

'But they haven't told us *who* they are yet…' Emmanuel began pacing.

'Maybe that's the grand finale,' Asher said. His face was flushed bright red. The kid was terrified.

'Did you manage to get into Mona's laptop?' Eli asked, an attempt to change the subject.

'Yes, not long ago though. I found her password scribbled in a diary. It was *MONAPOSSESSED*, and three exclamation marks.' There was a hint of a smile on Emmanuel's lips.

'Any luck finding anything?' Eli was grasping at straws. He knew it.

'No, not yet,' Emmanuel said. 'There're loads to get through. I'm going to carry on now.'

'Did you get any sleep at all?' Eli asked.

Sleep deprivation felt like almost as big of a threat as the demons. Their minds needed to be sharp if they were to stay safe, even though sleeping felt risky.

'No, but…'

'Get some sleep now. Just a couple of hours. I can go through the laptop,' Eli offered.

'You didn't find anything in the podcasts?' Emmanuel asked, without an ounce of optimism in his voice.

'No, I didn't. I'm not quite done yet. Asher can take over that, I'm sure.' Eli hoped it would help distract Asher from the dream. From what the demons had said.

Asher sniffled and withdrew from Eli. 'Yeah, I can.'

'Are you sure?' Emmanuel questioned, uncertain.

'I am,' Asher said. He exhaled slowly. 'I'm fine.'

'Okay then,' Emmanuel said. 'But I'm going to nap here, just in case you need me.'

Eli wondered if Emmanuel was scared to be alone. 'We'll be quiet,' he said.

'No need. I can sleep through anything,' Emmanuel replied. He laid down on the sofa and tugged a throw blanket up to his shoulders. Within minutes, he was snoring.

'Right, down to business?' Eli said to Asher.

'Yes, sir.' Asher brought his hand to his head in a salute.

A DEMON IN A BOX

The exorcist didn't arrive.

By 11:30 PM, Uncle Eli had given up. He told Asher to go to bed. If the exorcist arrived, he'd knock on the door and wake them up. They all needed sleep.

'No,' Asher replied. 'I'm staying down here. I think we should all stay together.' The thought of being in that bedroom made his skin crawl.

'If that would make you feel better, we can stay down here, but you can't tell Emmanuel what to-'

'I'm happy to sleep down here,' Emmanuel cut him off. 'Asher is right. We should all stay together. After what happened to Mona…'

As predicted, the police had said there was no trace of her on the moorland surrounding the house. They were monitoring her social media but, Officer Emmerson reiterated, they weren't concerned. Mona was young, had no family ties. And, given her occupation, it made sense that the video was a hoax to garner attention for her upcoming podcast episode. After all, the police couldn't conceive for a second that what happened in the video could possibly be real. And why would they? They had no reason to believe.

Uncle Eli had simply nodded. Convincing the British police force that demons were real was not on his list of priorities, Asher figured.

'I think I found something,' Emmanuel said after they'd each chosen a spot on the sofas and got settled. He'd taken the laptop from Uncle Eli after his nap and hadn't looked away from the screen all day.

'What?' Uncle Eli propped himself on his elbow.

Asher rolled too. The cast on his leg meant turning was quite a task, but he managed it.

'Have you heard of a Dybbuk box?' Emmanuel asked.

'No,' Asher and Uncle Eli chorused.

'Well, a *Dybbuk* is what we'd call a malevolent spirit in Judaism, or a demon, in other words. The lore around them says that, and I quote: "*A Dybbuk is thought to be the soul of a deceased person that has become dislocated and is now wandering. It is believed to enter a living person and control them until it is exorcised by a religious rite.*" A Dybbuk box is essentially a box that you trap the Dybbuk in. It's not scientifically accurate or proven, but that goes without saying, and it was made famous by the film *The Possession* in 2012, which was based on a real-life story of a guy who sold a Dybbuk box on eBay. The guy admitted the story was fiction, but many people have said they've experienced paranormal incidents surrounding Dybbuk boxes, even if they're not Jewish. The legend of trapping a demon in a box isn't new by any stretch of the imagination.'

'Wait, you're telling us we need to trap the demons in boxes?' Asher couldn't believe what he was hearing. It sounded insane. These demons had already killed Mona, and Emmanuel was talking about trapping them in a box. A box, for fuck's sake.

'Mona had a box upstairs, a little wooden box. I thought it was a jewellery box, but now I'm not so sure. I just read one of her files from a podcast episode a few years ago, called *The Dybbuk in a Box*, and it's pretty much a step-by-step guide on how to trap a Dybbuk in a box.' Emmanuel stretched out his long legs and stood up. 'One minute.' He vanished upstairs.

Uncle Eli shrugged at Asher, and Asher returned it.

Emmanuel came back less than sixty seconds later. He was panting.

'Everything okay?' Uncle Eli asked him.

'Yeah, I just… I didn't want to be upstairs alone, you know?' Emmanuel smiled sheepishly.

Uncle Eli dipped his chin in acknowledgement.

Asher focused on the wooden box in Emmanuel's hands. It was about the size of a postcard, wooden with brass hinges, and looked like a small treasure chest. Various symbols were etched onto the surface.

'How did you not notice that before?' Asher asked. The box was pretty noticeable.

'I did. I thought it was a jewellery box or something,' Emmanuel reiterated.

'So why do you think it's a Dybbuk box?' Uncle Eli asked.

'The symbols,' Emmanuel said. 'They're protection symbols from various religions. There's the Hamsa Hand, the Ankh, a cross, a pentacle, an evil eye...'

'What's the plan?' Uncle Eli said.

'We trap the demon in the box.' A ghost of a smile tugged at Emmanuel's lips.

'Now?' Asher said, manoeuvring himself so he was upright.

'No time like the present. With Mona's step-by-step guide...' He looked like a kid on Christmas, one who'd won the game of chess against his chess-pro father.

'Okay then.' Asher used his crutches to stand. 'Worth a shot. And Mona said that this worked?'

'She did. She said the family didn't experience anything malevolent afterwards,' Emmanuel confirmed.

The whole house was still. Quiet. Usually, at night, Asher could feel the demons. He'd expected talk of trapping them to bring them out of hiding. Unless they knew the box wouldn't work.

'First, salt,' Emmanuel said.

He went to the kitchen and took a container of salt from the cupboard. In the centre of the living room, around the coffee table, he poured the salt in a circle. He then placed the wooden box on the table. Specs sniffed the air and snorted in derision, watching Emmanuel intently.

'Okay, I'm going to read from this now.' Emmanuel held the laptop in front of him.

'Where do you want us?' Uncle Eli asked.

'Stand outside the circle, please.'

'Okay.' Uncle Eli stood beside Asher. Specs remained on the sofa between them.

'This may sound ridiculous. It's a dead language. Sumerian, I believe, but my ancient linguistics isn't great. Thankfully, Mona wrote it out phonetically,' Emmanuel said.

'Should you be reading something if you don't know what it says?' Uncle Eli asked.

'It worked for the family Mona spoke to.' Emmanuel shrugged.

'Let him do it,' Asher said. After the threats he'd received last night in his dream that he wasn't sure was a dream, he was ready to try anything. Even dead languages. It was the first ray of hope he'd felt in days.

'Maybe we should wait for the exorcist,' Uncle Eli suggested.

'No, I have a good feeling about this,' Asher said.

'Me too,' Emmanuel concurred.

Uncle Eli paused, arms crossed tightly across his chest. 'Okay, fine. Do it.'

Emmanuel began to speak. To Asher's ears, it sounded like some variant of Indian. Although he was fairly sure Indian wasn't actually a language. *Hebrew?* he wondered. *Bengali?*

The room felt empty. Not tense, or scary, or anything like that. There was no feeling of dread, or fear.

They're not here, Asher thought.

Emmanuel continued speaking. Growing in confidence. The words filled the space. It didn't feel empty anymore. It felt full. Full of static. Full of potential.

The lights flickered and began to dim.

Specs barked; it sliced through the space. Uncle Eli bent down to reassure the dog. Each bark snapped in the air, exploding like firecrackers.

Emmanuel read aloud from the laptop. The glow illuminated his face. The brightness syphoned out of the ceiling light, almost completely. A shroud of darkness covered the room. Not completely, just enough to dull its features, like a veil.

Inside the salt circle, shadows materialised from the floor.

The energy shifted. Terror trailed an icy finger down Asher's spine.

The shadows became something almost human. Something *wrong.*

They were children.

Three boys. Teenagers? Around Asher's age, possibly younger. Dressed in rags. They weren't solid but Asher knew if he reached out and touched them, he'd be able to feel them. This must be what his dad and Nanna saw when they saw spirits. It was grotesque.

Their faces were continually in motion. Moving and changing. Smiling, laughing silently, screaming. A stop-motion effect blinking and stuttering.

'Who are you?' Asher said, his voice barely more than breath. He was aware that Emmanuel was still talking, still reading the ancient words.

The middle one, the taller of the three, spoke. *We were his boys.*

'Whose boys?' Asher exhaled a shaking breath.

Damont. You took him from us. Now you must pay.

The coffee table shattered into a thousand pieces. The box clattered to the floor, the lid closed. Doors and windows opened. Cold air streamed in with so much force, it knocked Asher backwards. He couldn't breathe against it. It clogged his throat. The TV turned on. The radios. Their phones. Anything that could make a noise, did. Specs's barks turned into vicious howls.

Emmanuel attempted to speak over the brutal wind, the cacophony of noise. It drowned out his words. Asher looked around, frantically trying to figure out what to do. The box was closed on the floor.

'Did it work?' he yelled over the noise.

Nobody answered him.

Nobody could hear him.

He had to do something. He had to…

Everything stopped, still and silent once more. The windows stayed open. The air in the room was ice cold.

Emmanuel's mouth moved soundlessly.

Asher tried to speak. No sound came from his mouth.

He looked down at Specs who snapped and barked but made no noise. His eyes were wild, panicked.

Uncle Eli attempted to speak.

The air felt full of pressure, the way it did when an aeroplane ascended. His ears felt like they wanted to pop. The pain was excruciating. A trickle of blood spilled from Uncle Eli's ear.

Emmanuel raised his hands to his forehead, gasping in pain. He crouched down, putting his head in his hands and rocking. A vacuum. It felt like they were in a vacuum.

His body began to rise and straighten out, stretching and elongating until his feet no longer touched the floor. He screamed, although nobody could hear it. His mouth stretched wide, his eyes searching and panicked.

The pressure in Asher's head began to decrease. His ears crackled. Sound began to flood back in. Specs. Emmanuel. Uncle Eli. He could hear them all.

'His feet aren't…' Asher said, breath caught in his throat.

Emmanuel's body continued to rise. The veins bulged in his neck. His hands clawed at his neck. 'They're hanging me!' he choked. He hung in the air with his head almost touching the ceiling, desperately grappling with his neck. A rope of shadow circled it.

Asher froze, not knowing what to do.

Emmanuel's body careened across the room and was slammed, wildly, into a wall. He hit it face-first and crumpled to the floor.

Uncle Eli ran to Emmanuel, turning him onto his side so the blood could run out of his mouth.

'You say you're Damont's boys?' Asher yelled into the empty space. 'He killed you, right? Just like he tried to kill me. Why are you defending him? Why do you want revenge when he hurt you?'

Asher was shoved to the floor, pinned down. A shadow figure above him. It no longer looked like a boy. It looked every inch the demon it was. Crimson illuminated the eye sockets.

'Damont did not kill us.' The face was inches away from Asher. The mouth didn't move as it spoke. Long, blank fingers circled his neck. *'He saved us. He set us free. Gave us everything. You took him from us. You, your cunt of a father, and your psychic. Your grandmother's death was laughable. She thought she knew things. She thought she understood. How we laughed when the noose snapped her neck.'*

Tears pooled in Asher's eyes.

'He killed you. He raped you. Damont was evil. You were innocent, once,' Asher said, voice shaking.

'Do not speak his name!'

The fingers tightened around Asher's neck, dragging him into an upright position, and then continuing to raise. He couldn't get enough air into his lungs. He was choking. They were choking him.

'This is how your grandmother felt when she hanged herself, and how your psychic felt when we hanged her.' The words were whispered in his ear. His body rose up and up, his feet unable to touch the floor.

'Asher!' Uncle Eli ran to him and began trying to pull him down. Specs snapped at the spectre.

In stuttering sounds, while clawing at his neck, Asher said, 'We learned… about it… in school. He groomed… you. He hurt… you. He…' Asher's world began to go dark. '… was a bad man… We killed him.'

'Do not speak ill of him!' the voice screeched. The hand released his neck, but a noose made of something not quite solid slid into its place.

'Asher, no! Let him go, you bastard! Take me instead!' Uncle Eli wrapped his arms around Asher's legs, so the *rope* wasn't taut.

Finally able to breathe, through fits of coughing, Asher said, 'You stayed here for him. You should have moved to the other side. You shouldn't be here. It's not right. It's not the way things are meant to be.' His words were frantic, rushed, he didn't know how long he'd be able to speak for or what the demons had planned.

The demon's face was before him. Centimetres away. Behind the black shadows of the face, Asher could see the features of a boy.

'You do not know what you are talking about. Do not speak of things beyond your limited understanding.'

'I know a lot,' Asher snarled. 'My dad saw spirits. Nanna did too.'

'Stupid child!' the voice roared. Uncle Eli was thrown back from him. It sent him sprawling to the floor. His head bounced off the hard wood with a sickening thud. He stilled.

'No!' Asher screamed.

Specs barked and snapped at Asher's feet.

Asher's breath came in short, sharp exhales.

His stomach plummeted as he dropped to the floor. The noose around his neck vanished. The demon was toying with him. His broken ankle, cocooned in the cast, smashed into the floor. A dull aching pain shot up his leg. Asher tried to sit up but was shoved back to the floor. The demon's face circled closer to his own. So close their noses almost touched. It opened its mouth wide and roared.

The demon's fingers reached into Asher's stomach. He felt them slide within his organs. There was no pain, only violation.

The demon's fingers moved within him, trailing up his body and to his brain. They teased. Wanting. Searching.

'No!' Asher pleaded. He knew what they wanted. They wanted to possess him. To *become* him.

'Why would we want that?' the demon said. *'You're so… breakable.'*

Asher's wrist snapped back against his forearm. The noise preceded the pain. And then the agony set in: burning, searing, pain.

'You killed him,' the demon whispered. Its sinister voice felt like smoke against Asher's cheeks. *'We want to make you suffer before we kill you. We don't want to be you. We want revenge.'*

The face before Asher's vanished. He lay there, trying to catch his breath, trying not to focus on his broken wrist.

Asher turned his head, his body shaking too vigorously for him to move, and watched as the demon crawled into his uncle's body.

POSSESSED!

'Please, no. Please God, no…' Asher stammered, praying to any god who would listen.

Uncle Eli lay like a corpse, stiff and still.

Asher attempted to steady himself enough to stand. A broken ankle in a plaster cast and a wrist he was pretty sure was also broken made getting up difficult. He rolled to his side and braced himself on his good wrist, before pushing himself up.

Uncle Eli didn't move. He stared, open-eyed, at the ceiling.

Specs licked his cheeks. He didn't react. The dog looked at Asher and whined.

'I know,' Asher said. 'I know.' He knelt beside his uncle and put his fingers to his neck like they'd taught them in school, checking for a pulse. It was there. Regular and strong. 'Oh, thank God.' Asher sighed.

He turned his attention to Emmanuel. He wasn't where he'd landed. That meant he was okay, he'd stood up and moved, Asher reasoned.

'Emmanuel?' he asked. 'I think Uncle Eli is…'

'Possessed?' Emmanuel said, although the voice wasn't wholly his. There was a static quality to it.

'Run!' The word came from the TV. A single, short, sharp syllable.

Asher spun and looked at Emmanuel.

That's not him, he thought. Emmanuel had a grin plastered to his face. His head was tilted at a strange angle. His limbs hung in a way that looked wrong, like somebody wearing a body that was too big for them. He began to giggle.

'Oh, fuck,' Asher said through gritted teeth. 'Please, no.' He tried to scramble away. To run. He couldn't. His body was broken. He shuffled back using one hand and one foot.

Emmanuel stalked closer to him, peering down. Leering. He contorted his mouth wider and wider, laughter pouring from it. The cackling turned into a growl. 'We are going to hurt you like you hurt him. You will pay for what you did.' The words came from Emmanuel's body.

'Please don't,' Asher begged. 'I'm like you. Don't do this. He wanted to hurt me like he hurt you.'

'You will never be like us. Damont freed us. We owe him everything. Can you imagine what it was like to be an orphan on the streets of Paris back then?' Emmanuel leaned closer, reaching out with a stuttering hand toward Asher. 'Nobody cared. Nobody wanted us. Damont did. He saved us.'

Specs launched himself at Emmanuel's hand, latching onto it and shaking with all his might. Spit and blood flew from it. Asher took the opportunity to stand. He hobbled away, thanking God that he'd left the plastic boot on his cast.

He needed to get out of there. He needed to leave.

The car keys. He needed the car keys. And a phone.

But they'll follow, his brain reminded him. *And you can't leave Specs.*

Specs.

Asher turned to see the dog hadn't let go of Emmanuel. He still remained attached to the flesh of his hand.

'Specs, come!' Asher yelled.

Specs dropped the hand and ran to Asher.

'We need to go, now.' He bent when he reached Uncle Eli and pulled his phone from his pocket, stuffing it in his own.

That's not your uncle, he thought, looking at the still body.

The car keys had been flung on the radiator shelf by the doorway. Asher stumbled to them and shoved them into his other pocket.

He cast a glance back over his shoulder. Emmanuel was approaching with weird, stuttering movements. The demon struggled to control the body. Or maybe Emmanuel was fighting back. Either way, Asher needed to move. Quickly.

He was shoved towards the door. It sent him sprawling onto his wrist. It crunched.

A cry of pain and anguish escaped him.

Emmanuel towered behind him. The bloody mess of his hand dripped onto the floor.

'Got you,' Emmanuel drawled, savouring every syllable.

'Please don't do this,' Asher begged. He tried to pull himself to his feet. But a boot to the small of his back slammed him back to the floor.

Eli fought to control his own body. The demon wore him like an ill-fitting suit. His body sat up.

'I am going to make you kill your nephew, and then I am going to kill you.' The voice came from inside his head.

'Who are you?' Eli asked. He heard the words, but he wasn't sure whether he'd spoken them aloud.

'You know who I am.'

Eli stood.

'What's your name?' Eli asked. An attempt at distraction as he fought to stop his body from obeying a mind that wasn't his own.

'You know who I am. I am you.'

Every cell of Eli's body was on fire. He burned. His muscles cramped and contorted as the demon forced him to step towards Asher. Asher, who was on the floor, face down. Emmanuel, who was stepping on his back, holding him down. Specs, who was trying to tear Emmanuel away.

'Please don't do this,' Eli pleaded.

'We have to.'

'You don't. You can move on. You don't need to do this to us. Maybe Damont is on the other side,' Eli said. The pain of trying to stop his body threatened to cloud his thoughts entirely. He sincerely hoped Damont wasn't on the other side.

'Ha! Pathetic.'

Eli fought. He fought with every fibre of his being. His body moved forwards on reluctant legs.

Specs snarled at him and snapped a warning bark.

'Please, don't hurt them. Take me. Take Emmanuel. Don't hurt them.'

'You are begging to save a dog's life?'

'Yes.' The pain flooded Eli's nervous system. He couldn't stop himself from moving closer to Asher.

Another warning snap from Specs.

'It looks like the dog doesn't think too much of you.'

It wasn't working. Eli couldn't stop the demon. Fear coursed through him… What was the demon going to make him do?

'I am going to make you cut him to pieces and eat him raw.'

'You're not Damont,' Eli stammered. 'Damont does those things. Not you. You're just a kid.'

'Just a kid? Could a kid do this?'

Eli's brain went black. His mind exploded in unbearable heat. It encircled him. He couldn't think. Couldn't speak. Couldn't…

'Uncle Eli!' Asher's voice broke through the pain.

Eli wouldn't allow this to happen. He wouldn't allow the demon to hurt Asher, not after everything the kid had been through. It was his job to protect him. But how could he protect him from something he didn't understand? Someone he didn't know?

'Who are you?' Eli screamed with all his might. He could feel the demon's tendrils snaking through his brain, his body. He and the demon were one. If the demon could see his thoughts, then he could… Eli focused not on preventing his body from moving, but on the demon's presence inside him.

'Tell me your name!' he demanded.

Artur Desprez.

The name flashed in Eli's mind. He *knew* it. They shared the same mind. Whatever the demon, Desprez, knew. Eli did.

The boy was fifteen years old at the time of his death.

He watched the memory of what happened. Of Damont tricking him, coaxing him into his tailor shop and…

Eli blocked out the rest. He didn't need to see what Damont had done to the boy.

'Damont hurt you. He is a murderer, and far worse things too.'

Eli knew that Damont had murdered more children than he could count. He also knew that many of them had passed over to the other side. Only three were so heavily groomed that they stayed by his side and refused to cross over.

'You were warned not to speak his name!'

This was Eli's chance. Artur, the demon, was distracted. He lunged at Emmanuel, knocking him onto the radiator shelf. His head hit the ledge with a deafening crack. He lay still on the floor.

'Run, Asher!' he yelled. He could feel the demon regaining control. Tendrils leaked into his muscles, forming neural pathways. He didn't have long until the demon took over.

Asher climbed to his feet.

Kill the host, kill the demon. Eli slammed his body down on top of Emmanuel's, slid his hands around his neck, and squeezed.

AN INTERLUDE FROM THE BEYOND (1)

Felix and Lilith watched as Eli choked Emmanuel to death. They watched the demon's vapour dissipate and dissolve into the air around them. The 'Beyond' was a veil between the living and the dead. A limbo. A waiting place. They walked the same plane, for a short time, before crossing to the next plane of existence. They knew things now. With death came knowledge. An understanding of the universe. Of what they should do. The need to pass over to the next realm of existence was strong, desperate, a cord that tightened, dragging them to the other side.

Would they turn into demons if they stayed? Would they lose their humanity? Or were all demons inherently *bad* to begin with? That was knowledge they did not have. It was beyond their understanding.

They'd watched Damont's boys descend on Eli and Asher. They'd watched as Damont's boys terrorised them. They'd watched as Damont's boys murdered the podcaster, ripping her limb from limb and tearing her body into the smallest pieces before consuming them. Mona was collateral. Uploading the video of her death was their way of compounding Asher's pain and suffering. Although they were demons, they were still children. They did not care if they were seen. They did not give a second thought to the consequences of revealing themselves to the world. Their drive was singular: hurt the Eastwood family for as long as they could and then feast on their souls. Revenge. They wanted revenge.

Emmanuel was also collateral. As was Lilith's cellmate. Their targets were Asher and Eli, and Felix could do nothing to stop it. Nor Lilith. They'd tried relentlessly, observing as the demons that were once children tore Asher's life apart.

Felix could feel this. It was in the universe. The collective consciousness that ran through all spirits. Not ghosts; ghosts weren't real. You were either a spirit, newly dead and trying to find your way, or a demon; a spirit who'd refused to leave. There was nothing in-between, other than the occasional imprint of energy. That was what people often thought of as ghosts. Sentient ghosts weren't real, as he'd always suspected. The demon that left Emmanuel's body had once been a thirteen-year-old orphan son of a baker. He was called Jean Fortin. He'd been raped and then eaten alive, his body consumed by Damont. His centuries of existence after his death had turned him into a monster on par with his creator. And now he was no more. He ceased to exist in all planes of existence.

Felix knew all of this because the universe did.

Artur, wearing Eli's body, raised to his feet, looking down at the now still Emmanuel.

The third demon, once a boy named Jacob Dugain, was attempting to fill Emmanuel's body, to slip into it and bring it back to life. He was only nine years old when Damont murdered and cannibalised him.

'Don't,' Felix said. 'You don't need to do this.'

Eli walked towards the door. Felix's brother was still fighting, he could feel that. He remembered the agony of trying to fight the possession. Two consciousnesses fighting for control. How his muscles had burned so fiercely. How he'd silently begged the dog to end his life.

The shadow form of Jacob knelt next to Emmanuel's body. *'He is not quite dead. He died briefly. He is back.'*

'Let him be,' Felix said.

Lilith walked over to the boy and placed a hand on his shoulder. The demon could not hurt her. She was already dead.

Jacob reared, snarling like a rabid dog. *'I have to do this,'* he growled. *'For him.'*

'The man who murdered you. Who ate your body?' Lilith's words were soft, kind.

The man who set us free. Who gave us meaning.' Jacob tried to enter Emmanuel's mind once more but failed. The mind had to be *awake* to be possessed. Emmanuel wasn't conscious. He was barely alive. Jacob roared with frustration.

'No, he didn't. You were children. He hurt you. He abused you. Then he killed you. He didn't even allow you to find peace in death,' Lilith said.

This was the first time one of the demons had been receptive enough to allow Felix and Lilith to speak to them. To try and reason. They were formidable, powerful beings intent on making Asher and Eli suffer. Intent on torturing them. Intent on prolonging their misery. Felix and Lilith were nothing but an annoyance to them. Buzzing flies on the edge of their consciousness. One demon had died with Emmanuel. One was inside Eli, who had walked out of the door, following in Asher's wake. The other was in front of them, trying to possess Emmanuel's unconscious mind.

'I have to be with Asher,' Felix said. Artur would find him soon, and that would be the end of it. There was nothing Felix could do other than to be with Asher at the end. He'd tried to warn them. It had hurt. It had taken a lot of energy. Every now and then he'd been able to send a message. The Gameboy. The mirror. The TV. But he'd been useless afterwards. He'd all but fade out of existence. He didn't have the strength to communicate, to warn his son and brother of the demons who hunted them. Had Felix been alive, the anguish and frustration might have killed him. It was agonising to watch the people you loved being hurt and not being able to do anything. For them to not even know you were there.

Lilith had never managed to send a message. Not one. Only older spirits, those who'd hung around for years, decades, could influence technology in that way, and they had to be very, very angry or very, very desperate.

Felix fled, following behind Eli.

Lilith nodded in understanding. She knew what she had to do.

AN ESCAPE ATTEMPT

Asher ran. Well, *ran* wasn't the best description of what he did. He staggered. He'd dropped the crutch when Emmanuel had attacked him. Specs ran beside him. He had no idea where to go. What to do. The car keys were in his back pocket. As far as he could tell, he had two options… Run or hide. It was dark. Coal black. The only light was from the moon. He could hide in the car. Lock himself in, but the way the demons had blown out the windows quickly put a stop to that idea. He couldn't drive. He'd been kidding himself to think he could. What the fuck even was a clutch?

No. He had to run and hide.

Think. Think. Make a fucking decision! he chided himself.

There was a ramshackle shed around the side of the house. It contained a load of crap. Tools. Empty coffee jars. Paintbrushes. Maybe something he could use as a weapon.

And then what? the voice in his head said. *You can't protect yourself from the demons forever.*

He'd cross that bridge when he got to it. Asher made his way slowly to the shed. It smelled of mould and dampness. He yanked on the door. It stuck, swollen in the jamb.

'Come on,' he muttered, pulling again, only able to use his right hand. Frustration and panic swarmed in his stomach.

The door sighed open. Relief consumed him. He inhaled the full scent of rot.

He climbed in. Specs followed. Shutting the door tightly, he looked around. It was too dark to see anything.

The phone.

He patted his pocket. Of course, it wasn't there.

A rusty metal torch hung from a hook by the door.

It was heavy, but Asher managed to hold it aloft, shining the cone of light around the tight, cramped space.

A hammer.

A chainsaw.

A mallet.

Rope.

Asher picked up the mallet. He ignored the ache in his opposite wrist. The mallet was cold, wet, and heavy. It would have to do.

Crunching footsteps came from outside, growing closer.

Asher peeped through a gap in the door.

Uncle Eli.

He reminded himself that it wasn't his uncle. It was something else. Something old and evil. Uncle Eli would never hurt him. He loved him.

Specs growled towards the closed door. Blood dripped from his muzzle. He stood to attention. Ready to pounce. Ready to protect.

A voice that wasn't quite Uncle Eli's said, 'Asher. Come out, come out, wherever you are.'

Asher didn't dare breathe.

He could hear his heart beating in his chest.

'You are too old to play hide and seek,' the thing wearing Uncle Eli's body said. 'Do not make me come and find you. Then I would have to kill you…' The thing laughed. A high-pitched giggle.

Asher clenched his teeth to stop a scream from escaping.

He was trapped.

Three short raps sounded at the door.

'May I come in?' The thing giggled again.

Asher didn't move a muscle.

Specs groaned, hackles raised.

'I'll give you until the count of three, and then you are dead. One… Two… Three.'

Asher raised his hammer.

Uncle Eli yanked on the door, pulling it open. It flung wide and bounced off the shed wall.

'Found you,' he said, a wide grin on his face.

'Who are you?' Asher shouted. His voice came out dry and hoarse.

Uncle Eli tutted and sighed. 'You know who I am.'

'Please don't do this. Why are you doing this?' Asher's arm ached. The mallet grew heavy.

'It's your turn now. You need to pay for what you did. Now, be a good boy and drop the mallet, and let Uncle Eli rip you to pieces.'

Uncle Eli lunged. Asher swung the mallet downwards. It bounced off his uncle's temple. Specs leapt into action, clamping his jaws onto Uncle Eli's thigh without a second thought. Uncle Eli shook his leg, attempting to get the dog off him. His hands began to clamp around Specs's throat. Asher saw red.

He raised the mallet again, smashing it into the side of Uncle Eli's head, above his ear.

The crunch of bone made his stomach turn.

Uncle Eli dropped to the floor like a stone.

Kill the host, kill the demon.

What Uncle Eli had done to Emmanuel, Asher had to do to him.

Asher sobbed, tears spilling from his eyes and down his cheeks as he positioned himself over his uncle. He yanked the rope from the hook and looped it around Uncle Eli's neck twice, clamping his teeth onto one end and pulling the other tightly with his good hand. His muscles tensed, shaking with exertion.

Uncle Eli began to fight back. Bucking and shaking.

Asher pulled tighter.

The veins bulged in Uncle Eli's neck, as though trying to puncture the skin and break free.

'Stop fighting, please,' Asher begged. 'Please.'

The body below him slowed. The movements became more sporadic.

Uncle Eli lay still.

Asher remained as he was for another minute and then pressed his fingers to Uncle Eli's neck.

AN INTERLUDE FROM THE BEYOND (2)

The demon was exhaled from Eli's body, melding with the air and vanishing on the wind. It didn't go quietly. It evaporated with a cry of anguish.

Felix watched as Asher released the rope from around Eli's neck and started chest compressions with his one good hand. He pressed hard, rhythmic. He could hear the words to '*Nelly the Elephant*' under Asher's breath: a trick taught in schools to help them time their compressions properly.

Come on, Eli, Felix thought. *Come on.*

Eli's spirit began to separate from his body, rising out of it like a fog.

Asher continued chest compressions, oblivious to what Felix could see.

Eli looked around with terrified, searching eyes.

'You need to go back. Now. He needs you,' Felix commanded. There was no gentleness in his voice. No begging. Only instruction. The way it had been when they were children. Felix was the elder brother, the one in charge.

'I tried to stop him,' Eli said. 'I tried to…'

'I know, but you need to go back. Now. Don't leave him alone.'

Eli nodded.

Felix could feel all the questions, the emotions, leaking out of him.

'Mum passed over. She thought everything was okay. She didn't know,' Felix said, answering the unspoken question.

'Lilith?' Eli asked, aloud this time.

'She is here with me,' he said.

'Good, good. We did it, right? We did it.' Eli sighed, his head lolling, and dropped back into his body.

Felix could not cry, but his heart ached for Asher, for his brother.

Eli gasped a breath, choked and coughed. Asher sprung back, warily.

Specs licked him. A sign that the demon had gone.

'Is it you?' Asher whispered.

'It's me,' Eli said. 'It's me.' He raised a hand to his head, exploring the damage. He blanched. Cried out. 'I need an ambulance,' he gritted out then said, 'Emmanuel?'

Asher shook his head.

Felix watched the realisation wash over Eli. He'd killed a man. He was going to prison.

'He's not dead,' Lilith said to Felix, approaching slowly. Beside her, walked Jacob. 'And Jacob is coming with us.'

'Us?' Felix asked.

'Yes, us. It's time for us to go and see what's next. You feel the pull, don't you? We're not supposed to be here.' Her voice was full of authority.

'Okay. Felix exhaled. The thought of leaving Asher behind was a pain like he'd never experienced.

'We'll go together,' Lilith said. She reached out and took Felix's hand, slipping her other through Jacob's. He looked up at her with childlike focus.

'How did you...?' Felix said, but he knew. He knew that Jacob had been a child without a parent. A child doing as they were told. A child who'd been promised the whole world. A child who wanted to belong.

The step to the other side was only small. A decision, more than a movement. Lilith stepped forwards, taking Jacob with her. Felix released her hand and watched her vanish. He couldn't leave just yet. He had to know that Asher would be okay, but Lilith needed to leave. She deserved peace.

THE AFTERMATH

Emmanuel crawled to the shed. Asher's breath caught in his chest.

'Thank God!" Asher leapt forwards. 'Do you have your phone?'

Emmanuel nodded, and then winced, putting his hand to his head. His face was a bloody mess, and his nose was definitely broken. Asher reached into his pocket and dragged out the phone.

A thousand thoughts swirled around Asher's mind. He knew that the whole thing would look terrible and that the police would be suspicious and want to investigate, especially considering Mona's disappearance. They needed an explanation that wouldn't cause too many difficult questions.

'You were fighting, okay?' Asher said, looking frantically between Uncle Eli and Emmanuel. 'We can't mention the demon at all. I don't want to end up being taken away from Uncle Eli… If they think he's…' His breath caught in his throat. A sob shook free. He'd just got Uncle Eli back; he wasn't going to lose him now. 'You were blaming each other for Mona's death, right?' he continued. 'Neither of you wants to press charges.' It was a phrase he'd heard from an American TV programme. He wasn't entirely sure the rules were the same in England, but it was their best shot. They needed an ambulance now, and they didn't have time to think of anything better. 'You were fighting, and you both got hurt. It's all okay now.' He nodded to himself. Yes, that would have to do. 'And I fell and broke my wrist,' he added as an afterthought. He was so caught up in Uncle Eli almost dying that his own pain wasn't important.

'Yeah, okay, Ash,' Uncle Eli muttered. He sounded hazy. Drunk.

Emmanuel nodded and then leaned back against the shed. Uncle Eli had propped himself against the metal shelving unit. He dipped in and out of consciousness. 'He fell and banged his head on the mallet,' Asher said. 'We can't explain his head with you two fighting.'

'You're right.' Emmanuel breathed in shakily.

Specs curled himself into a ball in Uncle Eli's lap.

They sat like that in silence and waited until the flashing lights lit up the sky.

Two ambulances wove down the single-track road. They pulled up outside the house and Asher shouted them over. There were four paramedics in total: two from each ambulance. They split off in a well-practised fashion. Two going to Uncle Eli, and two going to Emmanuel. Specs refused to move from Uncle Eli's lap as the paramedic checked him over.

'It's definitely a trip to A and E, I'm afraid,' one of the paramedics, an older chap with a shock of white hair, said to Asher. 'Can you tell me what happened?'

Asher repeated their story. The paramedic looked sceptical but nodded. 'You're holding your arm funny. Are you hurt?'

'Oh, yeah,' Asher said. 'I fell over. I think it's broken.'

'Hmm,' he said. 'Usually, lads your age who'd broken a bone would be screaming their heads off.'

Asher shrugged. He didn't know what else to say.

'Let me take a look.' The paramedic peeled back Asher's sleeve and gently prodded the already swollen joint. 'Yeah, that doesn't look great. I think you might be right. Let's get you to the hospital with your dad.'

Your dad. The words knocked the wind out of Asher. The paramedic didn't notice.

'You'll have to put the dog inside. I have a feeling your dad will be in for a while. Have you got any family or close friends we can call?'

'Mrs Birch,' Uncle Eli said. 'Call Mrs Birch.'

Using Emmanuel's phone, he called Mrs Birch's home phone. The only number, other than Nanna's, that he knew by heart. She answered on the second ring.

Asher explained what had happened, very briefly. That Specs would need picking up from the house, and Asher would need picking up from the hospital, and could they stay with her until Uncle Eli was better, please?

She started fussing immediately and Asher felt terrible that he'd barely given her any thought since the whole Emmanuel thing had blown up. She was the closest thing to a grandma he had right now.

After very reluctantly putting Specs in the house and locking the door, Asher put the key in the key safe and texted Mrs Birch the code. It felt wrong leaving Specs behind, but Mrs Birch would be there in an hour and the paramedics said he wasn't allowed in the ambulance.

'The police will want to speak with you at the hospital,' Asher overheard one of the paramedics say to Emmanuel. His heart sank. Tears finally leaked from his eyes.

'Hey,' Uncle Eli said from the trolley he'd been loaded onto. 'It's over. We'll all be okay.'

Asher's wrist was taken care of in a couple of hours. He was given another red cast and was fairly certain he'd been placed on some kind of social services watch list. Mrs Birch had driven immediately to the Airbnb to collect Specs and had then gone straight to the hospital to collect Asher. Uncle Eli thanked her profusely for coming to their aid, again. He promised her faithfully that she could borrow Specs whenever she wanted, and that they'd see each other more often.

Both Emmanuel and Uncle Eli were monitored closely. Emmanuel was released after forty-eight hours, his nose in a splint and sporting two black eyes. His hand had looked a lot worse than it actually was. There was no long-term damage from Specs's bite, just a lot of stitches.

Uncle Eli was released a week later. His skull fractures had been serious enough to worry the staff, but not serious enough for immediate intervention. A 'wait and see' approach was taken and, thankfully, worked. After a full week of living with Mrs Birch, who flapped around both Specs and Asher, feeding them cookies and spoiling them rotten, Asher was ready to go home. He loved Mrs Birch, but he just wanted things to go back to normal again.

It was safe to go home now. Emmanuel had released a statement to the press, which meant that no reporters or weird internet stalkers should be turning up at their door.

AN APOLOGY

This is not a statement I thought I would have to give. However, over the past week, I have had time to reflect upon my actions and I believe this apology to be necessary. First of all, I had no right to release the video I did without the permission of the Eastwood family. I was repeatedly told not to by Elijah Eastwood but, unfortunately, my own greed and desperation to further my stagnant career clouded my judgement and I made a decision that I will regret for the rest of my days.

The video was doctored.

Most of it is deepfake/AI. The Eastwood family had nothing to do with it. They were not willing participants in this.

Lilith Lavelle came to me and said that she believed the Eastwoods were haunted. Sadly, the haunting in this instance was the result of undiagnosed mental illness – which is not my place to go into further.

I took a video Lilith sent that showed NOTHING and made it show PROOF. There was no proof. The whole thing was a lie. A deepfake, I think you'd call it. And, again, the Eastwood family had nothing to do with it. They are victims of my greed.

You may also have heard that I was working with podcaster Mona Koestler, who disappeared. This is true. I convinced her to showcase the Eastwood proof video as I was confident she would not be able to disprove it. As of today, Mona is still missing. If you have any information of her whereabouts, I will include the crime reference number at the bottom of this blog post. Please do contact the police.

With this apology, I am stepping back from my career, and my online presence will cease.

I am sorry for letting you down.

Emmanuel Stark.

Asher walked into the house, Mrs Birch and Specs on either side of him. Uncle Eli sat on the sofa, a massive white bandage around his head. Asher ran to him and hugged him tightly. After seeing him in the hospital, fastened to too many tubes and looking like death, Asher was beyond pleased to see him back home. His face was a patchwork of bruises, but he wore a big smile.

'Careful with him!' Emmanuel sauntered in from the kitchen. His black eyes had turned yellow, and he no longer had the splint on his nose. He handed Asher a can of Fanta, and Uncle Eli a coffee, and then he sat down on the armchair.

'What...' Asher started.

'I'm here to help out, until your uncle is back to normal,' Emmanuel said.

Asher looked suspiciously between the two of them. There was something they weren't telling him.

'Are you?' *Together.* Asher didn't say the final word.

'No!' they both said, too quickly.

Asher smiled and shook his head.

The house felt blissfully empty. Normal.

'Mrs Birch, do you want to stay for a coffee?' Uncle Eli asked. 'It's the least I could do...'

'Yes, I'd love to,' she said. 'I'd like that very much.'

Specs barked once. A happy bark of triumph.

If Specs was happy, Asher was too.

Getting the police not to take the case further had been a delicate dance. Both Eli and Emmanuel had told the police repeatedly that they didn't want to press any charges against the other. Part of the English judicial system, it seemed, was asking the victim what they would like the outcome to be. That being said, getting the officers to agree had taken both Emmanuel and Eli sitting in a room (together) and telling the officers that there had been a misunderstanding. They'd fought. It was a one-off. They were friends again now and it wouldn't happen again. Reluctantly, the officers nodded their heads. It was done.

'Can we ask for an update about Mona Koestler?' Emmanuel asked. He'd gone to the Airbnb and emptied it of all their stuff, technology and all, the second he'd been released from hospital. He'd also had the forethought to hide all the data they'd collected in an encrypted folder using his phone while in the hospital, just in case the police started sniffing around and wanted to see what actually happened.

The police had been happy to drop the case… Start talking about demons and there was a significant chance they'd change their minds.

'No update,' the police officer had said.

It was late in the evening and Emmanuel and Eli sat across the table from one another, laptop between the two of them.

'Can you believe the exorcist showed up the next day?' Emmanuel asked. They'd been in hospital when they received a phone call from the exorcist asking why the house was empty. Emmanuel had told him it was a false alarm, and all was well. The exorcist had huffed something about cutting his holiday short.

'I can't believe you hung up the phone on a bishop.' Eli laughed, shaking his head. He winced, his fingers coming to his temple.

'Ready to watch?' Emmanuel asked.

Eli nodded his head once, slowly and carefully. He couldn't bring himself to speak.

Asher hadn't asked to see the videos. If he did, Eli would show him. He wouldn't hide anything from his nephew, but he also wouldn't force it upon him.

Asher deserved to live a normal life. One where demons weren't the basis of his every thought.

Emmanuel pressed 'PLAY' and, together, they relived the worst night of their lives.

They'd decide what to do with the recording later. For now, they just needed to convince themselves that it had been real.

EPILOGUE

Eli sat in bed next to Asher. Specs snored at their feet.

'I have to tell you something.' Eli pursed his lips.

'If it's about Emmanuel, I know that…'

'It's not that,' Eli said, although that was a conversation they'd have to have, eventually. The *Emmanuel Thing,* as he'd come to think of it, had taken him by surprise. Poor Craig had been understanding, but that didn't stop Eli from feeling terrible.

'Then what?' Asher asked. He tucked the Gameboy into the duvet next to him and looked at Eli.

'When I died, when the demon left me, I saw your dad and Lilith.'

Eli had convinced himself in and out of having this conversation so many times, but he thought Asher had the right to know.

'You what?' Asher's lip quivered.

'They were there the whole time, but they weren't strong enough to…' Eli lifted his hands, opening his palms. 'They couldn't help us. Those messages on the Gameboy, I think that was Felix trying to warn us. He tried to help us.' Eli wiped the heel of his hand against his eye.

'Why hadn't they crossed over? And what about Nanna?'

'Nanna crossed over already. After she died, she thought our *problem* was fixed, so she crossed over. Your dad didn't. He stayed behind to check you were okay. To watch over you.'

'What about Lilith?'

'She was with your dad.'

'They were here. They tried to…' Asher stumbled over his words and dissolved into sobs.

Eli pulled Asher into his chest and let him cry. His own tears fell too.

'Where are they now?' Asher said into Eli's damp shirt.

'I don't know. Your dad told me to come back, that you needed me, and I couldn't die yet.'

Another sob shook Asher's body. He pushed himself away from Eli. 'Dad? Lilith? Are you here?'

Eli waited with bated breath for a response.

Asher picked up his Gameboy and asked the same question again.

Nothing.

'I hope that means they've passed over now,' Asher said. 'I don't want them stuck here. They need to move on.' He looked into the space of the room. 'Dad, if you're here. I'm okay. I'll be okay. You can go.'

Specs licked Asher's tear-stained cheek.

'Dumb dog,' Asher said, a smile breaking across his face.

ACKNOWLEDGEMENTS

Writing acknowledgements doesn't get easier with each book because the longer you're on this journey, the more people you have to be grateful for. They accumulate and snowball, and I am in constant awe of how selfless the people of this community are.

I'll start, as I always do, by thanking the creature this book is dedicated to. The great lump snoring next to me. Buster: the best decision of my life. You might not be as well behaved as Specs, but you are as loved.

Danny, my best friend, my tech-support, my partner. Thank you for allowing me the space and grace to write, and for putting up with the piles and piles of multiplying books around our home.

My mum and auntie for their ever eager support and beta-reading. How lucky am I to have you two? Your willingness to support my books – even the ones with nooses on the cover – is beyond appreciated.

My dad, who - now he's retired - has caught the reading bug, for his constant support. Joe, Shannon, and Alfie, for the same; although Alfie can't read.

The BIGGEST of thank yous goes to my Sassy Squad: MJ Mars and Leigh Kenny. It is impossible to put into words how much I appreciate their presence in my life.

The Slasher Queens, Alan Shivers and Emerald O'Brien, for always being so open with their experiences and knowledge.

The Asylum chat, with a special shout out to ML Rayner, for answering my ridiculous questions. The Instagram authors I chat to regularly. The British Authors group. There are just so many wonderful people that I want to thank, I'd run out of space if I thanked each of you by name.

Sharon Joy Reads for her consistent support and positivity, and Trish Wilson for changing the face of the British horror author events. Check out the Indie Horror Chapter group on Facebook for more details about the events.

My in-laws, my friends, my family who – although they're not horror lovers – go out of their way to support me nonetheless.

And a final thank you to YOU. If I've said it once, I've said it a thousand times, readers who support indie authors are f*cking amazing. You make what we do possible. You're a special breed of people. <3

A LITTLE PLEA…

I hate to have to do this (it annoys me more than it annoys you, I promise) but, if you enjoyed this book , I would very much appreciate it if you could leave a review on Goodreads and/or Amazon. Reviews are the lifeblood of indie authors. They help us to reach a wider audience. It doesn't have to be anything fancy, even just a star-rating will do. If you're not able to leave a review, but you still enjoyed the book, please tell the book-lovers in your life about it! Every little helps, and I am very grateful.

ABOUT SARAH JULES

Sarah Jules is an indie horror author from Yorkshire. She is a self-professed accidental hipster (who refuses to apologise for this). She is also the owner of Sarah Jules Writing Services, a job that allows her to work in her pyjamas, which she is immensely grateful for.

She has written three novels - YOU INVITED IT IN, DON'T LIE & FOUND YOU - and edited BLOODY HELL: An Anthology of UK Indie Horror, which includes stories from the best and brightest UK indie horror authors.

If Sarah isn't working (or writing), you can find her with her nose stuck in a book, travelling the UK with her partner, and her rescue pup, or sweating it out in the gym. She is a mental health advocate, coffee-addict, and loves all things spooky and/or creepy.

Sarah blogs (super-hipster, she knows) about all things books, writing and publishing on both her Instagram (@sarahjuleswriting) and on her website www.sarahjuleswriting.com.

CONNECT WITH SARAH JULES

You can find me across social media…

Website: www.sarahjuleswriting.com

Monthly Newsletter:
https://sarahjuleswriting.com/newsletter/

Facebook Page: Sarah Jules Writing

Instagram: @sarahjuleswriting

Goodreads: Sarah Jules

TikTok: @sarahjulesauthor